Cowboy and Killers

As he rode across the sandy wasteland, Pete sighted the soaring buzzards. They flew in smaller and smaller circles, swooping nearer and nearer their prey.

He spurred his horse closer—and stopped short, staring in amazement at the bullet-riddled body of the old man in the rocking chair, his guns by his side and his red riding whip lying nearby.

Pete stooped to pick up the crimson quirt when it happened. Suddenly, bullets bit the dust around his feet and he found himself a shooting target . . .

> *Here is another top Western by William Colt MacDonald, the action-packed tale of a cowboy and a mysterious crimson quirt that led him straight into a killer's ambush.*

Other SIGNET Westerns You Will Enjoy

☐ **LAW OF THE GUN by Lewis B. Patten.** Seven people driving a herd of cattle through Comanche country to Abilene discover that they hate each other more than they fear the Indians around them. (#P4625—60¢)

☐ **TROUBLE IN TOMBSTONE by Tom J. Hopkins.** A thrilling western where one man risks the woman he loves and a bullet in the back to hurl an ultimatum at the renegades who ran the town. (#P4590—60¢)

☐ **A BULLET FOR MR. TEXAS by Ray Hogan.** Following a lead to his lost brother, Shawn Starbuck signs on as bodyguard to a man everybody wants dead and puts his own life on the line. (#P4583—60¢)

☐ **WALK TALL, RIDE TALL by Burt and Budd Arthur.** In this dramatic western, one Texas rancher pits himself against the lawlessness of an entire town. (#P4523—60¢)

THE NEW AMERICAN LIBRARY, INC.,
P.O. Box 999, Bergenfield, New Jersey 07621

Please send me the SIGNET BOOKS I have checked above. I am enclosing $_____(check or money order—no currency or C.O.D.'s). Please include the list price plus 15¢ a copy to cover mailing costs.

Name_____

Address_____

City_____State_____Zip Code_____
Allow at least 3 weeks for delivery

the Crimson Quirt

William Colt MacDonald

A SIGNET BOOK from
NEW AMERICAN LIBRARY
TIMES MIRROR

Copyright, 1942, by Allan William Colt MacDonald

All rights reserved. No part of this book may be reproduced without permission. For information address Doubleday & Company, Inc., 277 Park Avenue, New York, New York 10017.

Published by arrangement with Doubleday & Company, Inc.

Seventh Printing

 SIGNET TRADEMARK REG. U.S. PAT. OFF. AND FOREIGN COUNTRIES
REGISTERED TRADEMARK—MARCA REGISTRADA
HECHO EN CHICAGO, U.S.A.

Signet, Signet Classics, Signette, Mentor and Plume Books are published by The New American Library, Inc., 1301 Avenue of the Americas, New York, New York 10019

First Printing, May, 1949

PRINTED IN THE UNITED STATES OF AMERICA

1   Death on Rockers!

IT WAS SHORTLY after he had struck the trail leading to Beauregard City that the rider on the rangy roan gelding noticed, silhouetted against the vast expanse of turquoise sky, the trio of soaring buzzards. On either side of the well-traveled trail was a wide stretch of slightly rolling country, covered with mesquite, cacti, paloverde trees, and creosote bush. To the east, at the rear of the rider, were the foothills of the Picadero Mountains, far to the west, their serrated peaks etched sharply in the bright morning sunlight, were the towering granite slopes of the Sierra Trabadura Range.

However, it was the buzzards, swinging closer and closer to the earth in their erratic flight, that held the rider's attention. One, more bold than its companions, suddenly zoomed down to disappear behind the foliage of a paloverde; it didn't rise again. The other two birds swooped nearer, swinging wide on curving, split-tipped wings. His curiosity thoroughly aroused, the rider touched spurs to his mount and moved off the trail, heading across the loose sandy soil toward the point where the first bird had vanished. The remaining two birds, noting his approach, spiraled abruptly once more and floated far above on motionless wings against the wide blue expanse.

The man on the horse mused, "It might be a dead cow or some other animal that's attracted those zopilote birds. Again, it might be a man."

The horse picked its way carefully through the semidesert plant growth, the shod hoofs now and then striking loose bits of rock imbedded in the soil. The rider knew he was nearing the buzzards' point of interest when the third bird rose heavily, almost reluctantly, from beyond the lacy branches of a mesquite not more than fifty feet ahead and took to the air on sluggish, flapping wings. The rider spoke to his pony and moved on a bit faster.

Then, rounding a tall clump of prickly pear, the man on the horse suddenly checked his mount and came to a halt, his keen gray eyes intent on the scene before him. "What the hell!" was the involuntary exclamation that rose to his lips. The sight was so incongruous as to be unbelievable.

"If this isn't the damnedest thing I ever saw, my name's not Pete Piper," the rider told himself.

In the first place, what was a rocking chair doing away out here, miles from everywhere? And in the second place, why should anyone come out here to sit in the rocking chair, surrounded by brush and cacti? There wasn't any house near by; there wasn't even a wagon that might have transported the sitter and his chair. It was all very crazy; that's what it was, Piper told himself.

But there it was, the rocking chair, placed in a cleared space, with its occupant's head resting comfortably against a small cushion at the back of the chair. The man sat quietly enough, without moving or even deigning to notice the arrival of the rider. Piper mused, "Maybe he didn't hear me. He's sort of turned away, so he might not have seen me either." Piper could see now that the man seated in the rocking chair was elderly: a long gray beard hung halfway down his chest. Tangled white locks straggled from below the rim of the black sombrero.

Piper raised his voice, "Hi-yuh, old-timer!"

The man in the chair didn't move.

"Probably deaf as a rock," Piper told himself and repeated the greeting in a louder tone. Still no movement from the old man in the rocker.

Piper frowned and slipped down from his saddle. His legs carried him in long strides toward the rocking chair. After a moment he saw that the elderly man's eyes were wide open. Then he saw something else: a dark spreading stain of crimson showed on the denim shirt beneath the straggling ends of the gray whiskers.

Piper stiffened, then relaxed again. His eyes narrowed as he approached the silent form in the chair. The elderly man was dead; no doubt about that. Piper said soflty, "No wonder you didn't see me, old-timer."

Piper put out one hand and touched the left arm resting on the arm of the rocking chair. The flesh was stiff, cool to the touch. Still *rigor mortis* hadn't set in completely. Death couldn't have occurred more than hour or so before. Piper stepped back and surveyed the silent figure in the chair. The right hand was clenched about the butt of a six-shooter resting in the dead man's lap. Leaning against the side of the chair was a .30-.30 Winchester rifle. The glassy eyes, wide open, stared vacantly at the surrounding brush and trees. The feet, in their shabby, run-down boots, rested on the gravelly earth.

Piper's gaze noted other details. The rocking chair itself, for instance. It had been constructed with a walnut frame and curving armrests. The high back and seat—what Piper could see of the seat—was of cane. A cushion for the head and one beneath the chair's occupant had been provided.

"If this isn't the dangedest," Piper muttered. "What did he do—bring his favorite rocking chair out here and then commit suicide? If so, where's the horse or wagon that carried the chair? Nope. It's not suicide. He wouldn't have brought out two guns, if that's what he'd been aiming at. One would have been plenty."

He stooped and sniffed at the muzzle of the rifle resting against the chair arm, then moved around and, stooping lower, placed his nose close to the barrel of the six-shooter held by the dead man. There was an odor of burned powder lingering about both guns: they had been fired fairly recently, sometime that morning at least.

Piper moved carefully around the back of the chair. Now he noticed something else: through the openings in the woven cane back he could see where a bullet had entered the old man's shoulder. Piper frowned and muttered, "At least that proves one shot was fired before he sat in the chair: the chair ain't hurt any."

Now Piper stepped back, watching carefully where he placed his feet, and commenced to examine the earth around the dead man. He moved in ever-widening circles, noting both hoof and footprints as his narrowed gray eyes sharply took in every inch of space. Several yards away from the dead form in the chair Piper saw tracks attesting that a wagon had passed recently. That didn't help much, though. It only increased the puzzle. What was a wagon doing off here in the brush and mesquite, instead of on the road that ran from Beauregard City?

Piper shook his head in perplexity and started to follow the wagon-wheel tracks, his head with its flat-topped black sombrero bent toward the earth as he moved. He was a tall, lean individual with red hair and a good jaw. His shoulders were wide in their tightly fitting woolen shirt. His corduroy trousers were tucked into the top of well-worn riding boots. A Bull Durham tag dangled from one pocket of his open vest. About his waist was a cartridge belt and holstered six-shooter. To his friends he was known as Pete.

For ten minutes he followed the wagon tracks until they joined the trail that ran to Beauregard City. But the wagon hadn't taken that direction, it had headed east. The hoofprints of the team drawing it proved that the vehicle had been pushed along at a sharp rate of speed. Why?

Pete Piper retraced his steps and, having reached the dead man once more, circled off in the opposite direction. Here, after a time, he saw the prints of three riders, also traveling fast. Two had been traveling together, apparently in pursuit of the third. The prints of the third horse abruptly swung off to the south. These Piper followed until they led him behind a tall clump of opuntia cactus where the carcass of the horse lay sprawled, dead, on the earth. It had been shot twice, though from the position of the wounds, Piper judged the animal had run some distance before dropping.

There were footprints near the body of the horse, too: wide-spaced footprints that conjured up a vision of a running man, footprints that, after a time, became less certain and took on a stumbling aspect. These footprints led Piper back to the rigid form seated in the rocking chair. Everything was as he had last left it. There seemed little more he could do.

"I'd sure like to examine those guns," Piper muttered, "but I reckon I'd better leave things as they are and get on to Beauregard City to report this. Might be a coroner wouldn't like me messing around a body found like this."

Still he was reluctant to leave. Again he glanced at the hoofprints near the chair. They led off to the north, in the direction of a high ridge known as a hogback, which reared its sloping sides well above the wide stretch of semidesert growth a quarter of a mile away. Piper glanced toward the top of the hogback; nothing but trees and brush to be seen up that way.

That seemed to be all there was to it. Piper glanced toward the sky; the buzzards were still hovering about up there, waiting for him to leave. "Damn stink birds," Piper muttered and started toward his horse to get a blanket to cover the body. He wasn't following quite the same path now as he had taken when arriving. Then suddenly a bright red object caught his eye where it nestled among the lacy branches of a mesquite tree. He paused and, reaching among the branches, drew out a riding quirt such as American cowboys and Mexican *vaqueros* often carry. What was this red quirt doing here? He examined it with growing interest.

The quirt had a heavy round handle, with a sort of braided leather knob at the top, covered with woven horsehair. Below the handle was a length of plaited rawhide, from which hung twin strips of heavy leather, about a foot and a half long, the sort that would urge a horse to a speedier gait or cut its hide to ribbons, depending on the mood and temperament of its rider. A rawhide wrist loop dangled from the handle. The quirt was about three feet long, over all; the whole had been dyed a vivid crimson.

"Hmmm! Wonder where this came from?" Piper mused. "Looks like Mexican handiwork. How did it get caught in the branches of this mesquite? Has it been here long? Nope, I don't reckon so. It doesn't look as though it had been exposed much to the weather—just shows ordinary usage, and not much of that. I've got a hunch there's some connection between this red quirt and that dead man."

He stood scrutinizing the quirt a moment or two longer, then resumed his way to the pony. Procuring a blanket, he hastened back and spread it over the silent form in the rocking chair, then prepared to continue the journey to Beauregard City.

Still reluctant to leave, he examined the crimson quirt again before slipping the wrist loop over his left hand. He stood idly slapping the twin lashes against his boot, brow furrowed in concentration. "Queerest mix-up I ever ran into," he muttered. Then it happened:

A swift breeze fanned his right cheek. Leaves from a tree near his shoulder fluttered to the earth. A sharp whining sound droned in his ears. All this before he heard the sharp crack of the rifle.

The sound wasn't difficult to locate. Piper instantly raised his gaze to the top of that hogback a quarter mile distant. There, drifting lazily upward against a background of brush, was a swiftly dissolving puff of powder smoke. Even while he watched, a second shot cracked out. This time the bullet threw up dust and gravel a few yards from Piper's feet.

2 Sharpshooting

PIPER WHIRLED and ran back to his horse, jerked his rifle from the boot on the saddle and screened himself behind a paloverde tree. With the rifle butt at shoulder, he peered through the branches of the tree toward the top of the hogback. Three minutes passed. Five. There weren't any more shots. Nor was there any movement to be noted on top of the hogback.

Piper slowly started to lower his Winchester. Then he paused. Up atop the long ridge he'd caught a silvery metallic gleam in the tangled brush. Again his rifle came up, one finger slowly tightening about the trigger of the weapon. The silvery gleam was gone now, but Piper fired, shooting in the direction from which the gleam had come.

The echoes of the shot died away. Piper waited, gaze intent on the top of the hogback. He couldn't be sure, at this distance, but he thought he detected a sort of agitated movement. A sound that resembled a curse of pain faintly reached his ears.

A slow grin spread on Piper's bronzed features. "If I hit anything or anybody at this distance, and without even seeing them, that's sure sharpshooting," he told himself. "Reckon I'll wait a few minutes more, then go see."

There weren't any more shots, nor was there any movement that he could perceive at the top of the long ridge. "Reckon I'd better go see," Piper told himself. Shoving his rifle back into its boot, he gathered up the pony's reins and climbed into the saddle, then set off in the direction of the ridge, guiding the pony carefully between the various growths that barred the way and never once removing his gaze from the hogback.

It was a foolhardy thing to do; Piper realized that, but he possessed an insatiable curiosity as to the reason for anyone shooting at him. "I don't know anybody in this neck of the range," passed through his mind. "If whoever did that shooting was trying to drive me away from that corpse in the rocker, I was leaving anyway—so there was no reason for shooting. Howsomever, when anybody shakes lead out of a barrel in my direction I want to know the reason why."

His pony reached the foot of the hogback and commenced the steep ascent. It occurred to Piper that somebody might be waiting to ambush him at the top, but he kept steadily on, though by this time the walnut butt of his six-shooter was gripped in his right hand. Twice the pony slipped and slid back a few feet, necessitating a search for easier paths to the top. However, the horse finally made it, puffing and blowing, its hide streaked with perspiration.

Here at the top was a tangle of brush and stunted trees. Piper drew to a halt to rest his mount, his eyes alert in all directions, his ears sharp for the first hostile sound. But there was nothing to be seen or heard except a few birds moving among the leaves and branches.

Piper relaxed a trifle, his eyes now sweeping the surrounding country below the hogback. Suddenly off to the northwest he spied two swiftly traveling clouds of dust. His gaze narrowed.

"Two riders." He spoke half aloud. "Those hombres are sure demolishing space. Must be they're shy on guts to let me run the two of 'em off that-a-way. Well, well!" He drew out his Durham and papers and slowly rolled a cigarette, his eyes still intent on the fast-vanishing riders. They were too far away for Piper to determine anything regarding their features or general getup. "And I never would be able to catch 'em now," he told himself, scratching a match for his cigarette.

He inhaled deeply and blew out a gray cloud of smoke. "Two against one," he repeated. "Why didn't they stay and fill me full of lead while I was climbing this ridge? They sure must have lost their nerve plumb sudden. Anyway, it still doesn't explain why they shot at me in the first place. Well, I'll give a look-see."

He dismounted from the pony and made his way into the brushy thicket, heading for the point from which he judged the shooting had come. There was a good deal of prickly pear up here, some scrub oak and other low growths, but finally he located a spot where the leaves and brush showed signs of trampling. There were the marks of booted feet, too, though none were plainly discernible. Farther back droppings showed where two horses had been tethered. After some further search Piper picked from the earth two empty .30-.30 rifle shells. These he slipped into his pocket.

Piper had started to head back toward his horse, when his toe stubbed against a heavy object only a few yards from the point where he had picked up the cartridge shells. He stooped down and retrieved a pair of field glasses. That is, the object had been field glasses. Now the binoculars were ruined; at least the lens in the right barrel was. Only a few splinters of glass remained at one side of the barrel's rim, and there were tiny flecks of lead adhering to the metal where a bullet had ripped through the outer half of the barrel.

A slow grin twisted Piper's lips as comprehension dawned upon him. "No wonder those two high-tailed it," he chuckled. "They sure must have thought I was doing some real sharpshooting. Gosh! Talk about a lucky shot! And one of those hombres must have been looking at me when it happened. Probably plumb forgot that these glasses would give off a glint of light. And said glint was gone, complete, by the time I fired my shot. I couldn't do this again in a million years—but those two didn't wait around for me to try." A low laugh suddenly welled from his throat. "I'd like to bet a plugged peso that the hombre that had these glasses up to his eyes sure got a heavy bump when my slug struck. He's just lucky it came at an angle. Otherwise he'd have had an eye put out."

Placing the binoculars to his eyes, Piper adjusted the lens in the left barrel and gazed down toward the spot where the dead man sat in his chair. The sight came into view with astonishing clarity and nearness. Almost Piper felt as though he could reach out and touch the still form in the rocker.

He lowered the glasses soberly. "Why, those scuts could watch every move I was making. Ten to one they were eyeing me while I looked for sign and when I found that red quirt. I wonder . . ." He paused, pondering the problem, frowning. Glancing down at the quirt dangling from his wrist, he continued, "Could those hombres have wanted this quirt? It could easily have been overlooked in that tree where I found it. It was quite a little distance from where the dead man sat. And are they the ones who killed him? Pete Piper, you sure got yourself tangled in a problem this time."

He gave a last glance around, then, taking the damaged binoculars with him, retraced his steps to the waiting pony, meanwhile speculating: "No, they couldn't have wanted this quirt. Men don't kill just to gain possession of a riding quirt. But those two sure didn't want me down there."

The sun had passed meridian by the time Piper and his pony once more reached the bottom of the hogback. It was hot, no doubt about that. Piper wiped perspiration from his face with the bandanna knotted about his neck, spurred his mount and moved on at a faster gait.

Within a few minutes he was back at the spot where the blanket-covered figure rested in the rocking chair. Nothing had changed since Piper left. The soaring buzzards still hovered high above the earth. Piper didn't dismount but pushed on until he turned right on the trail that ran to Beauregard City.

3   Trouble Ahead

IT WAS shortly after one-thirty in the afternoon when Piper rode into Beauregard City, which gave the impression of being a thriving cattle center. There were three or four streets paralleling the main thoroughfare and an equal number crossing these. Southeast of the town Piper had noticed a group of cattle pens arranged along a spur of the T.N.&A.S. railroad. Tall cottonwood trees, particularly plentiful in the residential section, furnished shade from the broiling rays of the sun.

Along Main Street, as he pulled the roan to a walk, Piper saw several saloons, two general stores, a bank, and a two-story brick hotel which bore the sign: COWMEN'S REST HOTEL. There were restaurants, a photograph gallery, a feed store, at least one barbershop, and two livery stables. Many of the buildings had false fronts from which the paint was peeling, due to the action of desert wind and sun. The roadway was dusty, unpaved, with a plank sidewalk on both sides. An almost unbroken line of wooden awnings projected from buildings above the sidewalks. Cow ponies and wagons waited at hitch racks on either side.

Pedestrians moved along the street. Mostly they wore sombreros, but a few sported derby hats. Apparently the fashion of the day had reached Beauregard. Men stood in the shade of buildings, talking idly, or pushed through the swinging doors of saloons. Piper passed two women carrying parasols. "Right likely up-and-coming town," he mused. "What's this Southwest country coming to? Parasols and hard-boiled hats! I'll bet there's a school and a church here too. It wouldn't surprise me none if a lot of folks in Beauregard wear their Sunday clothes every day."

The gelding reached another intersection. Here, just across the street, on the corner to Piper's right, was a long, low rock-and-adobe building, with barred windows along the rear wall. A sign had been nailed to the edge of the wooden awning, projecting from the building, bearing the words: OFFICE OF THE SHERIFF, TRABADURA COUNTY. Seated on the porch, chair tilted back against the front wall near the open door, was a lean, gangling man of about thirty years of age, with sleepy blue eyes and tousled hair the color of hemp showing beneath his gray sombrero that rested precariously over one ear. A gun sagged at the man's right thigh, and there was a badge pinned to his open vest.

Piper pulled over to the hitch rack and dismounted. The man with the hemp hair eyed him drowsily a moment, then again bent his attention to the short stick of yellow pine he held in one hand, while a keen-bladed Barlow knife peeled off a long, thin shaving. A small pile of shavings had collected about the man's chair.

Piper thought: "Just another hombre whittling away his life. It doesn't look too encouraging. I could be wrong, though." He rounded the end of the hitch rack and stepped to the porch. The whittler didn't look up. Piper said, "You the sherriff hereabouts?"

The sleepy eyes concentrated on the pine stick a moment longer, then lifted to meet Piper's. Now Piper detected a definite twinkle in those eyes as the man drawled, "Not yet," and resumed his whittling. After a moment he resumed, "I sort of had hopes a spell back, when Sheriff Perkins was took bad with lumbago, but he recovered, hang the luck," Whittle, whittle. "Me, I'm just a deputy. Name's Homer Pritchard." More whittling, then further talk: "Sheriff Perkins is down to the Lariat Saloon, gettin' a shot of tonic for his lumbago. I hope it don't cure him. Where and when did the killin' take place?"

Piper had started to grin; now he sobered. "How'd you know there'd been a killing?"

Deputy Sheriff Pritchard spat a long thin brown stream out to the roadway and whittled a couple of more shavings from the stick. "You're a stranger in Beauregard," he explained; "therefore, you don't run cows around here. You'd have no rustlin' to report. If you were lookin' for a job you'd be talkin' to hombres at one of our saloons 'stead of me. If you were lookin' for acreage or city lots you'd be conferrin' at one of our local realtors'. There's not many things brings a man to the sheriff's office, 'ceptin' crime. I figured there must be a killin'."

Piper laughed. "You're not as slow as you look."

The deputy tossed away the pine stick and put the Barlow knife in his pocket. "I couldn't be." He grinned and put out one hand. "Your name's——?"

"Pete Piper. I was riding toward town when I saw some buzzards circling around. I went to investigate and found a dead man in a rocking chair."

"Rockin' chair, huh? Folks get queer ideas now'days. Used to be, they'd bury dead men. Where'd you find him?"

"Just this side of a long hogback, about twelve miles east."

"We call that hogback Elephant Ridge."

"Good name, at that. Anyway, a couple of hombres took shots at me from the top of the ridge. I shot once and got one of 'em plumb in the binoculars——"

"If that's a vital spot I never heard of it."

"Field glasses. Here, wait, I'll show you." Pete Piper strode out to his pony and got the damaged binoculars and returned to the deputy. "It was a luck shot, of course——"

"Wait a minute," Pritchard interposed. "Here comes Sheriff Perkins now. It'll save tellin' your story twice."

A bulkily built man with thinning gray hair, wearing corduroys, was approaching the building. When he arrived the deputy introduced Piper, mentioned the nature of the business that had brought him to the sheriff's office. Piper liked the sheriff's looks and his firm handclasp. After a moment he told his story, leaving out only the part that related to the finding of the crimson-dyed quirt.

When he had finished Sheriff Ethan Perkins frowned. "Old codger, eh? Queer setup, ain't it? Rocking chair! How in hell did it get out there?"

"Maybe," Homer Pritchard suggested dryly, "it was rockin' its way across country and just happened to be convenient."

"Maybe," the sheriff retorted crisply, "you'd better hitch up a wagon, Homer, and go after that body. Get Doc Gillett. You'll find him down to the Lariat bar now if you hurry." Turning to Piper, "He's town coroner. Doc will be right glad you didn't disturb that body. Let me see those field glasses. . . . Hmmm! You shore scored a direct hit. These glasses look like a pair I saw Nick Traxler using one time."

"If those are Traxler's glasses," the deputy put in, "there'll be trouble ahead."

"Who is Nick Traxler?" Piper asked.

The deputy supplied the answer: "Owner of the Diamond-T spread. Nick would like to be boss of this country hereabouts, but so far he ain't convinced me and the sheriff. I tell you, Piper, The Pritchard & Perkins combination is hard to beat. But Traxler can be rattlesnake mean when he wants to."

"Quit running off at the head, Homer, and get yourself a wagon, Doc Gillett, and on your way."

"Maybe you're right at that," Pritchard drawled. He spat another long brown stream and ambled across the street in the direction of the Blue Star Livery, calling back over his shoulder, "I'll see you later, Piper."

Pete nodded and turned back to Sheriff Perkins. The sheriff stood thinking, narrow-eyed. "These may be Traxler's glasses, Piper, but Nick Traxler wasn't using 'em when your shot shattered this glass."

"How do you know?"

"Traxler wouldn't have turned tail and run the way you say those two hombres done. It'd been just the opposite. Nick Traxler would have been on you like a wildcat, lead spitting from his gun barrel. Whether you like the man or not, you got to admit he's not yellow." The sheriff considered a moment. "It might have been one of the other two, of course."

"What other two?"

"Nick's brothers—Luke and Ivan. In my estimation, those two are just a couple of handicaps Nick had saddled on him.

They're no good—not that Nick is either, for that matter. But, like I say, that's only my opinion. . . . I wonder who that dead man is. Only one I know hereabouts that fits the description you give is old Tiger-Eye Munson. But Tiger-Eye is one of Traxler's men."

"We're not certain Traxler is responsible," Piper reminded.

"True enough. I was just letting my imagination run wild. . . . I'm sorry, Piper, but I'll have to ask you to stay in town until this business is cleared up a mite more."

"That's all right with me."

"Mind my asking what you're doing in Beauregard?"

"Nothing in particular. I'm just looking over the country a mite. Got in mind to buy me some acreage and start a small outfit. I was down in Mexico. Just crossed the line this morning, not having found exactly what I wanted down there. The first trail I hit after leaving the border was the one that runs here. I figured to get a bite here and move on. Howsomever, I'm in no hurry."

Sheriff Perkins nodded. "If you're looking for an outfit we'll be glad to have you cast your eye around this range. As for food, any of the restaurants are pretty good. The hotel dining room is best, but that will be closed now. Kind of late for dinner. The hotel bar is first-rate. I like the Lariat bar, myself. Where'll I find you?"

"I'll get me a room at the hotel," Pete replied. "This Traxler you mentioned, have you seen him around town today?"

"Saw him going into Turk Raven's Saloon about two hours back. All the Diamond-T outfit hangs around Raven's place. Maybe you'd like it; maybe you wouldn't. I don't. But I've got to admit Raven ain't broke no laws that I know of—that I know of," the sheriff repeated meaningly.

"In other words"—Pete smiled—"the raven may be as black as his reputation.'

"That's something I've still to learn. Well, I'll see you later, Piper."

4   The Queen Bee

PIPER climbed back into his saddle and turned the pony east on Main Street until he'd reached the Cowmen's Rest Hotel. Here he arranged for a room on the second floor and evaded the clerk's curiosity regarding the business that brought him to Beauregard City with an inquiry regarding dinner.

"Dining room's closed until five-thirty," the clerk told him. "However, Mr. Piper, I can recommend the Busy Bee Restaurant. That's just three doors west of here after you cross Tonto Street. This hotel's right at the corner of Main and

Tonto, so you won't have any trouble finding it."

"Thanks," Piper said dryly. "I'll try the Busy Bee and hope I won't get stung. I don't know as I ever yet hit a town that didn't have a Busy Bee eating place. Some of them are certainly honeys!" sarcastically.

"I'm sure you'll find this is different," the clerk said.

"If it isn't I'll come back and comb your hair," Piper said humorously.'

He strolled out of the lobby, the crimson quirt dangling from his wrist, followed by the puzzled gaze of the hotel clerk. Getting his pony at the hitch rack, he walked it across the street and entered the wide doorway of the Beauregard Livery. Here he left the pony with instructions concerning its care, then departed and crossed the street in the direction of the Busy Bee Restaurant, which he quickly spotted from the neat blue sign above its entrance.

There wasn't anyone to be seen when he entered the Busy Bee. A long counter, equipped with stools, ran along one wall. The remainder of the room was given over to a number of oilcloth-covered tables and straightback chairs. At the rear was a pair of swinging doors leading to the kitchen. Piper seated himself on the stool at the counter nearest the door and waited. He waited for five minutes, ten. No one appeared.

"Must be the drones are in charge today." He laughed to himself. After a moment he rapped on the counter with his knuckles.

The summons brought an instant response. There came the sound of quick light footsteps from the kitchen; then the swinging doors opened and a girl entered. "Oh, I'm sorry," the girl said contritely in a throaty voice. "I was reading. I didn't know there was anyone in here."

Piper swallowed hard. Here, he told himself, was the queen bee of the hive—of all hives, as far as Piper was concerned. This girl was more than just pretty; it was the sort of beauty that took a man's breath away. Her eyes were deep violet with long black lashes. Her hair, like pale gold, had been plaited into heavy twin braids that encircled her head. She was tall, slim; something boyish in her make-up, as well. Her smooth skin was richly tanned, attesting the fact that a lot of her hours had been spent in the open. The mouth was too wide to be strictly feminine, but it merely lent emphasis to a firm chin that showed plenty of character. Beneath the neat white apron was a dress of checked gingham.

The girl spoke again. "Food, cowboy?"

"More than that," Pete Piper said enthusiastically. "Nourishment for the eyes of men——" He broke off suddenly, realizing what he had said. "I beg your pardon. I was thinking of—of—well, you see——" He broke off again, stammering for words.

The girl smiled. "What'll it be, a steak and fried potatoes, coffee, pie?"

"Anything you say," Pete replied. "Whatever is handiest, just so you don't have to be away too long. You don't have to cook it yourself, do you?"

The girl eyed him steadily. "I haven't had any complaints on my cooking yet. The regular cook won't be in for an hour or so yet."

"I—I—well"—Pete reddened—"I didn't mean your cooking wasn't all right. I just wanted to make sure you wouldn't be away too long. I think we should get acquainted."

The girl eyed him coolly now. "You wouldn't be trying to get fresh, would you, redhead?" she asked.

"Ah, look, don't get me wrong," Pete pleaded. "If you feel that way I'll leave pronto. It's just that I'm a stranger here and——" Again he broke off.

His manner was so earnest that the girl smiled in spite of herself. "All right, cowboy. And now if the steak is what you'd like I'll get busy."

"Thanks a lot. I'm—I'm Pete Piper."

The girl pretended to be impressed. "Not *the* Peter Piper! The one who picked a peck of pickled peppers?"

Pete grinned. He was commencing to regain his balance now. He shook his head. "No, I'm the Peter Piper who pertly pawned a pinkish pearl of pretty precious pulchritude for a petty pot of phony pesos. Now do you place me?"

The girl looked gravely at him, though Pete could see her eyes were brimming with laughter, and shook her head. "I'm afraid I don't," she told him, "but I'll be thinking it over while I'm getting your steak."

She disappeared into the kitchen from which, in a few moments, came the sound and odor of frying meat; once she stuck her blond head through the swinging doors to ask if Pete liked his steak rare or well done.

"The rarer the better," Pete replied, adding in an undertone, "It won't take so long that-a-way." After a few minutes he told himself he must remember to give the hotel clerk a cigar. "After all, he recommended this Queen Bee place. Maybe I'd better make it box of cigars."

The sound of drumming hoofs sounded in the roadway outside. Through the window of the Busy Bee Pete saw a rider in cowpuncher togs flash past on a sweat-lathered pony. The puncher looked as though he'd been riding hard and fast. He didn't remain long in Pete's mind; Pete's eyes were concentrated on those swinging doors leading to the kitchen; he was growing more impatient every minute.

His waiting was rewarded at last; the girl with the blond hair pushed her way through the swinging doors, bearing a tray heaped with steaming platters of food. This she placed before Pete on the counter and invited him to "Pitch in, cowboy."

The food was good and there was plenty of it. The coffee was strong and hot. The girl reached to a back shelf and procured a bowl of sugar which she placed on the counter close to Pete's hand. Pete grinned and started to help himself to the sugar. "Last thing I'd figure was needed around here," he said boldly.

"Salt might be more appropriate," the girl retorted, though Pete could see she wasn't angry.

"There seems to be plenty of pepper." Pete laughed. "Gosh, this food is good. I've a notion to start a restaurant, myself, if I could get a cook like you. Or maybe I wouldn't need to open a restaurant. Have you ever considered leaving?"

The girl nodded. "I'm leaving tonight."

"Giving up your business?" Pete asked, surprised.

"It's not my business. I'm just substituting for the regular girl while she's away on her honeymoon. She married the man who owns the place, Sam Birch. She's a friend of mine, and when she and Sam asked me to help keep the business running I took the job. They'll be home on the Limited tonight."

"And then what will you do?" Pete paused. "I hope you don't think I'm inquisitive. I don't mean it that way."

"Of course not," the girl said dryly. "Well, when I get through tonight I'll go back to the ranch with Dad. We run the C-Bar-A twelve miles west of here."

"I had a hunch you were real cow-country stuff, Miss Abbott."

"What gave you the idea my name was Abbott?"

"Didn't think it was." Pete smiled. "Only I figured it started with *A*, and the only thing to do was go right through the alphabet until I struck the right name."

"Persistent, aren't you?" The girl's smile matched Pete's. "I don't know as I'd want to wait around while you went through the alphabet."

"There's quicker methods," Pete suggested hopefully. "Course I could go on guessing, if you refuse to help me out. Let me see, there's Adams and Adair and Abercrombie and —Say, your name wouldn't be Alexander, would it?" Mentally he congratulated himself on having gathered previously information regarding cattlemen in this district.

"It would—and is." The girl eyed him suspiciously. "How did you know?"

"Hit on it by chance, that's all, Miss Alexander," Pete said blandly. "Let's see C-Bar-A. Of course the *C* would stand for your father's name."

"It would—and mine as well."

"Caroline, Catherine, Cecila, Cathleen—ring a bell when I

18

make a bull's-eye, will you—Chloe, Clara, Clarabel, Clementine, Constance, Cora, Cynthia——" Pete paused to catch his breath.

"You seem to be much better acquainted with girls' names than surnames," Miss Alexander interposed. "It smacks of a wide experience, Mr. Piper."

"Pure chance," Pete said glibly. "When I was a monitor in school I had charge of the *C* records. Let's see, there's Carmen, Camilla, Carlotta, Clarissa——"

"It must have been a school for girls," Miss Alexander put in. "I'll reward your curiosity because you'd never guess it in a hundred years. It's Cressida."

"Cressida! Wait! Shakespeare wrote a book about a girl named Cressida. She was a beautiful Trojan girl. Lady, you're well named. Bet your friends call you Cressy, though."

"They do." The girl laughed.

"Cressy Alexander," Pete said dreamily. "It all fits."

"What does?"

"Had my fortune told a spell back," Pete explained, chewing vigorously on potatoes and steak to avoid the girl's gaze. "This fortune teller allowed as I'd shortly meet up with a beautiful maiden who was quitting her job in a restaurant and that I would accompany her home the night she left. Can you imagine anyone hitting it right on the nose this way?"

"I certainly can't," Cressy said flatly. "Go back and tell your fortune teller he—or she—has made a very bad guess."

"Aw, Cressy—" Pete protested.

"'I said my *friends* call me Cressy. You haven't been here long enough——"

"I'm never going to leave though. Look, can you imagine me living here the rest of my days and going around with a long white beard when I'm an old man and meeting you on the street and saying, 'Good morning, Miss Alexander'? No, you can't! Anyway, by that time you'd be 'Mrs.' In fact, I don't know what's wrong with a town that lets you stay 'Miss.' And I always thought the only pretty girls in Western towns were the schoolma'ams."

"Probably an idea you picked up when you were a monitor in school," Cressy said dryly.

"But you won't let me see you home tonight?"

"I certainly won't."

"God gave all the hard hearts to women," Pete said in melancholy tones. "There's nothing so discouraging——"

He had no time to say more. A couple of men customers entered and found stools farther along the counter. Cressy went to serve them. Apparently they were friends, for the girl stood talking to them and answering questions relative to the C-Bar-A Ranch.

Pete finished his dinner in silence. He had no further opportunity to talk to the girl until it came time to pay for his meal, and one of the customers called her away an instant later.

Pete rose from his stool and started toward the door, vowing he'd make the next opportunity to see Cressy Alexander. The girl had just finished setting second cups of coffee before her customers and was gazing after Pete's broad shoulders as they moved toward the restaurant door. Suddenly she noticed for the first time the red quirt dangling from Pete's left wrist. For an instant the color left her cheeks; then her lips compressed firmly, parted again.

"Mr. Piper! Pete!" she called. "Wait a moment, please."

5   "Get That Quirt!"

TURK RAVEN'S SALOON didn't have a bad name, though it was the sort of place that didn't get the better class of business in Beauregard City. Traxler's Diamond-T men brought Raven their custom, which fact may have confirmed certain suspicions in Sheriff Perkins' mind. Aside from the Diamond-T, no one brought his trade regularly to Raven. Transients stopped on the way through, occasionally cowboys from other ranches dropped in for a drink if they happened to be in the vicinity of the saloon and the weather was too hot to walk another block or cross the street to the hotel bar, which charged a nickel extra on all drinks except beer.

At the present moment Raven was behind the bar, serving eight or ten customers on the opposite side of the mahogany. Raven himself was a small man with oily features, furtive eyes, and slicked-down black hair. His saloon was typical of its kind: a long bar, a few tables and chairs, pictures of race horses, burlesque actresses, and prize fighters on its walls; light entered, during the daytime, through a window at the rear and above and below the head-high swinging doors at the entrance.

Foremost among the customers at the bar was Black Nick Traxler, a swarthy-complexioned individual with beady black eyes, thin lips, and high cheekbones. He was well built, with wide shoulders and narrow hips. He wore a black sateen shirt, Oregon breeches tucked into boot tops. A rolled brim sombrero was shoved back on a head of curling ebony locks. He carried a well-worn six-shooter low on his right thigh. There was a certain animal magnetism about the man; when he turned at the bar to request another drink from Raven his voice was soft with a definite purring tone.

With Traxler were three of his men, Nevada Norton, Canary Sloan, and Ducky Drake. Drake was of medium height, in puncher togs, with a barrel-like torso. Canary Sloan had yellow hair and a chirping voice. In addition, Canary prided himself on singing sentimental songs in a wheezy tenor; Canary was the only one who took any pride in this accomplishment. Nevada Norton was the most important of the three: Nevada possessed a reputation as a two-gun man, though he was packing only one weapon at present, the butt of which carried several notches. Nevada was thin to the point of emaciation, his eyes were pale blue. He claimed to be a cowpuncher, but no one, not even his employer, had ever witnessed his engagement in such work. There were rumors of bank robbery and stage holdups attached to his name, but that was something else on which Sheriff Perkins had been unable to get proof.

The remaining customers were a miscellaneous lot: a puncher from the Ladder-D Ranch, another one from the Rafter-H, a whisky salesman who hoped to sell Turk Raven a bill of goods; the rest were citizens of Beauregard.

The Ladder-D cowboy, who was known as Bucky Billings, had been the last to enter. He had his drink, then spoke to the room at large. "Anybody heard anything of a killing over near Elephant Ridge?"

Nobody had, it appeared. Black Nick Traxler and Nevada Norton turned toward the speaker, but neither said anything. Turk Raven asked, "Where'd you hear that, Bucky?"

"I saw Homer Pritchard and Doc Gillett leaving town in a wagon a spell back. Asked where they were heading, thinking they might be aiming to pick up a corpse. Homer said a dead man had been found over near Elephant Ridge."

"Murdered or natural demise?" asked the Rafter-H puncher.

Billings shook his head. "You got me. Homer didn't have time to give details."

Raven said with grim humor, "Probably a killing. This climate is too good for anybody to die a natural death. Any of you Diamond-T hombres settled any old scores lately?" He grinned oilily.

Nick Traxler eyed Raven coldly. "That," he stated softly, "is distinctly not funny, Turk." The quiet words seemed to carry a threat.

"Sure, sure, Nick," Raven said quickly. "I didn't mean anything. You know me." His complexion turned sallow.

"Yes, I know you," Traxler said flatly.

Silence fell over the room for a few moments, broken only by the clink of bottles against glasses. Traxler said, "Let me have a cigar, Turk."

Raven quickly reached to his back bar and shoved a box across to Traxler. Traxler reached in, drew out a long, thin black cigar, bit off one end, and scratched a match. He blew out a long puff of gray smoke, then said in frigid accents, "I don't know why it is, but every time there's any crime hereabouts somebody mentions the Diamond-T. I don't like it.

Nevada Norton nodded. "There's only one way to shut up hombres that run off at the head that-a-way. An ounce of lead in the right place——"

"Hush up, Nevada," Traxler interrupted. "We're not doing any threatening of anybody. I was just stating a fact. There's a large number of people in Trabadura County, and the Diamond-T makes only a mighty small percentage of that number. It's time folks looked other places besides the Diamond-T."

Bucky Billings said a bit nervously, "That's so, Nick. Matter of fact, I saw a stranger ride up to the hotel just as I was riding in to get the mail."

Traxler said, "What sort of a stranger?"

Billings was vague. "Oh, I don't know. Redhead. Cowcountry stuff, judging from his legs which had been broncmolded. Probably wouldn't have noticed him, a-tall, 'cepting for the quirt he toted."

"Is that so?" Traxler's eyes had narrowed a trifle. "What sort of a quirt was it?"

"Red. Bright red," Billings replied. "That's what caught my eye——"

Nevada Norton said quickly, "Did you say this stranger was over to the hotel?"

"Will you hush up?" Traxler said sharply. "Nevada, there's no reason for us to be interested in this stranger just because he has a red quirt. They're plentiful. I remember there was some talk about Hugh Alexander carrying one before he was murdered. That was a dirty job. I just wish they could catch the hombre that did it."

Hoofs drummed in the street and stopped before the saloon. Running steps clumped across the sidewalk. A man burst abruptly into the barroom. He was slim and somewhat dandified in appearance. In many respects he resembled his brother, Black Nick Traxler, though his characteristics were weak, mentally and physically, where Nick's were strong. He wore a ring on either hand, there was a beaded Indian band about the crown of his fawn-colored sombrero. His six-shooter, in its hand-tooled holster, had mother-of-pearl stocks. The neckerchief at his throat was of bright blue silk.

Nick Traxler spoke sharply: "What's up, Ivan?"

Ivan Traxler's face filled with relief at the sight of his brother. "God! I'm glad to find you here, Nick," he panted. "I nigh killed a bronc——"

"Hush it up!" Nick snapped. "Cool down before you start spilling things. Now what's on your mind?"

He drew his brother off to one side of the room. Nevada Norton followed the two. Words tumbled frantically from Ivan

Traxler's lips. "I rode clear to the ranch. You weren't there—"

"Dammit!" Nick Traxler snarled. "Don't talk so loud!"

Thus admonished, Ivan lowered his voice. A frown gathered on Nick's face while he listened. Nevada's features took on a bleak aspect. Finally Nick said disgustedly, "You're a couple of fools. Where's Luke now?"

"He stayed home. His head ached."

Nevada Norton grunted disgustedly. "His head ached. Ain't that sad! By Geez! If he was my brother I'd make his head ache!"

Traxler said testily, "I ain't asking your advice, Nevada." He glanced toward Canary Sloan and Ducky Drake. "You boys better run along to the ranch now." They nodded and left the barroom. Nick turned back to Ivan. "Dammit! I don't see how that redhead found it when you two couldn't."

"It's a mystery to us," Ivan said earnestly. "I would have stayed and taken it away from him, but Luke insisted on leaving."

"Don't lie to me," Traxler said harshly. "You're both yellow! But we've got to get that quirt. Ivan, that redhead is in town now some place. You go locate him, then come back and tell me. Just do as I tell you. He was at the hotel. You can trace him from there. Now get going!"

6   "You're Covered, Redhead!"

PETE had already emerged from the Busy Bee when he heard Cressy Alexander call to him. He turned back as the girl quickly rounded the counter end and motioned him to wait where he was. She joined him outside, closing the door behind her.

"Change your mind about me seeing you home tonight?" Pete commenced. "That's mighty——" He stopped, noting her tense features and excited manner. "Why, what's up, Cressy?"

"Where did you get that red quirt?" the girl asked sharply.

Pete studied her agitated features in perplexity. "Why—what's wrong, Cressy?"

"That quirt! Where did you get it?"

"I—well, I found it. Why?"

"My brother owned one exactly like it. He—it—well, it disappeared. May I examine yours?"

"Help yourself." Quietly Pete slipped the wrist loop over his hand and handed the quirt to the girl. Cressy examined it minutely, eagerly; then disappointment crept into her face.

"I'm sorry, Pete," she said tiredly. "I guess I just jumped to conclusions. You see, my brother had a habit of putting his initials on everything he owned. I'd hoped to find——Well, when you said you found this quirt——It's all very foolish of me, isn't it?" She held the quirt out to him.

Pete slipped the red quirt back on his left wrist. "No, I don't know as it's foolish," he said slowly. "I don't think anything you'd do would be foolish. If you'd like to keep this—— No, I'd better not say that. I'll have to keep it for a while."

Cressy smiled faintly. "I'd completely overlooked the fact there could be two quirts, both the same. . ."

While they stood there, before the Busy Bee, Ivan Traxler had approached along the sidewalk. Ivan had gone first to the hotel as his brother Nick had suggested. From the hotel clerk he had learned that the redheaded stranger was probably at the Busy Bee Restaurant. Not being any too anxious to contact Pete, Ivan had dropped into the hotel bar for a couple of drinks before proceeding farther, excusing his delayed search on the ground that the dust from his long ride was affecting his throat, thus necessitating a thorough sluicing of that portion of his anatomy. Finally he had reluctantly continued his journey to the Busy Bee, arriving there just as Cressy Alexander was returning the quirt to Pete. He heard Cressy say, ". . . and I so hoped I could get the quirt that belonged to Hugh. . . ."

Instantly Ivan jumped into the conversation. "Hi-yuh, Cressy! This stranger got a quirt you want?"

Cressy glanced around. "Oh, it's you, Mr. Traxler. No, this is nothing that concerns you," shortly.

"Maybe it does, though," Ivan persisted. "If you want that quirt I reckon this stranger would be willing to sell it."

Pete had waited in silence. When Cressy made no attempt to introduce him he judged that this Traxler wasn't popular with the girl. She merely said tartly, "This doesn't concern you at all."

"Anything that concerns you concerns me," Ivan Traxler said, leering. "I admire your judgment, Cressy. It's a right nice quirt. If you don't want it I do. Maybe you'll change your mind later. How about it, redhead? What you asking for your quirt?"

"It's not for sale," Pete said quietly.

"Might as well put a price on it," Ivan insisted. "What us Traxlers want we get. Ain't that so, Cressy?"

"Miss Alexander to you, Mr. Traxler," the girl snapped. "And please move on. This is none of your affair."

"Maybe I'll make it my affair." An ugly tone had crept into Ivan's voice.

Pete said, steely-toned, "You heard Miss Alexander, Traxler. Move on. Get! Vamoose!"

Traxler pushed between the girl and Pete. "I ain't leaving without that quirt. I plumb admire it. Either you put a price on it, redhead, or I'll take it away from you and set my own price. Now think fast! What you aiming to do?"

"If you don't move on, Traxler," Pete warned softly, "I'll *give* you this quirt—but it will remain in my hand when I do."

"Oh, pretty hard hombre, ain't you?" Ivan sneered. Thrown off guard by Pete's quiet manner, he became overbold. "Dammit to hell! Give me that quirt. I'm telling you——!"

Without finishing his words he reached out one hand and tried to jerk the quirt from Pete's wrist. Involuntarily Pete's left arm came up. It was the most natural thing in the world for his hand to knot into a fist—a fist that ended solidly on Ivan Traxler's jaw.

Traxler staggered back across the sidewalk, tripped on his own spurs, and landed in a sprawling heap beneath the hitch rack at the edge of the roadway.

Behind him Pete heard Cressy's sudden wail of distress: "Oh, Pete, now you're in for it! Those Traxlers——"

"I'm not worrying about the whole Traxler crew," Pete said grimly. "Just as soon as this scut regains a couple of his few senses he's going to apologize for his language." He moved out toward the hitch rack.

Along the street ran cries of "Fight! Fight!" Men came running to gather into a crowd before the Busy Bee. Somebody yelled, "It's Ivan Traxler. Betcha there'll be some fur flying before long!"

By this time Ivan had grunted and slowly come to a sitting position. His eyes were vague, almost glassy. He shook his head violently, one hand tenderly fingering his jaw. Gradually his head cleared, and he raised an uncertain gaze to encounter Pete's grinning countenance.

A snarl of hate was torn from Ivan's throat as he scrambled up, right hand reaching to his six-shooter. Pete took one swift step forward. His left hand raised, flashed down, and the twin lashes of the crimson quirt slashed cruelly across Ivan's gun hand. With a sudden howl of rage Ivan released the grip on his gun and staggered back against the hitch rack, both arms lifting in the air now. A sudden laugh went up from the men crowding around.

"I could have shot you, Traxler," Pete said quietly. "Just remember that next time you reach for your shooting iron."

Ivan stood there, face white, blood trickling from his slashed hand. "I—I—I—" he stammered, then swallowed hard.

Behind him Pete heard Cressy's frightened warning: "Look out, Pete!"

Before he could turn Pete felt something round and hard jabbed against his backbone. He heard Black Nick Traxler's cold voice: "Raise 'em, feller. Nobody hits a Traxler and gets away with it. Raise 'em fast."

Pete stiffened, started to raise his arms. He felt the gun at his back move away. What happened next was too fast for

Nick Traxler's comprehension. Pete's right arm came around fast as he whirled to face Nick Traxler. The arm knocked Traxler's gun to one side, and Traxler was spun half around, almost off balance. By the time he righted himself Nick Traxler found himself looking into Pete's gun muzzle. A sudden yell went up from the crowd.

"Better do some reaching yourself, mister," Pete snapped.

Nick Traxler's swarthy features went white with mingled astonishment and anger; then something of grudging admiration entered his face. He said quietly, almost too quietly, raising his arms in the air, "That was neat, hombre. But there's more to it, than just this——"

Another voice snarled from Pete's rear, Nevada Norton's voice: "Claw for the clouds, redhead. You're covered complete. And I'm out of reach of your tricky ways. Raise 'em, pronto!"

Nick Traxler laughed coldly. "I warned you, mister, there was more coming. Nevada! Plug him if he moves even an eyelash!"

7 The Tables Turned

SLOWLY, gun still in hand, Pete lifted his arms. Black Nick Traxler nodded. "That's more like it, redhead. Keep him covered, Nevada, I'm aiming to get that red quirt that's caused so much rumpus. I wouldn't want it to cause more trouble."

"Don't touch this quirt," Pete warned grimly, trying to bluff his way out of the situation, "or I'll pull another trick that will make the other look like child's play."

"That don't work, hombre." Traxler laughed softly. "You won't be pulling any more tricks while Nevada's got his gun on you. Nobody ever bucks the Traxlers and makes it stick. We always come out on top. Nevada, keep him covered. Shoot at the first move!"

The crowd had backed away a trifle, half expecting bullets to fly when Traxler started to get the red quirt.

Ivan Traxler jeered, "You tell him, Nick. Nobody beats us Traxlers. Get his gun at the same time you get the quirt. I aim to teach this hombre a lesson. He got me off guard once, but——"

A slim form in checked gingham darted from the rim of the crowd, pushed Ivan Traxler to one side, and seized the six-shooter from Ivan's holster. The next instant the muzzle of that six-shooter was jabbed hard against Nick Traxler's spine.

"Hold it, Mr. Traxler," came Cressy Alexander's cool tones. "Call off your gunman or I'll pull this trigger just as sure as grass grows fresh in the springtime. Make it fast!"

"Good girl, Cressy!" Pete exclaimed.

Nevada Norton spat an oath and looked uncertain. Nick

Traxler stiffened, a dull red flush creeping into his high cheekbones. However, when he spoke his voice was steady enough: "Do what she orders, Nevada. She means what she says."

With an exclamation of baffled rage Ivan Traxler leaped toward the girl, but she was to quick for him. Momentarily the gun muzzle left Black Nick's spine to swing toward Ivan. Ivan halted in his tracks. Cressy again swung the gun back on Nick. Nevada, meantime, had lowered her own gun. Laughing, Pete leaped to Cressy's side, his six-shooter now covering Nevada and the two Traxlers.

"This is more like it," Pete chuckled. "Now if you hombres want to continue from here, just say the word——"

"Break it up!" came a sudden command. Sheriff Perkins pushed through the crowd. "Hey! What's going on here? Why, Cressy Alexander! Since when have you gone in for gun toting? Piper, put that hawg-laig away. There'll be no shooting while I'm here. You Diamond-T hombres take warning—keep your mitts away from your irons. You hear me!"

Laughter and cheers rose from the crowd. A man yelled, "Two Traxlers and Norton licked by a girl and a redheaded stranger!"

Sheriff Perkins raised his voice. "Keep quiet, all of you, until I get the straight of this. Cressy, you seem to know what's going on. You tell it."

Cressy's cheeks were pink while she talked. "There's not much to tell, Sheriff Perkins. Everything happened so fast. I had asked to see this red quirt Mr. Piper is carrying. While we were talking Ivan Traxler butted in on our conversation. He became pretty insulting, and Mr. Piper knocked him down. Then he tried to pull his gun and Mr. Piper slashed him across the wrist with the quirt——"

One of the crowd yelled out: "Piper had a right to shoot him. Ivan was going for his gun."

"Hush it!" Perkins snapped. "Cressy is telling this."

"Then," Cressy continued, "Nick Traxler came running and stuck his gun in Mr. Piper's back. Pete—Mr. Piper got the drop on Nick Traxler——"

"Wait a minute, wait a minute." The sheriff frowned. "You say that Pete got the drop on Nick after Nick had him covered. You're getting mixed up, Cressy."

Cries of protest went up from the crowd: "No, she ain't!"

Perkins' frown deepened. "I'm damn—danged if I understand how Pete could do that."

Pete grinned. "I took him by surprise, Sheriff. It was just a dirty, low-down trick. Anyway, that's what Traxler figures, I reckon."

"But I don't see how——" Perkins commenced.

"Take it for granted he did it," Nick Traxler cut in. "I'm admitting it, Sheriff."

Perkins nodded and said, "Get on, Cressy."

"Then," Cressy resumed, "Nevada Norton pulled his gun on Pete. I guess I got rather excited, because before I realized what I was doing I'd taken Ivan Traxler's gun and covered Mr. Norton. And then—and then you arrived." She looked with sudden distaste on Ivan's pearl-butted six-shooter still in her hand and handed it to the sheriff. Perkins tossed it to Ivan, who stuck it into his holster. "You see," the girl went on, "in a way the whole mix-up was my fault. I guess that's why I got into it."

"Just a moment, Miss Alexander," Nick Traxler said silkily. "I'm sorry this all happened. You see, I didn't know how it was. Now that we've heard your story I can realize my brother was to blame. Ivan, you've been drinking. You fool! Go back & wait for me at Turk's. I've got a few things to say to you. Get!"

Ivan slunk away like a whipped puppy. Nick Traxler continued, "Piper, I reckon I owe you an apology too. I made the mistake of jumping to conclusions." He held out one hand.

Pete shook hands. "Forget it," he said lightly.

Nick Traxler smiled thinly. "I'm not likely to forget the hombre who got the drop on me after I had him covered. I don't think you could do it again. But I'll remember it."

"Probably I couldn't," Pete replied carelessly, sensing the hidden threat in the man's smooth tones. "Howsomever, I'll be more on my guard hereafter. I wasn't figuring you'd have to take up your brother's scrap, nor that Norton would have to take up yours. Mostly, out in this country, men—real men, that is—do their own jobs——"

"Look here, you," Nevada Norton rasped. "If you're hinting that I can't handle anything that——"

"Hush up, Nevada." Traxler said sharply. "A girl put you out of the running a spell back, so you'd better not brag. Which reminds me, I must apologize to Miss Alexander for my brother's misdeeds."

But Cressy had already returned to the restaurant. Traxler spoke to Pete: "It's been a small misunderstanding all around, Piper. What say we have a drink and forget the matter?"

"It's forgotten as far as I'm concerned," Pete said lightly. "Thanks, no, I'm not drinking right now."

"Some other time then—if you're intending to stay in Beauregard," Traxler suggested quietly.

"I'll be staying all right." Pete nodded.

"I'm glad to hear that," Traxler said, small pin points of anger burning in his beady eyes. "Yes, I'll be seeing you again, Piper. . . . Come on, Nevada."

The two men pushed through the crowd which, at the sheriff's orders, started to break up and scatter along the street. Two or three men announced they were going to have cups of coffee and headed inside the Busy Bee to talk to Cressy and pay her further compliments. A few showed signs of staying near Pete and the sheriff, but at a word from Perkins they moved on.

The sheriff gave a long sigh and, removing his sombrero, mopped his glistening brow with his bandanna. "Every time there's a mix-up with Black Nick Traxler," he said earnestly, "I get to wondering why I don't give up law enforcement and buy me a nice little chicken ranch someplace. You don't seem to realize it, Pete, but those Traxlers are heap bad medicine."

"Haven't seen anything to bother me yet," Pete returned quietly. "Course, if Cressy hadn't jumped in when she did, I'd have been in a mighty tough spot. Sheriff, she's one peach of a girl."

Perkins looked at him scornfully. "Suffering bullfrogs! You'd think that thought was original with you. Cripes! Half the men in town want to marry Cressy Alexander, and there's another big percentage that have been thinking about divorce the past few years." He smiled wearily. "Not that it's as bad as that, of course, but you'll get the idea when I say she's plumb popular. Her father is A-1 too. So was her brother Hugh. Hugh was found killed out on the range about eight months back. That's another thing I never did clear up."

"Cressy mentioned that he was dead when we were talking about my quirt." Pete nodded. "I didn't know it was murder——"

"Say, that quirt of yours caused plenty trouble. Where'd you get it, anyway?"

"Found it," Pete returned noncommittally.

The sheriff waited for Pete to say where. Pete didn't give any details. The sheriff looked queerly at him but didn't further pursue the subject. Instead, "I'm still wondering, Pete, just how you managed to get the drop on Nick Traxler after he had you covered from behind. It don't seem reasonable— especially with Traxler."

Pete smiled. "It's a trick, Sheriff, one that has come handy on a couple of other occasions. I learned it from a man who always claimed it wasn't necessary to carry firearms for self-defense. He was a wrestler and knew more holds than anybody I ever saw; claimed he could disarm anybody with just the use of his hands alone. I reckon he could too. At present he's instructing a bunch of peace officers in his methods——"

"But Nick Traxler——" Perkins commenced unbelievingly.

"I caught Traxler by surprise, that's all. When I started to put my arms up I felt his gun withdrawn from my back. I knew he'd relaxed, then, figuring he was going to have everything his own way. He probably even let his hammer down, if he ever had it drawn back. I half stooped and whirled, my right arm knocking his gun arm to one side. That threw him off balance. By the time he'd recovered I had my gun out. I'll show you how to do it sometime."

Perkins shook his head. "It's a good trick to know all right, but, boy, you sure took chances."

"I had to." Pete grinned. "I'll never work that trick in this town again. Howsomever, maybe it won't be necessary."

"Let's hope not," Perkins said fervently. "It makes my throat all parched just to think about it. Let's drift into Beanpole Ridge's bar and sluice down. It's just next door."

"Thanks, no. I want to see Cressy as soon as those fellers leave in there. There'd probably be a crowd in the bar, all wanting me to explain how I got the drop on Traxler too. I never would get away."

Perkins laughed. "Sure, I understand, Pete. You have to catch 'em while they're young. Whisky is the only thing I know of that improves with age. If I was a mite younger, myself . . . Anyway, I know how it is. I'll see you later."

He left the hitch rack and turned into the saloon next door.

Pete hung around the front of the Busy Bee until the last customer had left, then entered. Cressy was waiting behind the counter, looking a trifle pale, but smiling.

"Maybe this Busy Bee place is appropriately named," she said.

"The queen bee is the busiest of the bunch"—Pete grinned—"for which I'm plumb thankful. I reckon you saved my life, Cressy. Now you have got a problem."

"In what way?"

Pete explained. "I owe you my life. What do you aim to do with it?"

"Give it back to you." The girl smiled.

Pete shook his head. "No sirree! You can't do that. It's against the rules. Cressy, you're a peach! Just the sort of a girl I've been looking for all my life——"

"Hush, Pete"—placing one finger to her lips—"the cook just came in the back way. Oh, Pete, I was scared, really. And it was all my fault. If I hadn't followed you out and asked to see your quirt——"

"Yes sirree." Pete turned suddenly belligerent. "You certainly got me into a fine mess. I don't see how you've got the nerve to stand there and think a few words will fix it up."

"But, Pete," Cressy protested, startled, "things just happen like that sometimes. I admit it was my fault, but there's no need of you taking that attitude." She stiffened angrily. "All right, I'm to blame. What do you want me to do now to square myself, Mr. Piper?"

Pete grinned suddenly. "That's more like it. Let me see you home tonight and your debt's squared."

"Persistent, aren't you?" Cressy smiled.

Pete nodded. "It's my middle name—Peter Persistent Piper." His voice took on a pleading tone. "Look, Cressy, we've been through fire together today——"

"I don't remember that part."

"Aw, you know what I mean. We clicked together like clockwork. Teamwork, that's us. You can't break up a combination like that. Besides, I've got to see your father on important business."

"You have?" Her eyes widened. "You don't even know him. What business could you have——?"

"The most important business in the world. Important to him too. The sooner he knows me, the better off we'll both be. A parent should know a man a long time before he consents to his daughter's marriage."

"Pete! You're going pretty fast, aren't you?"

"Yeah," Pete admitted brazenly. "I've got to make up for all these past years when you didn't know me."

The girl smiled scornfully. "I wonder if I missed much."

"You'll be surprised," Pete said confidently. "Look, I'm an impatient man: do I take you home or don't I?"

Cressy suddenly surrendered. "All right," she consented, professing weariness. "It's easier to give in than stand here arguing."

"Good!" Pete said eagerly. "Do I come here for you, or—?"

"Sam Birch and his wife will get in on the Limited around five-thirty. I'll meet you at the Beauregard Livery at six. Dad knows I'll be home tonight, so he and the boys will be waiting supper for me. We should make the ranch by eight or a little before. Is that all right?"

"Anything you say is all right," Pete said joyfully. "I'll have a rig all hired and ready to go. I'll get a fast-stepping team——"

"Mr. Piper, please!" Cressy protested. "Do I look too delicate to ride a bronc? My pony's at the livery."

"Better and better," Pete exclaimed. "Say, let me have a cup of coffee while I'm waiting."

"I'll do nothing of the sort. Go away from here. You bother me. I've got a lot to do. There's things to tell the cook and—well, I want things shipshape when Sam and his wife get in. On your way, cowboy."

Reluctantly Pete started to leave. "The minutes will sure drag until I see you again," he said sadly.

"Try to live through it," Cressy said heartlessly. "I'm looking forward to complete peace of mind for the next hour and a half."

"Better make the most of it then." Pete grinned as he paused in the doorway. "From now on things are going to move plumb lively!"

8   Holdup!

AT A QUARTER TO SIX Pete waited with his saddled horse before the hitch rack of the Beauregard Livery. He had also arranged to have Cressy's pony, a small buckskin, saddled and ready with his own, despite the skeptical glances of the livery-stable man.

The sun was dipping toward the distant peaks of the Trabadura Range, touching them with spots of golden light and making deep purple shadows in the draws and hollows. The town was quieter at this time: citizens, with their day's work done, were hurrying home to supper or dropping into the various saloons for the evening's appetizer. Pete waited, impatiently slapping the lashes of the crimson quirt, looped on his wrist, against his left boot top, his eyes intent on a point diagonally across the street where the Busy Bee Restaurant was located.

Once or twice he glanced east along Main Street toward Turk Raven's Saloon, and each time he saw a man standing on the porch, looking in his direction. After a time the man disappeared in the barroom; then Ivan Traxler came out and glanced toward Pete. Next, Ivan, too, disappeared, to be replaced by Nick Traxler. Black Nick nodded shortly to Pete, then withdrew inside the saloon.

Pete frowned. "Are those hombres keeping a watch on me or do I just imagine it?" he pondered.

While he was thinking over the question Ivan Traxler again emerged from the saloon, went to the hitch rail, and climbed into the saddle of his waiting horse. Turning the horse, he headed west along Main Street, then turned north at the first corner, where Tonto Street intersected Main. As he passed Pete he kept his face straight ahead. Pete was inclined to say something to him but felt he'd better let the matter drop. Once out of Pete's sight Ivan started his pony on a dead run for the Diamond-T.

Nothing more was to be seen of Nick Traxler, so Pete again bent his attention toward the Busy Bee Restaurant. The rumble of a wagon sounded in his ears, drawing his attention. He glanced along Main Street. A wagon, with Deputy Sheriff Homer Pritchard and another man on the driver's seat, was approaching, from east of town. Homer spied Pete as he drew abreast and pulled to a halt before the hotel. Pete made his way across the street. In the bed of the wagon was the walnut-framed rocking chair, and stretched beside it was a stiff blanket-covered figure.

"We got 'im," Homer announced. "Pete, shake hands with Dr. Gillett, Doc, this is Pete Piper, who found the body."

Pete shook hands. Dr. Gillett was a spare man with graying hair, dressed in citizens' clothing, boots, and a wide-brimmed sombrero. He said to Pete, "I certainly thought Homer was running a whizzer on me when he said the corpse was found seated in a rocker. Dangedest thing I ever saw. How do you figure it?"

"I don't." Pete shook his head. "Were those three buzzards still hanging around?"

"Yeah"—Homer nodded—"with some more of their relatives. Lucky that blanket didn't blow off. Oh, say, Doc will want you to testify at the inquest tomorrow mornin'. You'll be here, won't you?"

Pete grinned. "I don't think I'm ever going to leave this neck of the range."

"Glad to hear you like our country," Dr. Gillett said.

Homer was studying Pete suspiciously. "If you wait until we take this body around to the doc's I'll buy a drink, Pete. Then we can eat supper together."

"Thanks, but no can do, Homer. I've got important business to attend. We'll make it some other time."

Homer looked steadily at Pete. "Say, how come you got important business already? You haven't been in town a whole day yet. What's been happenin'? Any excitement in town while I was away?"

"Quietest day in a month of Sundays. Of course," Pete said modestly, "there was a little run-in with the Traxlers, but after I'd thrown the drop on Black Nick and a friend of mine had pointed a gun at a hoodlum named Norton, everything quieted down."

"T'hell you say!" Homer's eyes widened; then he started to laugh. "Cripes! I thought you meant that for a moment. But you got somethin' on your mind all right. You haven't even asked if we know that corpse you discovered."

"Do you?"

"It's old Tiger-Eye Munson, one of Traxler's crew. So this is one time we can't blame the Diamond-T outfit. But that rockin' chair is sure enough queer——" He broke off suddenly. "That's your horse in front of the Beauregard Livery, ain't it?"

"That's my pony."

"Sure looks like Cressy Alexander's little buckskin standin' alongside your bronc. Say—you son of a gun"—Homer's eyes bugged out—"you waitin' for Cressy?"

"Not any longer, I'm not." Pete laughed. He had just seen the girl leaving the Busy Bee. "I'm on my way, Homer. See you at the inquest tomorrow."

Homer gazed after his retreating form admiringly. "Fast worker, that redheaded galoot. Here I've been tryin' for five years to take Cressy Alexander ridin', and that hombre makes the grade his first day. There ain't no justice in the world, Doc. Let's get along and deliver this stiff on your doorstep. Giddap, team!"

Pete had cut across Tonto Street to meet Cressy. He looked admiringly at her. The girl had changed to denim overalls, riding boots, and a mannish flannel shirt. Her pale gold hair was neatly tucked up beneath a wide-brimmed tan sombrero. A dark blue neckerchief was knotted at her throat.

Pete greeted her admiringly: "Lady, you look like you could ride."

"Hi-yuh, Pete! Shucks, I could ride before I walked, or so Dad tells me. Golly, it feels good to get back into denims again."

They headed across the street toward the ponies waiting at the hitch rack. "I see you got Buckskin saddled for me," Cressey commented.

Pete nodded. "I had a tough time convincing that livery hombre, though. He acted like you never go riding with fellers."

"I guess I don't, very much," Cressy said a trifle wistfully. "Since Mother died I've stuck pretty close to Dad. We usually take rides together."

"Say, haven't you any dunnage to go back?"

"My trunk's at Mrs. Fogarty's boardinghouse. I'll have to send in a wagon."

"I suppose the bride and groom returned. Heard the Limited arrive a spell back."

Cressy nodded, laughing. "They've got an argument boiling already. Sam's wife wants to open a more elegant restaurant. I guess Cora picked up some ideas on her honeymoon."

"Brides usually do," Pete said dryly. "That is"—blushing hotly beneath his tan—"they get around and see how other towns live and—and so on."

"Cora surely did." Cressy laughed. "Some place she and Sam stayed, they served salads for dinner. Can you imagine the Busy Bee serving salads to Beauregard City?"

"I ate one once," Pete said reminiscently. "Lot of grass and other green stuff. If it hadn't been for the oil and vinegar they poured on I'd sure thought I had been turned out to pasture."

They reached the horses, mounted, and turned west along Main Street. A number of people passing spoke to Cressy and turned to stare after her and her companion. The sun was just dropping below the lower ridges of the Trabaduras by this time. The horses' hoofs thumped hollowly on a plank bridge over a wide, shallow stream just outside of town and turned slightly to the northwest on a well-worn, wheel-rutted trail.

"What river is that?" Pete asked.

"Rio Torvo—south fork of the Rio Torvo, to be exact," Cressy corrected herself.

The horses moved into a lope. The stirrups of the two riders were almost touching. "Quite a creek," Pete commented. "Does it cross C-Bar-A holdings?"

Cressy nodded. "We've plenty of water, thank goodness. It wasn't always that way, though. You see, the Rio Torvo heads up in the Trabaduras. The north fork cuts through Traxler's Diamond-T; the south fork crosses our property. At one time the south fork was much smaller—until Traxler's dynamite job—"

"Dynamite job?"

"I'll have to explain. Traxler did some dynamiting up where the river heads. Dad and I always felt that Traxler was trying to divert all the water to his fork. Anyway, something went wrong; I don't know what. Maybe inexperience in handling dynamite had something to do with it. When the blast went off it started a landslide that nearly blocked the north fork of the stream. Ever since, we've been getting most of the water, while the north fork runs dry some summers."

"That's a good joke on Traxler." Pete grinned. "Did he have any explanation to make?"

"Said he was prospecting for gold and all his dynamite went off through an accident. Of course we didn't believe him, but we didn't say anything. After all, we were the gainers."

It was growing darker. A soft breeze lifted across the range, waving the grass tops and bringing with it a faint scent of sagebrush. This was good grazing country hereabouts, Pete told himself. He had fallen silent the past few minutes, though his eyes were alert in all directions. "Maybe we'd better push up the gait a trifle," he suggested.

"Just as you say." Cressy sounded surprised. She touched spurs to her pony and bounded ahead. Pete whipped the twin lashes of the red quirt lightly against his mount's flanks and quickly caught up. They pounded steadily along the trail which traced a wandering course as it swung this way and that to avoid high outcroppings of granite, stray cottonwood trees, or wound between hills covered with brush on either side.

A half-hour more passed. Neither had spoken for some time. Cressy said lightly, "Penny for your thoughts, Pete."

"I wouldn't sell for less than a million." Pete laughed.

"They must be pretty valuable thoughts."

"They are. I was thinking about you."

It was Cressy's turn to fall silent. Night had descended by this time. Overhead the first faint stars twinkled into being. Cressy glanced toward her companion, eyes trying to pierce the gloom. Pete seemed to be fumbling with the buttons on his shirt.

"Whatever are you doing, Pete?" she asked curiously.

"Still thinking about you," he chuckled.

"You know I don't mean that."

"Not interested if I think about you?"

"Pete, don't be silly."

"Oh, I'm silly when I think about you, eh?"

"You don't understand me."

"I'm learning fast."

Again the girl was quiet. Sometime later she realized he hadn't answered her question. The ponies drummed on; now and then a hoof struck sparks from the gravelly footing. There were more stars in view by this time. Back of the riders a silvery glow was forming along the horizon. Pete said, "It's a good thing you know the way. I'd be lost if I ever lost you. The moon will be up in a little while, though."

"I expect to be home before that," Cressy replied. "Golly, I'm getting hungry. I hope you like Dad's cooking. We haven't a ranch cook at present."

They had slowed pace where the trail wound around a huge granite boulder, the size of a small house, when it happened:

A voice directly ahead spoke sharply: "Pull up and raise your hands. You're both covered!"

Both riders reined in abruptly. From the opposite side of the big rock came movements. Pete judged there were three men there. His hands were in the air, as were Cressy's.

The voice spoke again. "You got the idea right well! No tricks now. Just do as we say and everything will be hunky-dory."

"What's the idea of this——" Pete commenced.

"Shut your trap, mister. You'll understand in a minute. Young lady, no screaming now! You won't be hurt!"

"It'd take more than you to make me scream," Cressy stated defiantly. "Of all the cowardly, low-down——"

"Hold your temper, girl." Pete spoke softly.

Cressy fell silent. A shadowy form moved out to the roadway and approached on Pete's side. "Keep him covered, boys," he called, the tones sounding a bit nervous.

"Just what have you hombres got in mind?" Pete said easily. "I haven't enough money on me to make this worth your while——"

"We ain't after money." The shadowy form spoke from the darkness close by the side of Pete's horse. "I got my gun on you, mister, so don't go reaching for yours. Lower your left arm—gentle now."

Pete lowered his left arm until it hung by his side. He felt fingers touch his hand gingerly, then draw back. Pete didn't move. The fingers touched his hand a second time, this time more boldly. The next instant the wrist loop of the quirt had been slipped off Pete's hand; then the shadowy form stepped quickly back.

"That's all we want, Piper," the voice said triumphantly. "Just this quirt. You can go on now, you and the little lady, but next time don't put your nose into business that don't concern you. Get it?"

"I get it," Pete said quietly.

"Get going then, both of you."

Pete said, "Come on, Cressy, let's move out of here."

They touched spurs to their ponies and moved swiftly on. Back of them sounded the mocking laughter of the holdup men.

9. Cressy's Story

THEY RAN THEIR HORSES a half mile or more before slowing to a more normal lope. Cressy didn't say anything for some time. Pete said softly, "Well, that's that."

"Yes, it is, isn't it?" Cressy's voice sounded cold.

Pete said, "What's wrong? Weren't scared, were you?"

"Me, scared?" Scornfully her voice went on: "You're asking *me* that?"

"What's wrong then? Your voice sounds different."

"Look, Pete"—Cressy's tones sounded desperate now, as though she were trying to convince herself—"you really weren't afraid of those men, were you?"

"No ma'am," Pete said meekly.

"Well, then why in heaven's name didn't you do something? You didn't have to give in that easy!"

"You mean go for my gun and that kind of stuff?"

"Good grief, yes!"

"Look, Cressy," Pete said patiently, "that wasn't the time for gunplay. Shooting in the dark is pretty risky sometimes. If I'd gone for my gun there'd been plenty shooting. You might have been hit. I got you into one scrape today; I couldn't risk another. See how it was?"

"Pete! Why do you always have to think of me?"

"I didn't always," Pete answered mildly. "Never did it before until today."

"You know what I mean."

"Cressy, try to see things my way, will you? You're in my charge. I couldn't risk a gun fight. Bullets fly wild——"

"Bullets be hanged!" Cressy said hotly. "I'd sooner have been shot than let those cheap stick-up men get your red quirt. After all the trouble over that quirt, you surrender it like a lamb just because——Pete, you're the most exasperating man I ever knew!"

Pete grinned in the darkness. "They say the first ten years are the hardest. Try to tough 'em out, will you? I'll try hard to please—"

"Pete! Stop all this tomfoolery. You act as though you didn't care if the quirt were gone or not."

"Oh, it's the red quirt that's bothering you?" Pete pretended surprise. "Set your mind at rest, lady. Thy didn't get my red quirt. You know that saddle shop, sort of kitty-corner across from the Busy Bee? Well, I dropped in there this afternoon after I'd left your restaurant. The man sells quirts there. I bought a cheap one and stuck it inside my shirt. Tonight when we rode out of town I was carrying the red one on my wrist, but after it got dark I switched the two. You see, in the dark

37

those stick-up men couldn't tell any other color from red, I'll bet they'll be surprised."

Cressy was momentarily struck dumb with amazement. Then comprehension dawned on her. "Pete! You—you redheaded——"

"Don't you call me a redheaded devil. I've been called that before."

"You're pretty smart, Pete. And I thought, for a few minutes, you were afraid of those men. I'm commencing to think you have brains."

"Thanks, lady. I'm always grateful for donations."

"But how did you know that would happen? A person would think you'd been tipped off."

"Figured it might," Pete explained. "For some reason Traxler is mighty anxious to get hold of that red quirt. I just had a hunch, that's all. I felt pretty sure somebody would see me ride out of town with you. Our horses stood together at the hitch rail for quite a spell. It wouldn't be hard for Traxler to draw conclusions. Then, later, while I was waiting for you, I saw both Nick Traxler, Ivan, and a third man watching me from a saloon porch. A short time later Ivan Traxler went riding out of town. So you see, I was sort of expecting a move when it came."

"Was Ivan Traxler with those men tonight?"

"I don't know. I only heard one voice. Didn't recognize that, but I will next time I hear it, I betcha."

Another half-hour brought Cressy and Pete to the C-Bar-A ranch house. It was a big, rambling place, built of rock and adobe, set in a clump of ancient cottonwood trees. A windmill clanked in the night wind. Back of the house Pete could see the blocky outlines of a bunkhouse, corrals, and other miscellaneous buildings. Cressy's father heard them arriving and sent a cowboy to take their horses. Cressy introduced the cowboy as Pinto Grant, then ran up to the long gallery fronting the ranch house to greet her father. Pete followed closely behind and was introduced to Cyrus Alexander, a spare, sandy-haired man with steady eyes and a firm handclasp. Pete judged him to be in the middle fifties.

Alexander led the way into a long main room at one end of which a mesquite-root fire blazed in the fireplace. It was a comfortable room with large easy chairs and Indian rugs on the floor. "Just toss your hat and gun anyplace, Pete," Alexander said cordially. "We can eat as soon as you and Cressy get washed up. . . . Graveyard! Where are you?"

A tall, rawboned cowpuncher with a dour countenance entered from another room. "Wish you wouldn't yell at me that-a-way, Cyrus," he said in hurt tones. "A body's got enough sorrow in this world without bein' skeered plumb outten his wits——Oh, hello, Cressy. You back?"

"Knew I was coming, didn't you, Graveyard?" Cressy laughed. "Cheerful as always, I see. . . . Graveyard Gratton, shake hands with Pete Piper. Pete, don't get discouraged, there's no funeral taking place. Graveyard is always like this."

"Ain't nothin' to be cheerful about in this day and age," Gratton said mournfully. The handclasp he gave Pete was surprisingly firm. "Reckon I'm supposed to say, 'Pleased to meet you,' but I don't know yet if I am," he continued. "I'll just say howdy."

"Just taking me on trust, eh?" Pete laughed.

"Ain't sure yet," Graveyard said noncommittally.

"Graveyard," Cressy's father went on, "take Pete out and show him the washbasin. Meanwhile, I'll try to hurry up Cressy here. I'm starved fit to eat the Lord's supper."

Pete followed Graveyard out through the dining room, the table of which was all set, and washed in the kitchen. As he was drying his hands and face Pinto Grant returned from unsaddling the horses. Pinto proved to be a freckled individual with a cheerful manner and a wide grin.

"You two all the crew there is?" Pete asked.

"Yeah," Pinto replied. "We just about handle everythin' while Cressy's paw directs and does the cookin'. Now that Cressy is back, Cyrus will make a hand."

"I reckon it's just Cyrus' good heart that keeps me and Pinto on," Graveyard offered. "The C-Bar-A can't afford help right now." He checked himself suddenly and fell silent.

Pete and the two punchers returned to the dining room, where they were met by Cressy and her father. Alexander looked serious. "Cressy tells me you were stuck up on the way here, Pete."

"I knew it; I knew somethin' like that would happen," Graveyard said dolorously. "This country's gone plumb to the dawgs. I'm surprise you two got here at all."

"On top of that," Alexander said, "Cressy was nearly in a gun fight today."

"Blood will tell," Pinto Grant chuckled. "Just a chip off'n the old block. Well, relate it, Cressy."

"I'll talk while we eat," Cressy offered. "Let's sit down."

"We all sit down except Graveyard," Pinto said. "He has to serve us first. That's the agreement. Cyrus cooks; Graveyard serves, and I wash the dishes. Graveyard has to wait until all the food is on the table."

"I always get the worst of deals," Graveyard said in a discouraged voice.

" 'He also serves who only stands and waits,' " Pete quoted.

"Stands my foot!" Graveyard retorted. "I'll be settin', too, just as quick as I get the rest of this on the table."

They sat down. Pete noticed that Graveyard wasn't far

behind the rest. Cressy told the story of the holdup and what happened earlier that day in the mix-up with the Traxlers and Nevada Norton. Pete supplied details from time to time while they ate supper.

"Well," Graveyard said when she had finished, "I'm surprised you're not both dead."

"For once I agree with Graveyard," Cyrus Alexander put in. "I don't see yet how Pete got the drop on Traxler when Traxler had him covered."

"By cripes!" from Pinto. "That *is* something!"

"I guess I was just lucky and caught Black Nick off guard," Pete replied.

"You'll never know how lucky you were," Graveyard said, shoveling a forkful of food into his mouth. Despite his gloomy outlook on life, he seemed to eat three times as much as anyone else.

When Cressy had finished the recital of the day's doings her father said, "I wonder what it is about that red quirt that makes Traxler want it so much. Where'd you say you got it, Pete?"

"I found it." Pete hesitated. "I might as well tell you the whole business while I'm at it. I haven't even told Cressy yet about finding a dead man today——"

"A dead man?" Cressy exclaimed.

"Ten to one the Traxlers are back of it," Graveyard said darkly. "Was he anybody we know?"

"Old codger," Pete said. "Deputy Pritchard said he was named Tiger-Eye Munson——"

"Ol' Tiger-Eye!" Pinto exclaimed. "I guess that proves the Traxlers didn't do it. He was one of Black Nick's best men. Graveyard, don't ever tell me everythin' is bad in this world, if that old devil is dead."

"Pete," Alexander said, "don't let these two rannies interrupt. Get on with your story. We're anxious to hear."

Pete told of the finding of Munson's body in the rocking chair. That part of the tale brought exclamations of surprise and disbelief from his hearers. He finished up with the finding of the crimson quirt and of the men who had shot at him.

"Good grief!" Cressy said. "I never heard anything like it!"

"You've sure had a full-testing day." Her father nodded. "I'd like to take a look at this much-wanted quirt."

"It's in the other room with my hat and gun belt," Pete replied. "When supper's finished——"

"It's finished now." Pinto grinned. "All except Graveyard. He never does know when to quit."

Graveyard scowled and got to his feet. "Never know what meal will be my last," he said dolefully, "so I do my best when I can. Thank heaven for that lunch; some people might call it a meal."

They made their way into the main room of the house. The

men rolled cigarettes and examined Pete's red quirt. A few minutes later Pinto went to clear off the table and wash dishes. Graveyard followed to lend a hand. Pete and Alexander seated themselves before the fireplace, with Cressy between them.

Pete said, "Cressy, you felt quite certain that red quirt was your brother's when you saw it today. Ever since I've wondered why. There could be two quirts, you know, just alike. At the same time, I've a hunch this is the one your brother owned. I think you'd better keep it."

Cressy shook her head. "No, you keep it. It's already got me into a couple of scrapes today. No lady can go around indulging in gun fights day after day. I'll let you take care of it from now on. If it had been Hugh's his initials would have been on it someplace. I feel sure. He had a habit of initialing everything he owned. It was just that I'd never seen another one like it. I was in Beauregard City the day he bought it—"

"Cressy," Alexander put in, "why not give Pete the whole story? It all may tie in, somehow, with the trouble you've had today."

The girl nodded. "That's a good idea, Dad. You correct me if I tell anything wrong. To begin with, Pete, we're from Wyoming, originally. We came here eight years ago, after Mother died. A friend of Dad's had homesteaded this ranch, and we bought from him. After we had the place we learned that Nick Traxler had been after it but wouldn't offer enough. Once we had it he tried to buy from us. We liked it and refused to sell. That made a certain amount of bad feeling between us right from the start, as Traxler took it as a personal affront when we wouldn't let him have the holdings."

"That dynamiting you spoke of," Pete commented shrewdly, "commences to fit in. I've an idea that Traxler was trying to deprive you of water so you'd have to sell."

"Exactly my idea," Cressy's father put in. "It didn't work, though. Black Nick got the worst of that bargain."

Cressy went on, "We paid cash for the place when we arrived, but it required nearly all of Dad's money. The cattle that went with the ranch were a pretty scrubby lot, so when my brother Hugh heard of a good herd that could be bought cheap we decided to plunge. That meant that Dad had to sign a note at the bank for six thousand dollars. The note is still unpaid and falls due next month. We have managed to keep up the interest."

"How we've done it I don't know," Alexander put in wearily. "Graveyard and Pinto have had to take cuts in wages, though they offered to work for nothing. Unless a miracle happens, we lose the C-Bar-A next month. When I signed that note I never dreamed I'd have trouble repaying."

"We wouldn't have had, either," Cressy said loyally, "ex-

41

cept for a streak of bad luck. There were a couple of bad years. Cattle prices slumped for a time. We had some blackleg trouble too. A year ago Dad saw how things were shaping up. He went into town and talked to Banker Haines. Haines refused to grant him an extension. He was pretty cold-blooded about the whole business and advised Dad to sell out to Traxler. We would have, I guess, except Traxler wouldn't pay near what the outfit is worth. Well, we all pitched in and made an extra effort to raise the money. Hugh went to work on the T.N.&A.S. for a time. We raised the six thousand too, but we had to sell nearly all our herd to do it. About that time hard luck struck again."

Alexander explained that: "Like an old fool I got to messing around on a mean bronc. The critter threw himself backward and pinned me underneath. Broke my laig—not bad, but enough to keep me from moving around much. So there I was, flat on my back in bed, when I wanted to take that six thousand in and throw it in Banker Haines' face. Rather than hold up proceedings, though, we decided it would be best for Hugh to take the money in to the bank. He and Cressy started out that day eight months back. I never saw Hugh alive again." Alexander's voice faltered a trifle.

Cressy again took up the story: "The bank wasn't open yet when we reached Beauregard. I wanted to get some dress goods, and I knew that Hugh would want to drop in on Beanple Ridge for a drink while he waited. I went to the Emporium Dry Goods Store first, but they didn't have just what I wanted, so I started for Larrabee's General Store. It was still too early for the bank to open, and when I crossed toward Larrabee's I saw Hugh standing before Beanpole Ridge's, talking to a Mexican peddler. Hugh saw me and called out, 'Look what I just bought, Cressy.' He held up a red leather quirt. I called back and told him when he got through the business at the bank to call for me at Mrs. Fogarty's—she's an old friend of ours, you know—runs a boardinghouse in Beauregard. And that," Cressy finished quietly, "was the last time I ever saw Hugh alive."

"Gosh," Pete said contritely, "I hate to be asking more details, but I'm plumb intersted."

"I intend to go on," Cressy said. Her eyes were a bit moist. "As I came from Larrabee's I noticed the bank had opened. I took it for granted that Hugh was inside. I got my pony and went on over to Mrs. Fogarty's. She and I hadn't had an opportunity to visit for some time, so the minutes slipped past right quickly. Before I realized it two hours had passed. I commenced to worry. I got my pony and went to the bank. Banker Haines said Hugh hadn't been there. I saw Deputy Pritchard on the street and asked him if he'd seen Hugh.

Pritchard said he'd noticed him riding hard out of town about an hour or so before. I told Homer Pritchard I was worried, that Hugh had had a large sum of money on him. Homer offered to ride with me and see if Hugh had gone home.... We found his dead body about six miles from town, on the trail to the C-Bar-A. He had been shot."

Pete shook his head. "That's pretty tough."

"He'd been robbed," Cressy went on. "Why he never went to the bank I don't know, and nobody who talked to him that morning seems to know. It wasn't until sometime later that I thought of the red quirt he'd bought that morning. Nobody, apparently, had found that along the trail or anyplace else."

"That's the story," Alexander sighed. "So now you can understand why the C-Bar-A is pretty much up against it and why we have to raise six thousand dollars, or lose the place, in something less than a month."

"A lot can happen in that time," Pete said encouragingly, "so don't worry about it too much. I got a hunch your luck is due to change."

He had no time to say more. Pinto Grant and Graveyard Gratton entered the room with the news that the dishes were cleaned up.

"Dirtiest bunch of dishes we've had in a long time," Graveyard crabbed. "That's why I was helpin' Pinto."

Pete laughed. "Not holding that against me, are you, Graveyard?"

Graveyard said sourly, "Not you. Cressy. She never did learn to clean her plate proper. Now if she'd only take a biscuit and sop up her gravy, it'd cut our work in half."

"I'd make her do her own dishes from now on," Pete advised. "Well, I'd better saddle up and get back to town."

"No need for that," Alexander said quickly. "You stay the night, Pete. There's plenty room here or in the bunkhouse."

"He'll never get to sleep in the bunkhouse." Graveyard said. "Pinto snores somethin' terrible. I ain't slept more'n a wink since I don't know when."

"I'll risk it." Pete laughed. "Lead on. It's getting late, and Cressy and her dad probably want to do some visiting before they turn in."

10   Killer Unknown

IT WAS ABOUT NINE-THIRTY the following morning when Pete returned to Beauregard City. The ride from the C-Bar-A had been made with nothing unusual happening. Pete had loped easily along, looking over the country and not pushing hard. Now and then he had seen a few Hereford steers branded on the left flank with the C-Bar-A design, but there weren't many of them. Most of the time during the ride in his mind had been occupied with thoughts of Cressy Alexander, and it was with extreme reluctance that he had taken his departure from the ranch that morning.

Deputy Sheriff Pritchard was seated, whittling as usual, before the sheriff's office when Pete pulled up at the hitch rack and dismounted. Pritchard glanced up, grinned slowly, and put his knife away. "Dam'd if you don't surprise me," he drawled.

"How come?" Pete asked.

"I figured you'd probably forget all about the inquest on Tiger-Eye Munson. Don't know how any hombre could take Cressy Alexander ridin' and keep his mind on an inquest."

Pete reddened. "Cressy's a nice girl."

"Nice girl? If that ain't a masterpiece of understatement, I never heard one. You might show some enthusiasm."

"My mother taught me I should always conceal my emotions." Pete grinned. He came around the end of the hitch rack. "Anythin' new happened?"

"Not much. Say, you really did get the drop on Black Nick yesterday, didn't you? Dam'd if I didn't think you were joshin'. Sheriff Perkins told me all about it. I sure missed some excitement."

"You missed some more last night," Pete said. "Cressy and I were stuck up on the way home."

"T'hell you say!" Homer gained his feet, settled his sombrero more securely on his hemp-colored hair, and said, "I'm anxious to know. Let's go down to Beanpole Ridge's Lariat Saloon and get a morning brightener-up."

Pete nodded, and Homer joined him on the sidewalk. Pete said, "You didn't discover anything new when you went over near Elephant Ridge yesterday, did you?"

"Not much. Munson's body was like you said it was. You'll get the story at the inquest. But first tell me what happened to you and Cressy."

Pete related the story of the holdup while he and Homer strode along the plank sidewalk, Homer nodding now and then to passing acquaintances. When the story was finished he glanced admiringly at Pete. "And they never did get that quirt, then? That's what I call outfoxin' the dirty sons. Ain't no idea who they were?"

"Nary a one."

"Traxler is connected with it, I'm bettin'. I wonder why they're so anxious to get that red quirt of yours."

"That's what I'd like to know."

"Better put it someplace in safekeeping."

Pete shook his head. "So long as I carry it with me hombres maybe will keep trying to get it. If they try hard enough mebbe I'll get an idea of what's in the wind."

"You wouldn't be lookin' for trouble, by any chance?"

"No, but I'm not side-stepping any that heads my way, either."

"That's the old do-or-die spirit. C'mon, here's the Lariat bar."

They passed through the swinging doors into the saloon. The bar ran along the right side wall. An open doorway showed an alley at the rear. Back of the bar the mirror was speckless and the glasses on the back bar glistened in small pyramids. There weren't any customers at the bar, though three or four men were seated at tables across the room, reading newspapers; one of them was playing solitaire.

Behind the bar was probably the fattest man Pete had ever seen. He was huge, no two ways about that. His graying hair was neatly combed, and he wore a spotless bar apron beneath his fancy vest. There was a humorous twinkle in his eyes, and he shook hands cordially with Pete when Homer said, "Beanpole, this is Pete Piper, the hombre who gave Black Nick his come-uppance yesterday. Pete, shake hands with Bob Ridge—otherwise known as Beanpole. I can recommend anythin' he sells."

"Beanpole, eh?" Pete smiled, sizing up Ridge's imposing hulk.

"Yeah, Beanpole," Homer drawled. "We had to give him that name so we could distinguish him from Elephant Ridge."

"That'll be enough from you, Homer," Beanpole chuckled fatly. "I'm glad to know you, Mr. Piper. What'll it be, gents?"

"I'll have a spot," Pete said, "and a chaser of water—small spot and lots of water."

"Make mine the same"—Homer nodded—"but leave out the water and the small."

Beanpole served the men. Homer spun a coin on the bar. Another customer entered and went to the opposite end of the bar. Beanpole followed to take care of the man's wants.

Pete said, "Did you examine Munson's guns yesterday?"

"Yes." Homer nodded. "The six-shooter had two empty chambers. Munson carried his hammer on an empty shell. That means he'd fired the six-shooter only once. The Winchester was empty. That was natural. Tiger-Eye was first and foremost a dang good rifleshot. I reckon he got what was comin' to him; he was a hypocritical old blackguard. I hear Black Nick and his brothers are mutterin' threats as to what will happen if they catch the so-and-so that murdered their dear pal."

"The Traxlers in town this morning?"

"They came in for the inquest. They're probably down at Turk Raven's place now. Luke Traxler has a peach of a shiner."

The two were talking in lowered tones so as not to carry to the other customers in the saloon. Beanpole diplomatically stayed at the far end of the bar.

Pete said, "Homer, you knew Munson. Did you ever know

him to carry a red quirt like this one I've got?"

The deputy considered. "Can't say as I have," he said finally. "Why you askin'?"

"I found it resting in the branches of a mesquite not far from where I found Munson's body. I thought it might have been his quirt."

"More likely the killer's," Homer suggested, "if it belonged to either."

"Keep it to yourself until we see what develops. Incidentally, Hugh Alexander bought a quirt like this the day he was killed."

"By cripes! That's right. I'd forgotten that. I remember Cressy makin' some inquiries afterward. She told you about her brother's killin', eh?"

"Yes. I didn't want to go into details last night. It didn't make a pleasant subject. Maybe you can supply a few things I want to know."

"Any information I have is yours for the askin', Pete. Let's postpone it until later, though. It's just about time for the inquest at Doc Gillett's."

They said "So long" to Beanpole and made their way to the street. Pete said, "I reckon I'll get my pony and take him to the livery. No use letting him stand in the sun all day. Where's Gillett's place?"

"One block over, on Taos Street. But we're not in that much of a rush. I'll go along with you."

They procured Pete's horse, delivered it at the Beauregard Livery across the street from the Cowmen's Rest Hotel, then cut over Tonto Street until they reached the thoroughfare on which Gillett's house was located. The doctor's home and office proved to be a neat frame dwelling surrounded by a white picket fence.

A number of men stood in the doctor's yard. As many as possible of these crowded into the front room of the doctor's house, where there were still more of the curious as soon as Pete and Homer had entered. There were chairs for the jury of six men, which Sheriff Perkins had rounded up, and for the witnesses. The remainder was forced to stand. The three Traxler brothers—Nick, Ivan, and Luke—were on hand, as was the doctor, of course.

Luke Traxler was dark, like his brothers, but resembled them in little else, as far as physical characteristics were concerned. He was taller than Ivan and heavier than Nick; his features were coarser. He was a rather unkept individual. His left eye was black, like his brothers'. His right eye was also black, and bruised with a sort of purplish-green tint. It was shut and badly swollen. In short, Luke Traxler bore what is known as a shiner. He looked sulky about the whole business.

The three Traxlers glared at Pete when he entered, but none of them said anything. Dr. Gillett quickly got the inquest under way. He told briefly how he and Deputy Homer Pritchard had gone after the body upon hearing of its discovery by Pete Piper. Their evidence, the doctor stated, would be shown to agree with Pete's, as far as the position of the body in the rocker was concerned.

The walnut-frame rocker was there as exhibit A. Exhibits B and C were Munson's six-shooter and rifle. The rifle was empty when found; the six-shooter had two exploded shells in the cylinder, on one of which the hammer of the gun had presumably rested, thus giving credence to the doctor's statement that Munson had fired but one shot from his six-shooter, though he had completely emptied the chamber of the rifle of bullets.

At this point Homer was called as a witness. He corroborated the doctor's story to that point. The six jurymen listened with wide-open mouths. It was plainly difficult for them to swallow the story of Munson being found dead in a rocking chair out in the open country. They looked skeptically at each other. The foreman whispered to his companions, then arose to ask the doctor where the chair had come from.

"That, gentlemen," Gillett stated, "is, as far as we know, a complete mystery."

The doctor next explained the nature of Munson's wounds. Munson had first been wounded in the left shoulder, shot from behind, by a bullet from a .45 six-shooter. That had been done before Munson's form occupied the chair. That was plainly evident; the chair back was undamaged. The wound that had brought death—instant death, in Gillett's opinion—was also caused by a .45 slug from a six-shooter. The .45 slug had entered from the front, just over the heart. There had been considerable loss of blood from both wounds. At this point the jury was taken to another room to view Munson's remains. Within a few minutes it returned, wearing its same baffled expression. The contents of Munson's pockets had been examined; nothing there had revealed a clue to the mystery.

The three Traxler brothers were next called as witnesses one by one. Their evidence agreed on all points: they had no idea who had killed Munson, nor why; he had no enemies they knew of; he had left the Diamond-T Ranch early that morning to go to Beauregard City. No, they didn't know why; he hadn't stated. There was some snickering at sight of Luke Traxler's black eye. He glared balefully with his one good eye at his audience.

Sheriff Perkins next testified that he had interviewed other members of the Diamond-T crew and that they could throw no more light on the subject than had the Traxlers. The sheriff had also made inquiries about town, but no one had anything to offer.

Gillett had saved Pete's testimony until the last. Pete rose and told how he had found the body. He didn't mention seeing the tracks about, though he did tell of the shooting that had been done at him from the top of Elephant Ridge and of his own single shot in reply. He then related how he had gone to the top of the ridge and saw two riders fleeing toward the northwest.

"Could you identify them, Mr. Piper?" Gillett asked.

"No, they were too far away." Pete cast a glance at the Traxlers. Was it his imagination, or did they look relieved at the admission?

Gillett asked next, "Did you find evidence of any sort at the top of Elephant Ridge?"

"I found sign where two men had crouched in the brush. I also found two discharged .30-30 shells, probably the ones used in shooting at me." Peter produced the two shells and handed them to the doctor. The doctor looked at them, then passed them on to Sheriff Perkins with the remark, "I understand gun hammers sometimes leave distinguishing marks on shells, Sheriff Perkins. Would you say you could match the gun, or guns that exploded these shells, providing same could be found?"

Perkins scratched his chin meditatively, "We-ell, I'd hate to promise anything. Mebbe forty per cent of the rifles in this country are .30-30s, and it would be a whale of a job locating the right one. That wouldn't be easy to do."

Gillett nodded and turned back to Pete. Pete resumed and told of finding the damaged set of field glasses. "I'm not sure, of course," he said, "but it's my guess that my shot did the damage. Pure luck, naturally. The field glasses are in Sheriff Perkins' possession." He grinned. "I'll bet whoever was looking through those glasses when my shot hit sure got a bad shock. It was just lucky for him the bullet struck a glancing blow, otherwise the hombre might have been killed. At that, the wallop of those field glasses being jammed back against a man's head, when the bullet struck, would give him a black eye, I'm thinking."

A dead silence fell on the room. Suddenly Luke Traxler was on his feet, raving mad. "Damn you, Piper!" he roared. "Are you insinooatin' that I was the feller usin' them glasses at the time? Why, you——!"

"Shut up, Luke!" Black Nick spoke sharply. "And sit down!" He jerked Luke back in his chair. Everyone was looking at him now.

Pete assumed a look of surprise. "I hadn't thought of that, Traxler," he said smoothly. "Now that you bring it to my attention, maybe there's something in what you say. However, it's up to the sheriff to decide."

Instantly Nick Traxler was on his feet. "As I understand it, Dr. Gillett, this is an inquest to determine the cause of Tiger-Eye Munson's death, as well as his killers. No purpose can be served by making veiled accusations against my brother Luke. Both Luke and Ivan have testified they were at the Diamond-T yesterday. Luke stayed there all day. Ivan didn't come into town until long after Munson had been killed. I was in Beauregard nearly all day. It's about time folks stopped looking our way every time there's a crime committed. If they don't we're going to start fighting back in a way folks won't like!" He swept a savage glance over the six jurymen, who cringed before the hatred in his eyes, then continued in a softer voice, "My brother Luke got that black eye in a fall out to our ranch yesterday. His head struck a corner of the watering trough."

"Hope it didn't give him water on the brain," Pete said impulsively.

Laughter went around the room. Gillett smiled thinly. "I don't think this inquest is the place for humor, Mr. Piper." He turned to Black Nick. "I can understand your attitude, Mr. Traxler, and that of your brothers. No one has accused you yet. That is a matter for the jury to decide."

How the jury would decide wasn't any problem in Pete's mind. He had seen the six men cower under the lash of Nick Traxler's sharp words. Traxler, apparently, had the people of Beauregard pretty well buffaloed.

Sheriff Perkins said, "May I ask a question, Doc?"

"Certainly."

The sheriff turned to Black Nick. "Traxler, you used to tote a pair of field glasses. Where are they?"

"I wish I knew," Traxler said in bitter tones. "Some lousy two-bit buzzard stole them a couple of months back when we were all away from the house."

Perkins reached under a small table and produced the field glasses with the shattered lens. "Examine these and tell me if they're yours."

Traxler came forward, took one look, and said, "Hell yes! I'm glad to get them back, but I don't know if they can be repaired or not. I'll take them along and——"

"I'll have to keep 'em in my custody a spell, Nick," Perkins said, "until this business has all been settled one way or t'other."

"Just as you say, Sheriff."

That about wound up matters. The foreman of the jury asked a few questions; then he and his companions retired to another room to deliberate their verdict. When it came Pete wasn't surprised. They jury found that Tiger-Eye Munson had met his death through gunshot wounds at the hands of a party, or parties, unknown. There was no recommendation that the black-eyed Luke Traxler be held for questioning. Pete hadn't expected that, either. With glances of triumph the Traxler brothers rose and left the room. The gathering commenced to break up.

11   "I Aim to Help"

"WELL," Sheriff Perkins growled, "we don't know much more than we did." He and his deputy, accompanied by Pete, stood on the corner of Main and Tonto streets a few minutes after leaving Dr. Gillett's house. "Killed by an unknown! If Tiger-Eye Munson hadn't been so almighty thick with the Traxlers, I'd think they had something to do with it—but I reckon they're in the clear. At the same time, Luke's black eye and what you said about the binoculars maybe causing it, Pete . . ."

"Might as well forget that part now," Pete advised, "until you can get some sort of definite proof. As it stands, Luke seems to have an airtight alibi. Every man on the Diamond-T will swear Luke was at the ranch all day——"

"I just wish," Homer interrupted, "that Doc Gillett hadn't mentioned that rifle shells could sometimes be matched, through the hammer impressions, with the guns that fired 'em. I'd like to have sneaked a look at Luke's rifle sometime. And Ivan's too."

"Why Ivan's?" the sheriff asked.

"If Luke was atop Elephant Ridge that day, I'm bettin' it was Ivan with him. They pal together a lot, and Pete saw two riders."

"I dunno," Perkins objected. "We know that Ivan came tearing into Beauregard that day from the Diamond-T. Are you thinking that he could ride all the way from Elephant Ridge to the Diamond-T, then from there to town within that time?"

"It could be done," Homer maintained. "He could get a fresh bronc at the ranch, you know—and pound hell out of both horses."

"He always pounds hell out of his broncs anyway," the sheriff grunted disgustedly. "It's a shame the way that galoot treats good horseflesh."

"That's whatever," Homer said. "The point I'm makin' is that I'd like to check up on a few rifles here and there."

"It'd take too long," the sheriff said. "If we went direct to Luke and asked to see his rifle he'd probably say it had been stolen or something, the way Nick did about the field glasses. That is, if he's the one that fired the shots."

"Sheriff Perkins is probably right, Homer," Pete said. "That's something we'll just have to let drop for a spell. We can keep it in mind, though."

"We? We?" Homer drawled shrewdly. "How come? You aimin' to take a part in this investigation too?"

"I'm interested." Pete grinned. "I just aim to help where possible." He changed the subject. "Sheriff, did you ever know Munson to carry a red quirt like this one I've got?"

Perkins shook his head. "Not to my knowledge. By the way, where did you say you found that quirt?"

"I didn't say," Pete replied. "As a matter of fact, I took it out of the branches of a mesquite tree not far from Munson's body. I've got a hunch there's a connection someplace, but I don't know where——"

"The hell you did!" Perkins exclaimed. "What connection——?"

"I haven't the least idea yet."

"You should have reported it at the inquest," Perkins said.

"I would have if I'd been sure there was a connection of any sort. But, shucks, this quirt may have been there for days. But let's not mention where I got it for a time."

The sheriff gazed moodily down Main Street. "Dammit! One thing piles on another," he complained. "Ordinary crime I can handle, generally, but when it comes to mixing red quirts and rocking chairs into a killing, I'm about ready to give up. I never did go for mystery. Never got any fun out of working puzzles when I was a kid, either. I just ain't problem-minded, I reckon, but one thing I do know, and that's when to take a drink. The time is now. Come along to the Lariat and we'll have Beanpole do things with a bottle and glasses."

"Too soon before dinner," Pete refused, "as far as I'm concerned. Right now I'm planning to step across the street to the hotel dining room and get a bite."

"I'll go with you," Homer said. "My stomach's commencin' to think my throat met up with an accident."

They said good-by to the sheriff, crossed Tonto Street, and entered the hotel dining room on the first floor. The dining room opened off the lobby of the hotel and was about half full of diners, seated at a dozen or so tables, when they entered. A waitress took their orders for roast beef and other food. Neither had a great deal to say until the food was brought and they'd started eating. Pete opened the conversation:

"Homer, you were with Cressy when her brother's body was found, weren't you?"

"Yeah, and I don't want to go through that again. Not that Cressy went to pieces, or anythin' of the sort. She took it, chin up, like a little soldier. But I just hate to see some folks suffer, that's all."

"He'd been robbed, of course, but wasn't there any clue?"

"Not a one. Me and the sheriff worked as hard as we knew how on that case too. Ethan was pretty well broke up at the time. It's the first case that he'd failed to break. No, we never found trace of the money. Nor the red quirt, either, that Cressy failed to tell us about until several days later. Shucks! I hadn't even known he bought a quirt that mornin'."

"Just how was Hugh Alexander killed?"

"He'd been shot from ambush. There were some high rocks close to the trail. The killer had hid behind those until Hugh came ridin' along. The dirty buzzard was right foxy too. As far as we could judge from the sign, he'd blanketed his horse's hoofs and his own feet in strips of burlap, or somethin' of the sort, so no plain impressions would be left."

"Killed with a six-gun or rifle?"

"Rifle. Thirty-thirty, as near as Doc Gillett could judge. The lead he probed out was some battered."

"How do you account for the fact that Hugh didn't go to the bank that morning?"

"I don't. Neither does anybody else who knew Hugh. Hugh was a right reliable cuss. Likable as all get out and steady as a rock."

"You're absolutely sure he didn't go to the bank?"

"Hell, yes!" Homer took a deep swallow of coffee, forked up a mouthful of potatoes, and went on. "At the inquest Banker Haines and his cashier both testified that he hadn't come into the bank."

"Can you take their word for it?"

"Well, I can't say I like Haines so much; he thinks he's pretty important. At the same time, I ain't got no reason doubtin' his word, or Ward's either. Ward's the cashier."

"Those the only two you asked?"

"Cripes, no! We canvassed nigh everybody in town to see who'd been to the bank that mornin' after it opened. Nobody remembered seein' Hugh in the bank, though there were two or three not quite sure. On the other hand, any number of men remembered seein' Hugh around town, so it isn't as though folks aren't observant. We finally just had to conclude that Hugh hadn't gone near the bank."

"Why hadn't he?"

"Why ask me?" A trace of irritability crept into Homer's usually drawling tones. "I don't know—and I've laid awake many a night tryin' to figure out why. It just don't make sense, that's all. Here's a steady, reliable hombre comes to town with six thousand dollars to pay off a note. He waits around town until the bank opens, then suddenly, without even notifyin' his sister, he gets on his bronc and rides hell for Texas outten town. I was standin' in front of the sheriff's office when he went by, and I'm tellin' you he was sure pourin' it onto that bronc."

"Hugh wasn't inclined to gamble, was he?"

"Ain't I told you he was steady as a rock?"

"I've known rocks that rolled sometimes."

"I don't think I ever saw Hugh even get interested in a dice game."

"Did you notice if he had a red quirt when he rode by?"

"No. If the red quirt was as famous then as it is now I might have noticed, but naturally I wasn't thinkin' about anythin' like that."

"Naturally," Pete conceded. He continued eating for several minutes. Finally he said, "Traxler would like to get hold of the C-Bar-A."

"Hell's bells! That's not news. Traxler has never made any secret of his wantin' that outfit. You can't blame him for that. With an even break in luck, Cressy and her dad can build that place up into a sweet outfit; someday it will be valuable property."

Again Pete changed the subject. "Is there much rustling around these parts?"

"There's always rustlin' in the Southwest," Homer said promptly. "If you're tryin' to find out if the Diamond-T has been stealin' C-Bar-A cattle, I don't know. Cyrus Alexander makes no complaints to that effect. He's lost some stock, of course, from time to time, but I reckon it's just from natural causes. No, Trabadura County is pretty clear of rustlin'. I wouldn't say so much for Rhys County, though—that's the next county northeast of here. If it's rustlin' you're interested in, talk to Joe Dunlop at the Ladder-D Ranch. Joe's been havin' plenty trouble, I guess. He's kicked to us, but I feel right sure our jurisdiction is in the clear. We've done a lot of work and concluded the rustlers must be workin' in the Rhys County part of his ranch."

"I don't get you—exactly," Pete said.

"I'll explain. Maybe first I'd better give you the layout in this valley. We'll start with the C-Bar-A, with the home ranch twelve miles west of here—slightly northwest—right smack dab against the Trabadura Range."

Pete smiled. "You don't need to tell me where Cressy's place is located."

"I reckon not. North of the C-Bar-A, fifteen miles northwest of town, is Traxler's Diamond-T outfit. You see, all the outfits hereabouts spread, fanwise, west, north, and east of Beauregard. Next to the Diamond T is the Coffee-Cup Ranch, eighteen miles north of town; owned by Jake Maxwell. Seventeen miles northeast of Beauregard is Barney Higgins' Rafter-H spread. Now we come to Dunlop's Ladder-D, which

53

lies twenty miles in a northeasterly direction from here. It's more east than north, though. Part of the Ladder-D is in Trabadura County, part in Rhys County. The southwest corner of Rhys County touches just north of Elephant Ridge. Dunlop is really the biggest cattle raiser around here; mostly he ranges his stock along the Picadero Mountains. If you knew the layout of the draws and canyons in those mountains you'd understand why the rustlers are probably workin' over in Rhys County and not over this way."

"Do you think Traxler is rustling Dunlop's cattle?"

"I ain't got the least idea. I do know that Traxler would have a hell of a time workin' a Ladder-D brand into a Diamond-T. So long as the rustlers keep out of our county, that's all I care about. In addition to the ranches I've mentioned there are a few small outfits that don't amount to much and a couple of farms with fool hoe men tryin' to work a livin' from the soil. But this country is meant for stock raisin' and nothin' else."

"The day is coming, Homer, when you'll see plenty farms in this country. We need the farmers; they're the backbone of the nation."

"Mebbe so," Homer grunted, "but to hear some politicians talk, you would think they was the back*ache* of the nation. At any rate, I'm still maintainin' that dry farmin' is a tough racket. I've tried it and I know. If you don't get plenty of water you're out of luck."

They finished dinner and once more sauntered out to the street.

12   Shots in the Night

FOR A FEW MINUTES they stood on the hotel corner, rolling and lighting Durham cigaretts. "Where to now?" asked Homer.

Pete shrugged his shoulders. "I was just wondering what I'd do to pass the time. I reckon I'll just take a *pasear* around your town and look it over."

"I'll go with you," Homer offered promptly. "If you figure to be here for a spell, and it looks like you would, there's nothin' like gettin' acquainted with folks. Mebbe I can introduce you to some of the right kind."

For the next couple of hours they circulated around the business section of Beauregard City, talking to store and shop owners, and Pete discovered that his getting the drop on Black Nick Traxler the previous day had brought him considerable prestige in the eyes of the townspeople and lowered the Diamond-T's owner's stock to a similiar degree.

"Yeah," Homer commented as the two sauntered along

the eastern end of Main Street, their high boot heels clumping hollowly on the plank sidewalks. "I figure you're just what Beauregard needed. If them Traxlers can be took down a peg a few times folks won't stand in so much awe of 'em. It's really Black Nick they're shy of, of course. Ivan and Luke wouldn't amount to a row of spent ca'tridges 'thout Nick to back em.'

"I reckon,' Pete replied. "Say, isn't it about time we quit walking for a spell and dropped in for some of Beanpole's beer? A feller can get right dry pounding planks this-a-way."

"That's the brightest thought I've heard of today." Homer agreed. "But first I want to take you in and introduce you to ol' Jay Harvey, who runs the gun shop here. Jay knows firearms, and if you ever want any repairs on your shootin' equipment Jay can fix you up."

Pete looked ahead and saw a sign swinging above the door of a small shop a few doors beyond, on which were the words, JAY HARVEY, GUNSMITH. Just as they drew abreast of the shop and Pete turned in, Luke Traxler came barging out, his face red and angry. Before he could stop, or Pete could move aside to avoid the rush, the two collided, the force of the impact knocking Traxler momentarily off balance.

"I'm sorry, Traxler," Pete said quietly. "Didn't see you coming."

Traxler regained his balance, his features contorted with rage. "T'hell you didn't!" he roared. "You tried to knock me down on purpose!"

"Easy does it, Luke," Deputy Homer warned. "I don't want any fights—"

"What you want and what you get are two different things," Luke raged. "I ain't broke no laws and I don't intend to have"—and he called Pete a name no man will take —"push me around."

"Better take it back, Traxler," Pete snapped.

"I'll take nothin' back." And Traxler repeated the words.

"Suit yourself," Pete said coolly. "I've been thinking that your left eye don't match your right. Maybe I can do something about that."

Pete swung even while he was speaking, his right fist smashing against Luke Traxler's remaining good eye. Luke spun half around and sprawled on the sidewalk. He lay there for a minute, too stunned to move. Homer stepped forward, jerked the six-shooter from Luke's holster, emptied the cylinders of cartridges, and shoved the gun back into its scabbard.

"Just so you won't get any ideas that'll prove bad luck for you," Homer explained.

A small knot of men had gathered around. Luke groaned and stumbled to his feet. One hand strayed toward his gun before it occurred to him that it would be useless. He stood swaying uncertainly before Pete, muttering incoherent threats. His left eye was swelling fast. Suddenly, without another word, he turned and stumbled off, heading in the direction of Turk Raven's bar diagonally across the street.

"All right, scatter, you hombres," Homer said to the knot of men that had gathered. They scattered. He turned to Pete. "You sure move fast. Been here two days. Knocked down two of the Traxlers and threw a gun on the third. When do you start to slow up? Oh, hello, Jay!"

The gunsmith had emerged from his shop to witness the affair. He was an elderly man with spectacles. An oil-and-grease-stained apron covered his clothing. Homer continued, "I was just bringin' my friend, Pete Piper, to meet you, when we ran into Luke—at least Pete did. I reckon Luke ain't sure just what he ran into, but I'll bet he has visions of a fast freight."

The gunsmith invited them into his shop. They entered and closed the door. The shop wasn't large, but the walls were lined with racks of guns, rifles, shotguns, and six-shooters, both new and secondhand, mostly secondhand. At one side was a workbench to which was attached a small vise, at present holding a piece of gun mechanism on which Jay Harvey had been employing a file. Gun parts and stocks were scattered from one end of the room to the other. The men talked for a few minutes, explaining to Harvey what the trouble had been, then Homer asked:

"What was Luke doin' here, Jay?"

"He wanted to trade his .30-30 for a heavier-caliber rifle, a .38-.55."

Pete and Homer exchanged looks. Pete asked, "What's wrong with his old gun?"

"I don't know. That's why we didn't make a deal. But I do know Luke Traxler never did take good care of his weapons. Cleaning guns and him never did get along. He swears his gun is in tiptop shape, but I want to see it first before I tell him what I want t'boot."

"He didn't have his rifle with him, eh?" Homer asked.

Harvey shook his head. "No. Said it was out to the Diamond-T. Claimed he hadn't used it since last fall when it failed to bring down a buck he shot at. If he'd shot straight that .30-.30 would have brought down the deer all right."

"I'll betcha," Homer nodded. "Well, Jay, if he brings in his gun I'd like to have a look at it."

"I'll let you know." The old man added shrewdly, "I heard of some of the testimony that was given at the inquest today. I know what you got in mind."

"You're smart, Jay, but don't talk too much about it."

"Leave it to me. So long. Drop in again, Mr. Piper."

They stepped out of the gunshop and closed the door. Pete said, "Luke seems anxious to get rid of his rifle."

Homer nodded. "Howsomever, nobody but a damned fool would try to dispose of the gun here. Well, let's go get that drink we mentioned a spell back."

The remainder of the day passed uneventfully. Nothing more was heard of the Traxlers, somewhat to Pete's surprise. After eating supper with Homer at the hotel dining room the two men shot pool for a time at the local pool parlor. The evening slipped quickly past. By ten o'clock Pete had announced his intention of turning in, said good night to Homer, and headed for his hotel room.

The room was on the second floor of the hotel building, at the rear. Its single window overlooked a yard, back of the hotel, and a lean-to shelter, where temporary visitors could park their rigs and horses, the shelter being erected against the rear wall of the building. Beyond, the yard opened into an alleyway that paralleled Main Street.

Pete stepped into the room and bolted the door behind him. The room was scantily furnished with a threadbare carpet, an iron double bed, a dresser, and two chairs. Pete lighted the oil lamp that stood on the dresser. There was a packing-house calendar tacked to one wall. He slipped off the red quirt and hung it on a knob at the foot of the bed, then unbuckled his belt and gun and laid them on a chair next to his pillow. This last through sheer force of habit.

There wasn't any shade on the window. Pete blew out the flame in the lamp chimney and undressed in the dark. Then he opened the window and got between the blankets.

Gradually the noises of the town quieted down and Pete went to sleep. He breathed evenly, deeply, in the cool night air that swept in through the open window.

Just how long Pete had been asleep he didn't know, when something aroused him. He only knew he was abruptly wide awake, but whether the awakening was due to some strange noise or to some subtle, warning extra sense was uncertain. His eyes were opening staring into the blackness overhead. He shifted his gaze toward the open window, distinguishable only by a square dark gray. There wasn't a sound in the room, as far as he could tell.

He strained his ears in the darkness. Minutes passed. Finally there came a faint scraping sound near the foot of the bed. Pete shifted slightly. The noise ceased. Pete opened his mouth and a long-drawn snore emerged. He grunted sleepily and turned on his side, then resumed the snoring sounds. Between snores his ears were alert for the slightest movement in the dark room.

Again came that faint scraping near the foot of the bed.

Stealthily Pete put out one hand toward the holstered gun near his pillow. His fingers closed softly, firmly, about the walnut-butted weapon. Slowly he commenced to draw the gun from its scabbard. He turned his head slightly so as to look about the room. Somebody was there, standing at the foot of the bed; Pete, between his own snores, caught the sound of suppressed breathing.

His gun was free of its holster now. Pete shifted carefully, slowly drew his body erect, without being detected. A floor board creaked suddenly; there was a faint footstep. Then, against the lighter square of darkness at the window, Pete saw, through the gloom, the dark figure of a man in the act of departing.

Pete swung his gun toward the dim form. "Halt where you are, mister!" he snapped.

The man at the window paused, then turned, one foot over the ledge. A sudden brilliant flash of gunfire blinded Pete's eyes!

13   Alibi?

BLINDED as he was by the sudden glaring flash, Pete was forced to fire by instinct rather than aim. He heard the intruder's bullet rip into the wall at his rear. Fortunately, upon giving the order to halt, Pete had flung his body ot one side. He knew his first shot had missed when a second jarring explosion from the vicinity of the window shook the room.

Pete's reply was instant, savage. He thumbled another quick shot from his six-shooter and followed it in swift succession with two more bullets. The man at the window was halfway through when one of those three bullets found its mark. An agonized cry of pain was torn from the fellow's throat; then came the sound of a tumbling body on the lean-to roof outside.

The room was swimming with powder smoke. Pete leaped from the bed, rushed to the window. By this time his eyes had become accustomed to the darkness again. He thrust his head through the opening. Just a couple of feet below was the roof of the lean-to, and sprawled silently a short distance from the window, on the roof, Pete could make out a dark huddled figure.

"Got enough, hombre?" Pete said grimly.

There wasn't any answer.

"I reckon he has," Pete told himself. He quickly drew on his trousers and boots, slapped his sombrero on his head, plugged out the empty shells in his .45 cylinder, and reloaded. All this time there hadn't been a sound from the lean-to roof. Pete cast another glance from the window, then lighted the oil lamp.

Outside the room footsteps came hurrying up the stairs from the hotel lobby. There came a loud pounding on Pete's door.

Pete slipped back the bolt and opened the door. The hotel clerk stood there, clad in a long nightshirt and slippers. His face was pale, his hair tousled.

"Th-th-that shooting up here?" he quavered.

"It was," Pete replied laconically. "Reckon its all over now, though.'

"But—but what happened?"

"I'm not sure yet." Pete cast a look about the room and noticed that the red quirt was missing from the foot of the bed where he had placed it. Nothing else seemed to be missing. "Woke up and heard somebody here," Pete explained. "He was just crawling through the window. I ordered him to halt, and he opened fire. I did the same."

"But where is he?"

"If I'm not wrong, he's stretched on the roof of that lean-to below my window. With that lean-to roof so close to that window I should think you'd have a lock for the window."

"Was your window closed?" the clerk asked.

"You win," Pete said. "I opened it before I went to bed."

"Then," the clerk demanded triumphantly, "what good would a lock have been?"

"That's neither here nor there," Pete said grimly. "Let's forget it. Were you asleep when you heard the shots?"

"Certainly."

"It's a wonder the night clerk didn't get here before you. Where is he?"

"There's no night clerk. I sleep in a room off the lobby. If anybody wants a room after I've locked up for the night they have to knock on the door and awaken me."

"You sort of lead a twenty-four-hour existence, eh?"

By this time there came the sounds of other awakened guests in the hotel. The clerk went to the door, explained that a gun had been exploded by accident, and closed it again. Whether the guests believed him or not, the explanation satisfied and the sight of the clerk assured them there couldn't be much wrong, so they returned to their beds. Pete handed the oil lamp to the clerk with the explanation:

"Hold this light. I'm going out on that roof."

The clerk took the lamp. Pete crawled through the window and stepped the necessary three feet to the lean-to roof. At the first step his foot struck something. He stooped and found his red quirt. "I'll bet," he muttered to himself, "this hombre I shot proves to be one of Traxler's men."

However, when he lifted the head of the man who was sprawled face down, the face was unfamiliar. Pete said to the clerk, "Hold that light out a mite farther." The clerk thrust out the lamp at arm's length. The flame wavered in the chill night breeze.

"Is—is that man hurt bad?" the clerk gulped.

"Not any more," Pete replied. "He's dead."

"Dead? That's bad."

"Couldn't be worse," Pete admitted. "But it was him or me. You should be glad it's turned out this way. Think of the bad name your hotel would get if I was found dead in my bed. All folks can say about your hotel now is that it burgles easily but unsuccessfully."

"If that's meant to be funny," the clerk said reproachfully, "I don't think this is the time for humor."

Pete straightened up and thrust the six-shooter in his hand into the waistband of his trousers. "It's not the time to be fooling around, taking care of dead bodies, either," Pete said grimly, "but I don't reckon we can leave this feller on your roof."

"I'll have to notify the sheriff before we can move him," the clerk said.

"Well, get busy and notify him then. I'm coming back in the room."

The clerk drew back and placed the lamp on the dresser. Pete started to gather the rest of his clothes and put them on.

"I'll go get the sheriff, if you like," he offered.

At that moment there came a loud knocking at the door of the hotel lobby. "There's somebody now," the clerk said. "I'll go let him in." He scurried from the room. Pete heard his running steps on the stairway.

Within a few minutes he returned with Deputy Sheriff Homer Pritchard right behind him. "Hi-yuh, Pete," Homer said. "Charley tells me you shot a hombre breakin' into your room." It was plain to see that Homer had dressed hurriedly.

"Yeah," Pete nodded. "The body's out on that lean-to roof. The only thing he took, though, was my riding quirt. Funny, eh?"

The two exchanged meaning glances. "Darn funny," Homer said. "Just what happened?"

Pete told him, concluding, "The clerk was about to go get Sheriff Perkins."

"I don't reckon it will be necessary to wake up Ethan," Homer replied. "You don't know the feller you shot, eh?"

"Stranger to me. Cowpuncher, though, by his togs."

"I'll take a look at him."

Pete held the lamp while Homer crawled through the window. The deputy crouched by the side of the dead man and examined him. After a minute he said, "It's George Winchell."

"Who's he?"

Homer said carelessly, "Just one of the Diamond-T crew,

that's all. I happen to know that Winchell served a term in a pen, back in Colorado, for burglary. I reckon he must have had a hankerin' to return to his old trade." He climbed back through the window, then stopped and retrieved Winchell's six-shooter where it had fallen and slid under the dresser. He examined the gun; then, "Looks like he'd fired twice."

Pete nodded. "I emptied four slugs from my hawg-laig. The flash of his first shot sort of blinded me for a moment, and I had to throw my shots by guess."

"Sure good guessin'," Homer complimented.

"How'd you happen to come here?" Pete asked.

"Thought I heard shots. I'd got up to get a drink of water. They sounded pretty faint, so I couldn't be sure."

"The shots all exploded in this room before Winchell tumbled from the window," Pete said. "That's probably why they didn't sound loud to you."

"Probably," Homer agreed. "Anyway, I got dressed as soon as I could and headed down this way. I saw a light in the hotel lobby, which is plumb unusual this time of night, so I knocked to find out why."

Here the clerk put in, "How about Winchell? You going to leave him lay out there all night?"

"Why not," Homer asked gravely. "He won't catch cold."

"I'm thinking of the good name of the Cowmen's Rest Hotel," the clerk responded indignantly. "The sooner that body's removed, the better I'll like it."

"Think we ought to tell the sheriff?" Pete asked.

Homer shook his head. "No use wakin' him up. He's got a small house over on Taos Street. No need of us goin' over there. Ethan pretty much leaves things to my judgment. We'll wait a spell, then take this body to the undertaker's———"

"Figure we should notify the coroner?"

"Naw, I'll tell Doc Gillett how it was, and you can tell your story. You ain't denyin' you killed Winchell—in self-defense, of course—so there's no doubt how he come by his finisher. There won't be any inquest necessary. Charley"—to the clerk—"you go on back to bed. Pete and me can take care of Winchell's body. It's not far from the edge of the roof of the lean-to to the ground. I figure we can lower and then carry it between us down to the undertaker's. That's not far; almost across from the sheriff's office."

The clerk nodded. "That will be much better than bringing the body back through this room and down through the lobby. Please take care of it before daylight. I wouldn't want anybody to see a dead body being removed from here."

"It'll be taken care of." Homer nodded. "By the way, leave the lobby open, so Pete can get back to his room."

The clerk departed, closing the door. Homer laughed.

"Poor Charley. He's only been out from Wisconsin about a year. He's not yet used to the sight of sudden death, like we see it around here now and then." He paused; then, "Well, let's see what we can do about moving that body."

Gray light was commencing to glimmer in the east when they crawled through the window to the roof of the lean-to. It was an easy drop to the earth from the lower edge of the roof. Homer dropped to the ground, and Pete lowered Winchell's body. Together they bore the dead form through the silent town and, arriving at the undertaker's, awakened the man in charge and carried the body inside the "Funeral Parlors."

On the street again a short time later Pete said, "Was Winchell in town yesterday with Traxler and the other Diamond-T men?"

"I don't remember seein' him," Homer replied promptly. "By the way, I was talkin' to Black Nick last night after you left for bed."

"What did Traxler have to offer?"

"Stopped at the office on his way back to the ranch. Wanted to protest your blackin' Luke's other eye. Insisted I arrest you for disturbin' the peace. About that time Sheriff Ethan stepped in, after makin' his last round of the town. Ethan told him where he could go. I also brought out the point that it didn't look too good, Luke tryin' to get rid of his rifle."

"How'd he take that?"

"It shut him up pronto. Apparently Luke hadn't said anythin' to Nick about the rifle business. Nick's face got like a thundercloud, but he had damn little more to say after that. I guess it gave him somethin' to think about. Leastwise, he started bawlin' out Luke the instant he left the office. You know——"Homer paused, frowning.

"What's on your mind?"

"I was just thinkin'," Homer said slowly, "that it was kind of funny that Traxler waited all day before makin' his protests. There was seven of the crew in town, includin' the three Traxlers. They stopped before the office, and Black Nick came in. It struck me then that they wanted to be sure that I saw them departin' from the town. Now maybe that's exactly the impression they wanted to give me."

Pete nodded. "In other words, when I discovered my quirt was gone this morning—as it was intended to be—I couldn't blame any of the Diamond-T crew, because they'd swear they'd all left town before midinght. Just alibiing themselves. Maybe they're not as smart as they think."

"They couldn't be," Homer said. "I'm just wonderin' what Traxler will have to offer when we confront him with Winchell's death. I'll betcha he's waitin' right now for Winchell to return with your quirt."

"It could be," Pete agreed. "We'll see what this day brings forth. Meanwhile, there's a few hours of sleep left in my carcass. I'm goin' to take care of that right now."

"You and me both." Homer nodded. "Good night—or mebbe I should say good mornin'. Anyway, sleep tight."

14   Traxler Thinks Fast

IT WAS CLOSE TO TEN-THIRTY that same morning. In the Diamond-T bunkhouse Black Nick Traxler sat in a tilted-back chair, against one wall, facing several of his men: there were his two brothers, Nevada Norton, Canary Sloan, Ducky Drake, and a tall, stoop-shouldered cowboy named Hump Auringer. The bunkhouse was a long, flat-roofed building constructed of adobe. Along one wall ran a double tier of bunks. There was a desk just inside the doorway, near which Nick Traxler was seated. Farther down the room was a long mess table with a wooden bench on either side. Beyond that a doorway opened into the kitchen, where Soggy Horton, a skinny individual wearing a flour-sack apron, was mixing a mess of bread dough. There was a regular ranch house on the Diamond-T, but Nick Traxler rarely entered it, preferring to sleep and live with his outfit in the bunkhouse.

There was an air of gloomy expectancy on the faces of those present, with the exception of Black Nick's; it was as though they realized some calamity had fallen but hoped against hope it couldn't be so. Nick sat smoking a long black cigar, his features immobile, while his men waited for him to speak. Finally he knocked the ash from his cigar and said, "I've got to do some fast thinking. In fact, I have been doing it."

"But, Nick," Ivan protested. "Maybe there's a chance yet. Maybe George has just been detained."

"Detained, hell!" Nick snapped. "Sure he's been detained. He failed, that's what. I sent George Winchell to do a job. If he'd done it he'd have been back here with that quirt. He hasn't returned, so he's either been captured—or he's dead."

"I don't see," Canary Sloan asked in his chirpy voice, "why you're so anxious to get that quirt."

"What you don't know won't hurt you, Canary," Nick said coldly. "You'll know in plenty time. Just take my word for it; it's for the good of the outfit." His temper suddenly rose. "You got a lot of nerve, asking, anyway. You failed me too. If—"

"Aw, chief," Canary protested. "how could I tell? It was at night. When we held up Piper and the girl how was I to know that wa'n't the right quirt I took off'n his wrist? He was seen to be wearing the red quirt when him and Cressy Alexander left town."

"Haw! Haw! Haw!" Luke Traxler's boisterous laugh filled the room. "You sure looked funny, Canary, when you come ridin' in night before last, yellin', 'I got it, Nick! I got it!' And then when you produced that quirt in the lamplight and seed it was only an ordinary quirt, your face sure took a tumble. I like to died laughin'—"

"'Tain't funny, Luke," Hump Auringer growled. "Me and Canary and Ducky done our best. We at least took risks facin' Piper's gun. That's more than you can say. If you want to see somethin' really funny, give a look at yourself in the lookin' glass. Those two shiners of yours——"

"Damn you, Hump!" Luke started from his chair.

"Damn *you*, Luke!" Black Nick snapped testily. "Sit down and shut up. You're all boast and brag. Always shooting off your mouth at the wrong time. If it wa'n't for you we'd mebbe not be in the fix we're in at present."

Luke sat down. "Aw, Nick, I ain't done nothin'," he said in a half whine.

"You and Ivan didn't do what you should; that's a cinch," Nick said testily. "First you took my field glasses without my say-so. Then when a shot comes near, you drop 'em and run."

"But my eye, Nick——" Luke commenced.

"I wish it had been your neck," Nick said brutally. "The idea of you two seeing Piper with that red quirt and not going after it. Won't you ever get any guts? No, you have to turn and run. Two of you running from one man——"

"I noticed you back down some that same day," Ivan put in sullenly, "when Piper throwed a drop on you. Yes, and Nevada, too, when Cressy Alexander grabbed my gun. A little fast thinking——"

"Leave me out of your family squabble," Nevada snarled. He tried to change the subject. "Nick, when will Steve and Larry get back?"

"You know as well as I do," Nick said shortly. "You heard me tell 'em to stay over in Ladder-D country until they'd made a complete survey, so we'd know just where each herd was being held. When we hear from them we'll get busy again, but right now we got more serious things to think about."

"Meaning Winchell, I suppose," Nevada said. "Hell, he might show up yet."

"God! Such a dumb crew!" Nick glared around at his men, than again gave his attention to Nevada. "You're all hoping for the same thing, that Winchell will show up. Well, I'll tell you I gave up hopes of that quite a long spell back. If he'd been successful he'd have been back by dawn with that red quirt. If he'd been captured there'd been somebody here from the sheriff's office asking for me."

"Why for you?" Ivan looked startled.

Black Nick explained. "I told Winchell if he got in a jam to send somebody for me and I'd get him out."

"How do you expect to do that?" Ivan asked.

"With my brains, stupid," Nick snapped. "That's something you wouldn't know about. Anyway, I had to tell Winchell something so he'd go through with it. He wasn't keen on the job."

Ivan looked troubled. "I don't know as that was using brains, Nick. Suppose George really did get caught and he sent for you? That would tie us up with the scheme to steal the quirt. That's mighty risky."

"God damn it!" Nick swore. "We have to run risks, the way we operate. That's part of the business, but you'll admit it pays dividends." His voice became calmer. "But I guess we won't run any risks where Winchell is concerned. He didn't return with the quirt; no word has come from the sheriff about him. That means just one thing: George Winchell is dead."

"Who'd kill him?" Luke asked dumbly.

A look of extreme exasperation crossed Nick's swarthy feathers. His voice, when he spoke, however, was deadly calm, like that of a schoolteacher querying a small pupil. "Luke, whose room was George Winchell told to enter?"

"Why—why, Piper's room."

"All right, there's your answer," Nick said shortly. "If he hasn't been killed by Piper I miss my guess."

"That redheaded son———" Luke growled.

"You got to admit he's smart, anyway," Nick said grudgingly. "I'd like to know for sure if the sheriff sent to have him come here."

"I still think you got a wrong hunch on that, Nick," Luke said placatingly. "Why should Perkins have him sent here?"

An angry flush mounted to Nick's features. "Luke, will you please shut up? All you do is ask questions. You *think* I've got the wrong hunch, do you? What in the name of cripes a'mighty do you think with? If your brains were dynamite you wouldn't have enough to give you a bad hiccup if they exploded. I get so damn mad at you every time I think of you going to Jay Harvey to make a trade for your rifle. Jeez! Didn't you realize you'd give the whole show away? First thing you know, they'll be matching your rifle with those shells Piper picked up. We've got to forestall that sort of move; it'd prove you were on Elephant Ridge that day. And I think I know how to forestall———"

"All right," Luke cut in sullenly, "I won't trade my rifle."

"Moses on the mountain! The damage is done now. What would you say if Sheriff Perkins demands to examine that shooting pole?"

"I'll tell him it was stolen," Luke proposed brightly.

Nevada Norton shook his head despairingly and cast a thin smile around the room. The crew made no bones of the fact that Luke was the dunce of the outfit and treated him accordingly.

"You'll tell him it was stolen, will you?" Nick said sarcastically. "Dammit! Luke, you're hopeless I got by with that story on my field glasses. You can't expect the sheriff to bite twice on the same story."

"Maybe," Luke commenced, "I could tell the sheriff I lost my rifle."

"If you don't tell the sheriff anything I'll be thankful," Nick said irritably. "Every time you open your mouth you put your foot in it. Just keep out of the sheriff's sight—and Piper's. I even wish you'd keep out of my sight for a spell. No, you just leave all talking to me."

"Yes, Nick," Luke said meekly. "But what will you tell the sheriff?

"Look"—Nick spoke to the room at a whole—"I told you boys I'd been doing some fast thinking. Here's what I've decided. . . ." He talked steadily for several minutes. A couple of times Luke or Ivan tried to interrupt, but he shut them up with a look. When he had finished he said, "What do you think?"

The men looked rather dubious. Ivan protested vigorously. "That puts us right on a spot," Luke said. "Me and Ivan——"

"You put yourselves on the spot," Nick said coldly. "Now I've got to get you out of your mix-up, as usual. All you got to do is back me up if Perkins questions you. No matter what happens I'll get you two out of it. I always took care of you before, didn't I? You can either take my plan, Luke, or get out of it the best way you know how. I'll wash my hands of you."

"I'd be careful about saying that," Ivan commenced. "You won't wash your hands of us, Nick. After all, we know as much about that quirt as you do. One word from us——"

Like a flash, Nick leaped out of the chair and across the intervening yards between himself and Ivan. His fingers closed about Ivan's throat, and he shook his brother viciously. His eyes blazed with rage. "Oh, you'd double-cross me, would you? You may be my brother, but by God——!"

He broke off suddenly, regained his temper, and released his grip on Ivan's throat. Ivan choked and gasped, regained his wind. "You—you didn't have—to do that—Nick," he said with difficulty.

"I reckon I did," Nick said coldly. "It takes something like that to make you and Luke realize what we're up against. So long as I'm running this outfit my word is law; remember that. And I don't want to hear any further word of bucking me. You may be my brother, but I refuse to let your ideas buck mine. I'm doing what is best for the whole bunch, and

I can't afford to let you, or Luke, do anything that will imperil our own skins." He backed a couple of paces and glanced at the others. "How about it? Are you with me on the plan or aren't you?"

Nevada Norton was first to speak: "Ordinarily I'd be against it. Nick, but if anybody can handle it, I say you can. You never yet failed us, so I'm with you."

Nevada's words put the idea across. The others quickly agreed, except Luke and Ivan. Ivan nodded after a few minutes. "I still don't like it, though," he said weakly. "That sheriff isn't any fool. Neither is his deputy or that redhead. They'll see through you maybe."

"I don't give a damn what they see"—Nick laughed shortly——"so long as they can't prove anything. You've got to have proof to convict a man."

Luke, as always, threw the responsibility of his own troubles on Nick's shoulders. "Go ahead, I leave it to you."

"Good." Nick smiled thinly. "We're agreed, then. I'm riding for town right now. Nevada, Canary—you'd better come with me."

"You don't want me, do you, Nick?" Luke asked.

"No, nor Ivan, either. You stay here and sit tight. I'll tell you what happens."

Both Luke and Ivan looked considerably relieved when he left the bunkhouse, accompanied by Canary Sloan and Nevada. Within a few minutes they heard the thudding hoofs of the departing ponies.

15   Spiked Guns

SHORTLY AFTER TWO O'CLOCK that afternoon Black Nick, Canary, and Nevada rode into Beauregard City. They slowed their horses to a walk as they drew near the sheriff's office. Nevada said, "Want we should stay with you, Nick, or do you want to see the sheriff alone?"

"You and Canary go on ahead. I'll meet you in Turk Raven's place as soon as I get through with the sheriff."

Canary wiped moisture from his brow with the neckerchief at his throat. He looked worried. "Supposin' the sheriff puts you under arrest? What do we do then, try for a jail break?"

Nick smiled thinly. "Don't brand your steer until you've got him throwed, Canary. I don't reckon the sheriff will put me under arrest. If I don't miss my guess, what I tell him will knock his props out. Hell's bells! He wouldn't have anything to arrest *me* on."

Nevada nodded. "I hope not. Well, good luck, Nick."

He and Canary loped on ahead. They noticed as they

passed the sheriff's office that Piper and the deputy sheriff were standing on the sidewalk, their backs resting against the hitch rail.

The two men turned to see who was riding past. At that moment Black Nick reined his pony into the rail. "Howdy, Piper. Hello, Homer. Sheriff Ethan about?" He alighted and came around on the walk.

Pete nodded coolly. Homer said, "H'are you, Traxler? Yeah, the sheriff's inside his office, doin' things with his monthly swindle sheet. You got to see him?"

"Yes," Nick replied. "Though you might as well stick around, Homer, and hear what I got to say. You too, Piper."

Pete said dryly, "Thanks."

Homer lifted his voice. "Hey, Ethan, Nick Traxler is out here. Says he's got to see you about an alibi or somethin'."

Traxler reddened. "Someday, Homer," he said, trying to hold his voice to an even tone, "you and I are going to tangle. I haven't broken any laws, yet you're always throwing out veiled remarks suggesting that I'm in some sort of crooked business."

Homer grinned. "If that was veiled, I'm a monkey's uncle."

"Now I'm certain," Nick Traxler said tartly. "It *was* veiled. I've often noticed the family resemblance."

Homer's jaw dropped. Traxler smiled smoothly. At that moment the sheriff came out of the office, donning his sombrero. "You want to see me, Nick?" he said coldly. "Well, I want to see you too. I was just about to send Homer with a message———"

"Good thing I came in, Ethan," Traxler said quickly. "We'll get to my business first, if you don't mind. Mine will probably take less time—at least part of it. I just wanted to ask you to pick up George Winchell if you happened to run across him. The dirty thief lit out from the ranch last night, taking seventy-five dollars of mine, after I'd fired him———"

"Wait a minute," the sheriff interposed. "Are you trying to tell me you discharged Winchell last night?"

"I'm telling you. We caught him cheating in a friendly game of poker in our bunkhouse———"

"Seems I remember you bein' in town last night," Homer put in.

"This was after I got back," Traxler said smoothly. "The game was already going when I came in. I took a hand. About then Winchell pulled his crooked work. We caught him at it. He tried to laugh it off. I told him a thing or two. His language got sort of abusive, so I paid him off and told him to get out. He got out, but I didn't discover until this morning that he'd taken seventy-five dollars from my desk. I don't suppose there's much chance of catching him—he's probably jumped over the state line—but I just wanted to tell you, in case you did run into him."

Pete smiled coldly, a ceratin admiration for the man's boldness and quick thinking taking hold of him. He didn't say anything. Homer, in openmouthed amazement, just stood and stared. The sheriff's face grew red with anger. Finally he found his voice:

"Are you telling me, Traxler, that you fired Winchell last night?" Perkins asked in a strangled tone.

"Exactly. Is there anything strange about that?"

"And you're asking me to arrest him if I——?" the sheriff started.

"Why not?" Traxler frowned. "It's a crime. The sheriff of the county runs down criminals. I realize we haven't been exactly good friends, Ethan, but I'm asking no more than any taxpayer would. Oh, I don't expect you to load up with supplies and get on his trail. I meant in case you happened to run across him——"

"This," the sheriff roared, hurling his sombrero to the sidewalk, "is the limit! Of all the nerve I've seen, Traxler, yours takes the cake!" Angrily he stooped and retrieved the hat.

"Why, Ethan"—Traxler looked puzzled—"what's the matter? I'm not asking anything unusual."

Homer asked sarcastically, "You wouldn't have had a hunch that Winchell might be dead, would you, Nick? Not tryin' to cover anythin' up, are you?"

"Cover up? Dead? Dead!" Traxler's assumption of innocent surprise was about convincing. "Homer, you don't mean——?"

"Yeah, I do," Homer said flatly. "Winchell's dead—if you haven't already guessed it."

"Good lord! How should I have guessed anything like this? Winchell must have been taken suddenly ill after I kicked him out. Maybe I was too hasty. If he was sick it may have influenced his actions. I should think before I——"

"Too hasty! Too hasty!" The sheriff sputtered. "By Gawd! You've got a nerve, Traxler. No, Winchell wasn't taken ill."

"Call it lead poisoning," Pete said quietly.

Homer added, "Pete caught Winchell in his hotel room this morning, early. Winchell shot first. Pete finished the job."

The sheriff faced Traxler indignantly. "What sort of bluff is this you're trying to run on us, Nick?"

Traxler shook his head, unbelievingly. "I can't understand it. Winchell must have gone back to his old trade. He once served a term for burglary, you know, but he swore he was all through with that——" He paused, then said stiffly, "What do you mean, Sheriff accusing me of running a bluff?" Suddenly he smiled scornfully. "I get it! You believe I had something to do with the job Winchell tried to pull. Sheriff, you know me better than that. Cripes! How could I have had anything to do with it? I fired Winchell last night."

"You've got proof of that, of course?" Pete said quietly.

"Certainly. My whole crew witnessed my actions."

"That settles it, I reckon." Pete smiled coldly. "Ethan, we can't connect Traxler with the business." Both Ethan and Homer started to protest, then decided to drop the matter for the present.

Traxler heaved a sigh of relief. "I'm certainly glad that misunderstanding is cleared up. What did Winchell try to take from your room, Piper?"

"What would you think?" Pete asked.

"Money, I imagine," Traxler replied, watching Pete narrowly.

"Right," Pete responded, much to Traxler's surprise, though the man managed to conceal it. "He dropped my wallet when I plugged him. Nothing else was touched."

"Glad it came out like that," Traxler commented. "I reckon it's a good thing I fired the dirty crook off my pay roll. Oh yes, Ethan, you said you had some business with me, something about wanting to send Homer with a message."

"Forget it," Perkins blurted, angry at the way Traxler had evaded connection with the Winchell affair. "It didn't amount to anything."

A mocking smile played about the corners of Traxler's mouth. "You hadn't planned to bring me in for questioning in regard to this Winchell business, had you, Ethan?" he asked blandly.

"Whether I did or not makes no difference now," Perkins replied grumpily. "You *seem* to be in the clear. Forget it, unless you got some other business with me."

"That's just it; I have," Traxler stated. "Rather touchy business, in fact. I don't know just how you're going to take it." He assumed an expression of embarrassment.

The sheriff looked puzzled. "Well, spit it out," he growled. "What's on your mind?"

"Well, I—well, you see——" Traxler laughed, nervously, as though uncertain how to begin. Pete figured the performance as a piece of good acting. Traxler finally got it out: "Ethan, I want to make a confession— that is, a confession on the part of Ivan and Luke. I'm here on their behalf. This is what I really rode in to see you about."

"A confession?" Perkins said warily. "About Ivan and Luke?"

"What they been doin'," Homer asked, "stealin' chickens?"

Traxler flashed an angry look at Homer but held his temper. "Fact is, Sheriff," he said smoothly, "Ivan and Luke were up on Elephant Ridge that day Tiger Eye Munson's body was found. It was Ivan and Luke who Piper saw riding away——"

"Well, I'll be damned!" the sheriff exploded. "You mean they're the ones that killed Munson?"

"That's exactly what I do *not* mean. I'm here to——"

"Well, suffering wildcats! What do you mean?" the sheriff demanded angrily. "So help me, if you don't talk up I'll see that you're made to. You've said too much or too little—enough, leastwise, to warrant your arrest——"

"Not *my* arrest," Traxler suavely pointed out. "When I've finished you may see fit to get a warrant for Luke and Ivan."

"I'll get out warrants for your whole Diamond-T outfit if you don't come clean," the sheriff threatened angrily.

"Look, Sheriff," Pete proposed quietly, "suppose we let Traxler tell the story in his own way." The man's sheer audacity held a certain fascination for Pete. He was curious to hear what Traxler would offer.

"All right," Perkins grumbled. "Get on with it, Traxler."

Traxler nodded to Pete. "Thanks, Piper. I can well understand the sheriff's attitude." He smiled wryly. "I can't say I blame you, Ethan. My brothers made a mistake; I made a second mistake in backing them up. To start with, I'm admitting we were all wrong. What you'll do is up to you."

"Look, Traxler"—Homer yawned—"I think Ethan is anxious for you to start talkin'. I know damn well I am."

Traxler drew a long breath. "That morning Munson was killed Luke and Ivan had started across the range to the Ladder-D. Time was hanging heavy on their hands, so they figured to visit a spell with Joe Dunlop. As they neared Elephant Ridge they thought they heard shooting and rode over to investigate——"

"I'm surprised they didn't run the other way," Homer muttered in an aside to Pete.

Traxler cast an angry glance at Homer and continued, as though there'd been no interruption. "After some searching around they found horse tracks that led them to Munson's body, but there wasn't the sign of a rider——"

"In the rocking chair?" the sheriff asked becoming interested.

"In the rocking chair." Traxler nodded. "There they found things exactly as Piper described them at the inquest. No sign of a wagon, but wagon tracks were to be seen. Anyway, Luke or Ivan—I forget which—saw tracks leading up to the top of Elephant Ridge. They decided to see what could be found. Shortly after they reached the top Luke employed my field glasses to look down toward Munson's body. He saw Piper down there——"

"Thought you said your glasses had been stolen?" the sheriff put in shrewdly.

"I know," Traxler said humbly. "I admit I lied about that,

Ethan, but you'll understand when I've finished."

"I hope so," the sheriff said skeptically.

"Anyway," Traxler continued, "Luke saw Piper down there and jumped to the conclusion he was Munson's murderer returned. You can understand, Luke and Ivan were pretty well wrought up about finding their old pal, Tiger-Eye, killed. Without stopping to think, Luke threw a couple of shots at Piper—luckily, both missed—then grabbed up the field glasses again. About the same time Piper fired a shot in reply, making a lucky shot that ruined my glasses and scared hell out of Luke. You know, he's sort of rattle-brained at times. Him and Ivan had an idea that Piper had a couple of pals near, so they decided to make a run for it. Ivan would have stayed, but Luke insisted on getting away fast. You can't blame Ivan for leaving too. He wasn't going to stay and face, all alone, the man he thought was Munson's murderer—especially when he believed Piper had a couple of pals near."

"This," said Homer dryly, "is one honey of a story."

"Oh, I know it all sounds fishy to you," Traxler admitted readily. "I'm just telling what happened. Anyway, my brothers lit out for the Diamond-T, looking for me. They always run to me with their troubles. I guess you know that, Ethan. You see, by this time they realized they'd acted suspiciously in running away like that, and they knew they might be suspected of Munson's murder. That really scared 'em. In short, they just plain lost their heads, like we all do at some time in our lives. When they didn't find me at the ranch Ivan came on to Beauregard. He found me at Turk Raven's Saloon and told me what had happened. I bawled him out plenty but decided we'd better keep quiet about what we knew until we saw how things shaped up. That's why I've acted the way I did. I was wrong; I admit it. But I hope you'll credit me with coming clean. Now you've got the whole story."

"I'll be damned!" Perkins said. "You three lied at the inquest for fear Luke and Ivan would be accused of the murder?"

"That's just about it," Traxler said soberly.

The sheriff eyed him angrily. "I'll have to take this up with Doc Gillett, Traxler."

"I expected that, Ethan. It may be Doc will want to hold another inquest. I expect that too. But I'm telling you this right now: if the jury finds against Luke and Ivan, and warrants are issued for their arrest, I aim to fight the trial from start to finish. I stand ready to furnish bond the instant they are arrested. Those boys are innocent; I'm not going to stand by and see them convicted of another man's murder."

"You meaning me?" Pete asked softly.

"You're not in the clear, you know," Traxler said promptly. "A jury might ask what you were doing near Munson's body. Frankly, Piper, I don't think you did it."

"Thanks," Pete said dryly. "You maintain, of course, that Luke and Ivan are in the clear."

"Exactly. Hell, Piper, we thought a heap of old Tiger-Eye. Best friend we had. He's worked for me for years." He turned to the sheriff. "Well, Ethan, the problem is in your lap. What you aim to do?"

The sheriff looked troubled. "I don't know yet, exactly, Traxler. I'll have to talk to Doc Gillett and see what he says first. After I have his decision I'll go ahead on my own, whatever way suits me, regardless. But he's entitled to know what I know."

"And you'll let me know?" Traxler asked.

"I'll let you know all right," Perkins said grimly.

"Thanks," Traxler replied and moved out to his pony. He nodded to Pete and Homer. "I'll see you some more, gentlemen."

They watched him mount and turn his pony east on Main Street. After a minute the sheriff ripped out a sudden curse. Homer said puzzledly, "Now if that ain't the damnedest!"

Pete smiled. "There," he stated, "goes one smart hombre, and I'm meaning Black Nick Traxler. He's sure spiked our guns. By cripes! You almost have to admire a man like that. He thinks fast."

"Too fast for me," the sheriff sighed. "He riles me so, I lose my temper every time I talk to him. Say"—suddenly—"what do you mean he spiked our guns?"

"He's checkmated us all along the line," Pete explained. "He guessed that something had happened to Winchell, so he hurried to tell us he'd canned the man, so we couldn't tie the Diamond-T to that business."

"Do you believe he canned Winchell last night?" Homer asked.

"Certainly not," Pete replied promptly, "and neither do you and Ethan. But we can't prove otherwise, with Traxler's crew all ready to swear to what Traxler says. And we can't hold Traxler responsible for what an ex-employee does. I'm telling you, Black Nick is foxy."

"That's whatever," the sheriff growled. "His foxiness ain't going to prevent me from getting warrants for the arrest of Luke and Ivan for Munson's murder. I owe it to Doc Gillett to give him a chance to arrange another inquest first, but after that I'm letting my own judgment dictate my actions. Bah! That's the damnedest story I ever did hear."

"Yeah, it is," Pete agreed, "but there's just enough truth in it, Ethan, to make it appear plausible. Say you do arrest those two and bring them to trial. In the first place, Nick Traxler will get his brothers out on bail. The next thing is to get a jury to convict. Sure, any judge and jury would give them hell for covering up evidence, but that's no sign they'd be convicted of murder. Just think a trifle—what real proof have we that Luke and Ivan killed Munson? Not one shred!"

"By cripes!" Homer said. "That's true. We haven't, Ethan."

"Traxler has beaten us to the punch," Pete continued. "He was afraid we might ask to check up on Luke's rifle; if Luke refused to produce the weapon it would make him appear guilty. So Nick comes to you and makes a clean breast of things, admits he was wrong. That sort of stuff has a good impression on a jury, Ethan, and Traxler knows it. Nope, you'd never get a conviction, particularly in view of the way Traxler has folks buffaloed hereabouts. It's not what *we* think, Ethan, that counts. Traxler doesn't give a damn what we three think. It's what the people think, what a jury will think, Ethan, that will tell the story. Our best bet is to forget arrests until we can get more proof. To me, Traxler's story ties his brothers into Munson's death."

"I'd agree with you, Pete," Homer said, "if Munson and the Traxlers hadn't been such good friends."

"I'm just surprised"—Pete frowned—"that Traxler didn't accuse me of the crime and want me arrested."

"Mebbe I can explain that," the sheriff said. "I pick up information in my wanderings around town. Traxler has told two or three people he suspects you of being a deputy U.S. marshal."

Pete smiled. "And as such, he couldn't get me convicted. Let him keep on thinking so. It might help in the long run."

"Are you?" Homer asked bluntly. Both he and the sheriff watched eagerly for Pete's reply.

Pete shook his head. "No." There wasn't any doubt about it, the way the tones left his lips. The two peace officers looked disappointed. "Anyway," Pete continued, "Traxler has us stopped cold for the present. But there may be a flaw in his argument. I aim to find one."

Down in Turk Raven's Saloon, Black Nick had a cold, crafty smile on his face as he lifted a glass to his lips. Canary and Nevada Norton listened to him eagerly. "And they believed you?" Canary asked in his chirpy voice.

Nick Traxler laughed. "Hell, no! But they can't do a thing without proof, and they're smart enough to realize it. Don't worry, boys, I got them hog-tied plenty tight. I knew it would work!"

16   A Loophole

THE FOLLOWING DAY was Sunday. After shaving and getting into a clean shirt Pete rode to the C-Bar-A where he visited all day with Cressy, her father, Pinto Grant, and Graveyard. Much time was given over to telling what had happened in Beauregard City the past two days. They all argued and speculated regarding Black Nick Traxler and the sort of schemes he was promoting. Pete got some time alone with Cressy. The two walked around the various ranch buildings, at which time Pete noted that lack of ready cash had resulted in somewhat of a run-down condition on the ranch. Paint and repairs were badly needed at many points.

While the prime reason for the visit was a desire to see Cressy again, Pete had wanted to talk to her father and learn as much as possible about the various ranch owners who used Beauregard City as their headquarters for supplies. Alexander spoke of each man individually, and by the time Pete started back to town he felt he knew the country's cattlemen as well as a stranger could without actually meeting them. Cressy and her father asked Pete to stay for supper, but he had refused with thanks.

"You gave me my dinner," he had laughed. "I can't push a good thing too far. Besides, I've got one or two ideas I want to take up with Homer Pritchard. I'll come back for that supper some other time, if the invitation stands good."

"The invitation stands good—so long as we're here," Cyrus had replied moodily. "But it doesn't look like we'd be here very long. The time grows shorter every day."

"Don't take that viewpoint, Cyrus," Pete said earnestly. "I've got a hunch that this business is going to clear up all right. You know"—he paused and then went on—"before I came to this country I was looking around for a ranch of my own. I'd been down into Mexico but couldn't find just what I had in mind. Well, I've still got my money, and if worst comes to worst perhaps you'll let me offer a loan."

Cressy didn't say anything. Neither did her father for a few moments. When he spoke his eyes looked moist. "That's almighty decent of you, Pete, and I appreciate it a lot. But I can't afford to borrow more money. I've got to pull out of this hole by my own strength."

Pete nodded. "I reckon I know how you feel. Well, keep it in mind, anyway."

They'd been standing in the doorway of the house. Now he moved across the gallery and stepped to the earth as Pinto Grant rounded the corner of the building leading Pete's saddled roan.

Pete said, "Thanks a heap, Pinto."

"No thanks necessary, Pete. I'm glad to saddle up for you any time you can come out. Make it again soon."

Cressy left her father and joined Pete as Pinto departed. She placed one hand on Pete's arm. "I don't know how to say it, Pete, but you're good, awfully good. Your offer has lifted a load from Dad's mind. Oh, he won't take a loan, but he feels somebody, aside from his own outfit, is back of him."

"Didn't figure he'd take a loan"—Pete nodded—"but I wanted him to know if he got—well, sort of desperate for cash, I'd be within easy hailing distance. Of course I had in mind security for the loan."

"That's just it," Cressy said. "Banker Haines already holds the C-Bar-A as security. Dad has nothing else to offer."

"Yes, he has," Pete laughingly contradicted the girl. "I was figuring to hold you as security—or any other way—just so I could hold you."

"Pete!" Cressy smiled. "Can't you be serious about anything?"

"By cripes! I am. What could be more serious?"

Cressy shook her head and backed away. "Anyway, Pete, you're a great cheerer-upper. Come back and see us again."

"I'll do that." Pete laughed and climbed into his saddle. "When you figuring to get into Beauregard again."

"I want to drive in some day this coming week and get my trunk at Mrs. Fogarty's. Will I see you?"

"If you don't, drop by the sheriff's office. Either Ethan or Homer will know where I am. Come early and I'll buy you some dinner. Is it a go?"

"It's a go." Cressy promised. "Good-by, Peter, me lad."

"Oh, by the way," Pete said gravely, "you know I'm not the Pumpkin-eater Peter who had a wife and couldn't keep her." He sat looking gravely down at the girl, face upturned beside his horse. "I never even had a wife, but if I ever had one I'd sure keep her well. None of this pumpkin-shell stuff for my wife. Just keep that in mind. I don't go in for shell games, especially where my wives are concerned."

The girl was nodding and laughing and looking after him as he doffed his sombrero and rode away from the house. . . .

It was commencing to grow dark when he entered Beauregard City. Here and there lights were already starting to shine from doorways and windows along the street. Being Sunday, there weren't many pedestrians abroad. Pete stopped at the Busy Bee Restaurant for a quick supper, then started out to look for Homer. He found the deputy in Beanpole Ridge's Lariat Saloon, staring moodily into a glass of beer. Pete edged up to him without Homer noticing and said, "If you don't want it I'll drink it. Anyway, it might be bad for you."

Homer, startled, looked up; then his features broke into a lazy grin of welcome. "I can drink it now," he stated "It's just that I hate drinkin' alone. Beanpole!"

But Beanpole had already spotted Pete and came hurrying up from the farther end of the bar. "Evening, Mr. Piper. I reckon I'd better light up a couple more lamps. Didn't see you enter until you'd reached the bar. What'll it be?"

"Give me a bottle of that foamy stuff like Homer's drinking. I always did wonder what it tasted like."

Homer grinned. "I warn you, it's nothin' like milk."

"Do you know anything that is?" Pete accepted the bottle and glass Beanpole placed on the bar and poured his glass half full. "What was wrong with you when I came in? You looked like you'd lost your last friend."

"I've been thinkin' how Black Nick tossed a strangle hold on our plans. I've talked it over with Ethan. We've argued and argued, but we both come to the same conclusion. In spite of all the stuff Traxler confessed yesterday, we don't really know one damn thing we could bring him or his brothers to trial on."

Pete smiled. "I told you that yesterday. Ethan could make some arrests and we could kick up a fuss, but there's nothing a jury would bring in a murder conviction on."

"I know it," Homer said heatedly. "That's what makes me sore every time I think a blackguard like Traxler could stop us so neat-like. We're plumb hamstrung! We're decent Americans, you and me and Ethan and Cressy and her father and—and— oh well, most of the people in this town. What kind of a civilization is it that allows men like Traxler to operate in safety?"

"I got a hunch he won't operate much longer," Pete said quietly. "Trouble with us Americans, we're too easy going. Crooks put over a lot of stuff before we become aroused. But once we're aroused, there's hell to pay until said crooks have got their just deserts. Don't worry, we'll lick Traxler and his whole crew."

"I reckon"—Homer nodded—"but when?" He changed the subject. "Have a good time visitin' with the beauteous Cressy?"

"And with her father and their two hands." Pete nodded. "I get a laugh out of that feller, Graveyard Gratton. He sure is one pessimist. To hear him tell it you'd think the world was going to hell in a handcart."

"Ain't it the truth! But don't make any mistake about Graveyard. He's one sweet fightin' man. I don't know anybody I'd sooner have at my back in a ruckus. And he's loyal as all get out to the man who pays his wages."

"I gathered as much. Yeah, I had a nice visit, Homer. I spent part of the time getting a line on the beef raisers hereabouts from Cyrus."

"I could have told you anythin' you wanted to know."

"I'll get your opinions too. But to get back to Traxler: he claims that Luke and Ivan saw tracks leading up to Elephant Ridge. I saw tracks, too, but they were Ivan's and Luke's. If there were any others I didn't see 'em."

"Provin' what we already know—that the Traxlers are a lyin' bunch of no-good so-and-sos."

"Correct. But I'm reminding you, we've got to have proof of said lies before we can act."

Beanpole had moved down the bar a few minutes before. There were only a few customers in the place. Pete and Homer talked in low tones while they sipped their beer.

"Somethin' that occurred to me," Homer said. "Luke must have seen you with that red quirt, through the binoculars, that day. How come they hadn't found it before you?"

"It wasn't right near the body, remember," Pete explained. "I just stumbled on it in that mesquite by accident, you might say. Maybe they weren't anywhere near that mesquite."

"That's what I'm afraid of." Homer frowned. "Look at it this way: first, the Traxlers want that red quirt; second, if Munson had it with him why didn't Luke and Ivan get it when they killed Munson?—if they killed him."

"That's the point—if they killed him."

"It's a big point. Much as I'd like to think Ivan and Luke are guilty, if they were the ones that did it they would have grabbed the quirt then and there. Nope, we're back where we were. The Traxlers didn't do it, because Munson was a friend of theirs. Pete, Black Nick has tied his rope around us mighty secure-like."

"Maybe I've found a loophole," Pete replied.

"You have? Spill it."

"Homer, I've got Cyrus Alexander's opinion of Joe Dunlop that runs the Ladder-D. What's yours?"

"What's Dunlop got to do with this red-quirt business?"

"I don't know as he has anything, yet. I'm just asking a question. What sort of a hombre is he?"

"Nice enough feller, I reckon," Homer said slowly. "Like I told you, he's the biggest stock raiser in this country. He don't come to Beauregard much, nor does he mix in. I don't mean he's standoffish, or anythin' like that, though. In the first place, he's an Easterner who came out here for his health a good many years back. Pretty well educated, from all I hear. He had money, so he went in for cows and made a success of it. He goes in for breedin' on a scientific basis. A lot of folks resented it, in the beginnin', when Dunlop wouldn't let them run his business for him. Howsomever, I reckon he knows what he's about. When he ain't workin' on his stock he does a lot of readin'. I've even heard he writes poetry. Never believed it, though."

Pete nodded. "Your opinion agrees pretty much with what Cyrus told me. I just wanted to be sure before I started building that loophole I mentioned. Now, think carefully—what would Dunlop and Luke and Ivan Traxler have in common?"

Homer screwed up his forehead, considering. He laughed suddenly. "Well, I don't reckon Luke or Ivan ever wrote any poetry. Cripes! Pete, I can't think of one dang thing they'd have in common—not even stock raisin'. Luke and Ivan leave all that to Nick! I doubt if they actually ever worked cows much. Why, them two Traxlers are as different from Dunlop as night is from day."

"Exactly. And I think that's where the Traxlers slipped up in their story."

"How do you mean?"

Pete explained, "In making his so-called confession, Nick Traxler had to think of some reason why Luke and Ivan were over near Elephant Ridge the day Munson was killed. Do you remember the reason?"

"Why—er—why, yes. I remember distinctly, now, that Nick said time was hangin' heavy on their hands and they'd decided to visit with Dunlop for a spell—"

"Wait, now," Pete interposed. "Does that sound reasonable? Can you imagine Luke and Ivan visiting a man like Dunlop?"

Light suddenly dawned on Homer. "No, by Gawd! I can't!" he exclaimed. "There's the weak link in the chain, I'm bettin'. But they had to have an excuse for bein' over that way, and the Ladder-D ranch house is situated just north of Elephant Ridge's northeast end. By cripes, Pete! We've got 'em!"

"Don't go too fast, Homer. It's just an idea. Luke and Ivan may have intended to visit Dunlop that day, but it doesn't sound plausible. It's a weak link in Traxler's story all right, but he probably figured we'd never check on him close enough to notice it. Anyway, I'm going to ride over and talk to Dunlop tomorrow and get acquainted."

"Want I should go with you?"

Pete shook his head. "I don't want to take you away from your duties here, Homer. I'll let you know what I find out, though."

Homer looked disappointed, but he didn't say anything.

"Here's something else I've been thinking of," Pete went on. "How large a crew does Dunlop have on his pay roll?"

Homer considered the question. "He's the largest stockman around here, like I told you. He's got a sizable crew. I don't know exactly how many, but I'd say at least twenty."

"That's about what Cyrus told me too. Now how much of a crew is there on the Diamond-T?"

"We-ell, there's the three Traxlers. Nevada Norton, Auringer, Sloan, Drake—there was Winchell—the cook, Soggy Horton; a waddy named Barton who always pals with a feller called Larry Somethin' or Other; then there's—" He broke off, looking puzzled. "You know, it's kind of difficult addin' 'em up. It seems there's Diamond-T punchers comin' in and out of town all the time. It's hard to keep track of 'em. However, I've been out to the ranch on a couple of occasions, and there seemed to be quite a gang. I never thought of it before, but Traxler must hire close to twenty men too."

Pete smiled and spoke one word, "Why?"

"Why?" Homer frowned. "To work for him, of course."

"Doing what?"

"Working Diamond-T cows, I reckon. That's what most punchers do. Pete, what are you drivin' at?"

Pete asked a question. "Homer, from all I gather, I figure that Dunlop runs four times as many cows as the Diamond-T. Is that correct?"

"Four times, at least," Homer said promptly.

"Then why," Pete asked, "doesn't he have a crew four times as big as Traxler, or at least a great many more men? In other words, why does Traxler require the same size crew on a much smaller outfit? Give me a sensible answer to that and I'll buy you another beer and throw in a whisky chaser to boot."

Dawning comprehension showed in Homer's features. "By cripes! You've hit somethin', Pete. And I never gave it a thought. What does Traxler do with all his men?"

Pete studied the beer in his glass a minute. "Well," he said with soft finality, "somebody is rustling Dunlop's cattle, regardless what county it is being done in, Rhys or Trabadura. In other words, there's more than one way to rope a steer, and if we can't dab a loop on Mister Black Nick Traxler in one way, we'll do it another."

"Pete! You've got somethin' now!" Homer explained enthusiastically. "Mister, you've got a real head on your shoulders."

"Such flattery calls for me to buy the beer we mentioned." Pete grinned.

At that moment the swinging doors parted to allow the entrance of Sheriff Perkins. He headed for the bar. "Back, eh, Pete?"

"Back," Pete nodded. "The town quiet tonight?"

"Usually is on Sundays." Perkins nodded, then added, "The Diamond-T rarely comes in on Sunday."

"Probably spend all day Sunday recovering from Saturday's drunk," Pete chuckled. "There's nothing like a hangover to tame a man down."

"You said it," the sheriff replied grumpily, "and I'm still suffering from that hangover Nick Traxler hung on me yesterday. The more I think on it, the more I realize I can't do nothing."

"Maybe we can," Pete said. "I'm riding to see Joe Dunlop in the morning. I've just been telling Homer my idea. I'll see what you think of it. Ethan, you arrived at a particularly appropriate moment. I was just about to buy a drink, and you're included. Hey, Beanpole, how about some service?"

"Coming," Beanpole said. "Service is my long suit."

"I'll bet," Pete chuckled, watching the fat man range along the bar, "your suit is as wide as it is long."

17   Pete Goes Down

"So you see," Pete was saying the following day, shortly before noon, "I had to get a sort of line on things before I could get down to real work."

He was seated on the long gallery of the Ladder-D ranch house, talking to its owner, Joe Dunlop. Dunlop was a lean, spare man in his late fifties, with iron-gray hair and a bony face. He wore whipcord riding breeches, flat-heeled riding boots, and a soft flannel shirt open at the throat. The two men held long, cold drinks in their hands.

"Anyway," Pete went on, "that's the situation. This red quirt I'm carrying seems to have sort of tangled into the whole business. I'd like to know the reason why."

"It's very interesting"—Dunlop nodded—"a problem that will require, I should say, considerable shrewd detective work before you learn just what is at the bottom of the affair. As for my own difficulties"—he paused to take a sip from his glass—"I don't mind a few of my cattle being picked up now and then if the beef is required to feed people who are —well, what you call up against it. I expect to lose a few head that way. But the wholesale stealing that's going on— I have to call it stealing, as there seems to be no other explanation for the disappearance of my stock—is something that must be stopped."

"I don't figure there's any doubt it will be."

Dunlop smiled faintly. "Your assurance gives me confidence. I've gone into the breeding angle pretty deeply. It's cost a great deal more money than I can really afford if I'm to have my profits whipped away from under my nose. I've crossbred with good success. Also, I've improved the strain in my other herds. I keep the various breeds isolated —the Durhams in one pasture, the Polled Angus in another, and so on. Twice now my pasture fences have been cut. There's been some intermingling with my Herefords on the open range. When that happens my experiments are set back just so much. You see"—he smiled deprecatingly—"cattle raising is a hobby with me as much as a business."

"I heard you wrote poetry too." Pete laughed.

Dunlop flushed. "I imagine Beauregard doesn't quite understand that. It's something I do for my own pleasure."

A gong sounded inside the house. Dunlop explained, "Time for lunch. I imagiine it will be welcome, Piper. You made quite an early start from town."

"Lunch?" Pete looked startled.

"You'd call it dinner." Dunlop smiled. "I assure you there will be quantity as well as quality, despite the name."

They went into a long room lined on all sides with shelves of books. It was comfortably furnished. There were deep window recesses in the thick adobe walls, on the ledges of which were some potted plants. Dunlop went on, "I'm sorry my wife isn't here to welcome you. She's in the East, visiting her family, at present."

A table had been laid with silver and linen at one end of the long room. The two men seated themselves and were served by an efficient Chinese servant who moved noiselessly about the room. Despite Pete's expectations the food was wholesome—thick steaks, hot biscuits, pie, and coffee. At the end of the meal cigars and brandy were brought out. Pete leaned comfortably back in his chair while the Chinese cleared away the table. "You've given me a mark to shoot at," Pete commented.

"How is that?"

"This is the way a cow ranch should be run. One of these days I'll have a spread of my own. It's going to be as much like this as possible."

"Even to writing poetry?" Dunlop smiled.

Pete laughed. "I'm afraid that's beyond me. Maybe I could read some of yours."

"It's kind of you to say that."

Pete worked the subject back to the business in hand. "Mr. Dunlop, have the two Traxler brothers, Luke and Ivan, made a practice of visiting you?"

Dunlop raised his eyebrows in surprise. "Can you think of any reason," he asked dryly, "why any of the Diamond-T men should visit me?"

"No, I can't," Pete replied. He explained why he had asked the question.

"Oh, I understand. So they were supposed to be on the way to visit me that day of the Munson killing." Dunlop laughed softly. "I think I should place that statement in the realm of the improbable. Frankly, I feel sure they lied. I'll tell you why. I've never been friendly with the Diamond-T. For that matter, I keep pretty much to myself. I've met most of the cattlemen in this part of the country at one time or another, of course, when I happened to be in Beauregard, but I'm probably what you'd call a very unsociable neighbor. The two men you mention, Luke and Ivan Traxler, came here once —just once. At that time my wife was entertaining visitors from the East. Luke and Ivan heard we were having some sort of party and insisted on coming out here. I made them as welcome as possible, gave them drinks, and so on. That was where I made my mistake. They both got drunk and became very insulting to some of the women guests present. I asked them to leave; they refused. In short, I had to call on a couple of my men in the bunkhouse to throw them out bodily. They left, uttering threats, but that's the last I ever heard of them."

"That seems to clinch it." Pete nodded. "They certainly wouldn't have been coming to see you that day—unless—Say, they wouldn't be friendly with any of your hands, would they?"

Dunlop shook his head. "My crew, from the top hand right down to the cook, have no use for the Diamond-T men. I know that. I've a good crew. I've picked my men carefully. They're a sober, industrious group. I've had them with me for some years. I think, if I'm not mistaken, the youngest man on my pay roll has been with me eight years."

"I reckon we've proved Luke and Ivan are liars regarding that statement about visiting you."

"Undoubtedly. . .That Munson killing was a queer business, from all I've been able to gather. Found the dead man in a chair, or something of the sort—"

"A rocking chair, Mr. Dunlop. It certainly is queer."

"Rocking chair, eh? Do you mean it was a regular household rocker or—?"

"Just an ordinary rocker." Pete nodded, "Walnut frame, high back. Cane seat and back. It even had a head and seat cushion tied onto it."

"Wait! I remember seeing a rocker of that type—some place. Where was it? Oh, I remember. Let me see, it was early last Thursday morning. I happened to be up and—"

"That's the day Munson was killed. Where'd you see the rocker, Mr. Dunlop?"

"It was roped to the back of a big covered wagon that came through here. A man named—I think he said Joadie Tate—was driving the wagon. It was a full vehicle, loaded with all his worldly goods, such as they were. I remember seeing a mattress roped on the back, and tied next to that was a rocking chair. The wagon stopped here."

"Did he say why he stopped exactly?"

"Told me about it. I was rather busy at the time; perhaps I should have paid more attention. Joadie Tate's wife was sick inside the wagon. So he said. I didn't see her. I did see a little girl he had with him. Pale, wan little thing, looking half starved, as did Tate. It seems Tate and his family had moved up north of here, about eight months back, to take up farming land. The idea hadn't worked out. The crops failed. Then his wife got sick. They had relatives back in Rhysville, so they'd pulled up stakes and started for there.

They'd intended to stop that night at Beauregard City. I told Tate he should be heading more to the southwest or he'd miss Beauregard. I guess he'd become confused in his directions. Anyway, I saw that he filled his water bags. I gave him some other supplies as well. It was my suggestion that he stay the night. I offered to get a doctor for his wife, but he wouldn't hear of it. Said his wife was anxious to get back to her relatives and they'd push right on. I gathered that she was pretty sick, though, as I say, I didn't see her."

"You didn't see them again?"

Dunlop shook his head. "Tate climbed back on the wagon a few minutes later. That's the last I saw of them."

Pete frowned. "It might have been the tracks of Joadie Tate's wagon I saw near Munson's body, but how would Tate and his family fit into the business?"

"That"—Dunlop smiled—"is something I wouldn't know. You'll have to be the detective on that case."

"But you're sure Tate said they were heading for Rhysville?"

"Oh yes, I'm certain."

A short time later Pete had his saddled pony brought up from the corral. He thanked the cowboy who brought it, said good-by to Dunlop, and rode away from the ranch.

Once out of sight of the ranch house, over the first rise of land, he turned his pony north, exactly the opposite direction he would have taken to go to Beauregard City. To his right, as he rode through a series of foothills, towered the peaks of the Picadero Mountains, their rugged ravines and ridges standing out sharply in the bright afternoon sunlight. There was scarcely a cloud in the wide expanse of blue sky. From time to time he passed large bunches of Hereford cattle, bearing the Ladder-D brand. Here it was good grazing country, but nearer the mountains the grass gave way to a different growth, mesquite, prickly pear, some barrel cacti and greasewood, yucca and cholla. There was a great deal of broken rock about which in ages past had moved down from the tall peaks above.

Pete's eyes were alert as he rode, watching the contours of the mountains as he moved higher into the foothills. "Homer sure said something," he muttered, "when he said this was ideal country for rustling operations. A man could hide quite a respectable bunch of steers in some of these box canyons—and it would take some time to ferret him out—then move his stolen cows during the night."

For another hour he rode. By this time the sun was swinging far to the west and tipping the heights of the Trabadura Range almost hazy in the distance, with bright spots of fire. Finally Pete checked his pony and came to a halt while he rolled and lighted a brown-paper cigarette. "Maybe I'm mistaken," he said to himself; "maybe I didn't see a rider heading over this way this morning, when I was on the way to the Ladder-D. Or it might have been one of the Ladder-D riders cutting across to one of the many fenced pastures. Anyway, I feel better for having looked around instead of heading straight back to town."

His eyes were still straying along the foot of the mountains. His gaze passed what from this distance appeared to be a narrow crack in a red granite bluff, then came back again. A faint grayish spiral was drifting slowly from the crack. Pete's eyes came back to the curling smoke and stopped. Now he knew there was a canyon there and that the seemingly narrow crack in the rock would widen into a respectable entrance when he drew near.

"Somebody there all right." He nodded. "A Ladder-D puncher would be high-tailing home for supper by this time, more'n likely. I reckon I'll have to investigate."

He got down from his horse and seated himself on the earth. The sun dipped lower and lower and in time dropped below the Trabadura Range. Darkness commenced to envelop the sky. By the time the first faint star had appeared in the east Pete was ready to move. He rose stiffly from the earth after his long wait and climbed back into the saddle. Then he directed the pony's head in the direction he had last seen that smoke appearing.

He moved forward cautiously for the next three quarters of an hour. He was much nearer that canyon by this time. Finally he stopped about a hundred yards from a point where he saw a reddish glow against the face of a rock bluff. Here he dismounted and went forward on foot, moving stealthily over rocky soil.

Within a few minutes, glancing through the cactus-and-mesquite-studded country, Pete spied a small fire with two men seated near it. He dropped on his stomach and wiggled slowly along, with all the silence of an Apache. It required half an hour or more to bring him close enough to hear what the two men were saying.

From behind the screening shelter of a greasewood bush growing just within the entrance to the cracklike canyon Pete saw two men in punchers' togs taking their ease on spread blankets. Two ponies were tethered deeper within the canyon. Beyond the ponies Pete could make out the huddled shapes of a bunch of cows. One of the men was of burly build; the other was tall but much lighter in weight. Their sombreros were thrust on the backs of their heads; they were smoking cigarettes and appeared to be having an argument. The voices reached Pete clearly in the still night air, broken only now and then by the crackle of a burning twig in the campfire.

One of the men was saying, ". . . and I don't know, Larry, if Nick would like it or not."

"Cripes, Steve! He should kick! We've done what he ordered We can push this bunch of steers over the county line, dispose of 'em, and get back to the ranch. Nick ought to be glad if we can make some extra money."

The burly man was Larry; the other, Steve.

Steve went on, "I just remember what Nick told us. Remember? We weren't to touch any cattle. We were just to make a survey, as he called it, find out the location of the best canyons, the distance between water holes, and how much of a guard Dunlop keeps on the pastures where his blooded stock is. We've got that information. We'd better head back. If Nick ever got the idea we were knocking off money on the side he might—"

"You've got the wrong idea, Steve," Larry protested. "I expect to cut in Nick and the rest of the boys on the money we'd make. It just seems a shame to come 'way over here, spend as many days as we have, and then return with not a cent to show for it."

So interested had Pete become in the conversation between the two men that he failed to note the approach of a shadowy form sneaking up at his rear. The dark form closed swiftly in. The first intimation Pete had of approaching danger was the sharp sound of a stick broken underfoot. Pete turned, started to his feet. At the same instant something landed heavily against his head, knocking him sprawling to the earth. The last sounds he remembered, before becoming unconscious, were the startled cries of alarm from the men at the campfire as they leaped erect.

18   "Nevada's Bad Medicine!"

PETE GAINED CONSCIOUSNESS within a surprisingly short time. The blow on the head—he judged it had been made with a gun barrel—had been cushioned considerably by his heavy felt sombrero. In addition, he had been moving when the blow struck, and the gun barrel had not landed squarely. However, it was bad enough as it was. His head thumped violently, and until it cleared a trifle more he felt nauseated. Awakening, he had found himself stretched on the earth, with his wrists bound behind him. He heard voices and opened his eyes a slit.

Seated near the campfire were the two men, Larry and Steve, to whom Pete had been listening when his assailant crept up behind and dealt him the blow. Across the fire, in a sitting position, was Ivan Traxler. It was Ivan who had struck him, then. Pete cursed himself for letting Ivan sneak up unnoticed that way. "I sure must be slipping," Pete mused bitterly. "This is certainly one pretty fix I'm in." Then he sighted something else that added to his irritation: on Ivan's left wrist was the crimson quirt. Mentally Pete gave himself a "cursing out."

Ivan seemed to be in particularly good humor. "Hell, no!" he was saying. "Piper will be out for some hours yet. I really poured my gun barrel on him. Lucky Nick sent me over here to check up today. Thought I spotted him late this afternoon; I trailed him here. He was sure listening in on your conversation. Hope you two hombres weren't spilling anything. Not that it would make much difference, though," he added carelessly.

Steve said uncomfortably, "Ivan, I don't like the idea of killing a man in cold blood. And I ain't going to sleep here all night so near a dead man. I don't like it, I tell you."

"Don't be so squeamish, Steve," Larry scoffed. "You know what would happen to us if Piper went free. It would mean the pen if we were caught. If you insist, the killing can wait until morning."

"Dammit," Steve protested, "if Ivan wants him shot, why don't he do it himself? He admits he doesn't want to be here when——"

"Why should I be a witness?" Ivan cut in. "It's your concern. It's you two he'd grab if he was free. I'm talking for your own good."

"We've got to face it, Steve," Larry said coldly. "It's Piper or us. This is no time to be fussy. Geez! You turning yellow?"

"All right." Steve surrendered sullenly. "But you'll have to do it, Larry. I won't. And I won't stay here with a corpse——"

"I told you it could wait until just before we break camp in the morning," Larry said in ugly, impatient tones. "And I'll do it, I ain't lost *my* nerve. All I ask of you, Steve, is to keep your mouth shut later. After all, what's Piper's life mean compared to ours? We got too good a thing here to lose out now."

"It won't be risky," Ivan pointed out. "Look, Steve, Larry will use Piper's own gun, then place it in the redhead's hand. His horse is back there a spell. We'll bring it here, leave it near the body. In time the horse will wander off; somebody will find it. A search will be started for Piper—eventually the body will be found, apparently a suicide. It's all so simple."

"Don't talk about it so much," Steve said irritably. "I agreed, didn't I? But you got to wait until morning." He shivered slightly. "Ivan, why were you so glad to get that red quirt?"

Ivan smiled. "Someday maybe you'll learn. I'm aiming to make a pretty penny selling it. That's all you need to know."

Larry asked, "If I had it to sell, could I make some money?"

Ivan shook his head. "You wouldn't know where to sell it, Larry. So you needn't to get any ideas."

"Hell! You know me," Larry said. "I didn't have nothing in mind."

"Sure you didn't," Ivan said good-naturedly. "At the same time I'm glad you don't know as much as I do. . . . Well, I'm going to turn in. Throw me a blanket."

"Think we should examine Piper first?" Steve asked.

"Naw," Ivan grunted, wrapping himself in a blanket. "Like I told you, he'll be out for some time yet—and even if he was awake he wouldn't get loose of those rawhide thongs. I tied 'em plenty tight."

Pete had already learned the truth of that statement. The thongs around his wrists were tight. He had already tried their strength and found he could scarcely budge his wrists. With his hands behind him in such fashion it was an extremely cramping position.

Within a short time Larry and Steve also rolled into blankets. It wasn't long after that before the snores of three men sounded through the camp. The fire died down, leaving only a dull glow of embers. It was growing cold too. Overhead the stars shone down into the canyon.

Then Pete got busy. His arms strained against the bonds, relaxed and strained again. For some time he kept this up until his wrists were raw and he was almost exhausted. By this time he felt certain the rawhide had stretched a trifle. That was all he wanted: just a little play for his hands. The stars wheeled across the heavens, and still Pete struggled on. Three times during the night he was forced to stop when Ivan, or one of the other men, rose to see if he was still quiet. They made no attempt to examine the rawhide thongs, but once Ivan stood over him a long time, and Pete heard him say, "When I hit 'em, they stay hit."

When he had returned to his blanket Pete started again. The moon had come and gone by now. A sudden thrill of excitement ran through Pete. He could wiggle his left hand a trifle. He rested a few minutes, then, after some difficulty, succeeded in sliding the left hand into his right hip pocket, where he kept his jackknife. Fortunately they hadn't taken it away from him. Inch by inch he edged the knife from his pocket, until it lay in his sweating palm. Getting it open was still another difficult task, but he finally succeeded. After that things went a little easier. It was clumsy work, slow work. The sky brightened, grew gray. Then, just as Pete felt the bonds were nearly cut through, Ivan awakened and rose from his blanket. Ivan glanced at Pete, saw that he lay as before, then awakened the other two.

Steve glanced toward Pete. "Say, that hombre is still out. You must have hit him harder than you figured."

"Gave him all I had." Ivan laughed. "At the least a fracture, I'm hoping." They moved around the camp. When they weren't looking his way Pete continued the slow process of sawing at his bonds. If he could only have held the knife firmly, for it kept wiggling around, he would have been free by this time.

Ivan saddled his horse, as did Steve. They both mounted. Ivan said, "Steve will be back with Piper's horse in a few minutes, Larry. You'd better have the job done by the time he returns."

"It'll be done," Larry said cold-bloodedly. "Hurry it up, Steve. We'll get through here and push the cows north."

Ivan and Steve rode off without a backward glance. Larry went to saddle his own mount. It was growing lighter every minute. Farther on in the canyon some of the steers had commenced to bawl, anxious to be driven to water. Meanwhile Pete was now working furiously. Suddenly he felt the bonds loosen, drop off. He gave a long sigh of relief and relaxed to gather his strength for the test to come. Blood flowed back into his numbed wrists.

By this time Ivan and Steve were out of sight. Through thinly slitted eyes Pete saw Larry approach, leading his horse, reins in left hand. In his right he carried Pete's belt and gun. As he drew near he dropped the reins, drew the gun from the holster, leveled it at Pete. Pete heard the click of the hammer as it came back.

In that moment Pete moved like lightning. The gun roared once, but Pete had flung himself to one side before the shot came. Startled by the sudden swift movement of his intended victim, Larry's mouth dropped open, and he paused, too surprised to move quickly. By this time Pete was up, charging toward Larry. Larry again lifted the gun, but before he could draw back the hammer and pull trigger Pete's fist had landed with crushing force on the side of his jaw.

Larry went down like a poled ox. Pete was on him like a tiger, wresting the gun from his hand. He raised the gun, brought it down sharply on Larry's head once. Larry groaned and collapsed. Pete said grimly, looking down at the unconscious man, "That one shot will mean more to Steve than it meant to me, thank God!"

Ten minutes later Steve came riding back, leading Pete's

horse. Ivan wasn't with him. He looked nervous, tense. His gaze shifted furtively about the camp; then his eyes widened, bugged out. One hand started toward his gun as his gaze fell on Larry's prone figure. At that moment Pete spoke from behind a mesquite tree which Steve had just passed. "All right, Steve, me lad," he said softly, "raise 'em high and fast, or you'll get what I gave Larry."

Steve gulped; his hands came into the air. "Is—is Larry dead?" he gasped. "Look, Piper, this wasn't my idea——"

"Cut it short. Where's Traxler?"

"He—he went on to Beauregard. Look, Piper, I ain't——"

"Ivan didn't have enough guts to stay and see me finished off, eh?" Pete said grimly. "I got a score to settle with that hombre. Has he got my red quirt with him?"

Steve nodded. "Said—said he knew where he could get a pretty penny for it." He had recovered his nerve.

"Who's back of the rustling going on over here?"

Steve was scared, but he was still loyal to his employer. "Nobody," he said stubbornly. "You can't blame Ivan Traxler."

"Black Nick, eh?"

Steve said, "I don't even know anybody named Nick."

Pete smiled. "You'll talk yet, hombre. No, your friend isn't dead. You're going to tie him into his saddle; then I'm going to tie you into yours. Then the three of us are going places. And I want you to move fast, Stevie. I'm plumb short of patience this morning. Get off that horse. Hurry it up!"

It wasn't yet eight-thirty in the morning when Pete flashed into Beauregard, his horse sweat-streaked and dusty. The animal swayed a trifle as Pete pulled it to a halt at the hotel hitch rack, and stood droop-headed. "Good hawss," Pete muttered. "You sure earned your keep this morning."

Across the street Ivan Traxler had just emerged from the doorway of Turk Raven's Saloon. His face went white as his gaze fell on Pete, and he quickly leaped back inside the building, unnoticed by Pete. Pete's attention was on the hotel entrance, from which Homer Pritchard had just stepped to the street.

Homer's face lighted up. "Hi-yuh, cowboy? Where were you ——?" He broke off. "Cripes! What's doin? You been ridin'——"

"I'll tell it later, Homer," Pete said swiftly "Have you seen Ivan Traxler in town this morning?"

Homer nodded. "Came in early. Went to the bank first. It wasn't open. I think he's waitin' in Raven's Saloon across the way. What you want him for?"

"He stole my quirt. I'm figuring to put him under arrest."

"He didn't have the quirt when I saw him—— Hey, what do you mean, you're puttin' him under arrest?"

Pete put one hand in his pocket, drew it out and showed

Homer something shiny in his palm. Homer's eyes widened. "Like that, eh? But, wait, you'd better let me help you with this arrest."

"Nothing doing, Homer. What I want him for took place in Rhys County. We don't want any legal technicalities cropping up."

"I don't mean that. Nevada Norton is with Ivan. Nevada got drunk last night, stayed at the hotel. He's feelin' pretty ugly this mornin'. Nevada's bad medicine any time, but when he's got a hang-over——"

"It's still a job I want to do alone, Homer. It's best that way. You're sworn to keep the peace. You'd better move on, where you won't be a witness to any shooting that might happen. As I see it, it's my job alone. If Nevada takes a hand, that's too bad for somebody." Pete drew his six-shooter and spun the cylinder.

Homer said, "Nevada carries two guns. It'll be your weapon against three. You'd better let me——"

Pete reached over and whipped the six-shooter from Homer's holster, then stuck it into the waistband of his own trousers. "This'll equalize things," he said grimly. He turned and started across the street, his legs moving in wide strides.

Homer looked after him, worried. "Pete sure moves into action when he gets mad. I just hope Nevada keeps out of it. Pete can handle Ivan—but against Ivan and Nevada both. Cripes! Why did I let him have my gun? He'll need me!" Panicky, Homer started at a run, across the street, toward Raven's Saloon.

19   Roaring .45s

NEVADA NORTON GLANCED up as Ivan came plunging back into Raven's Saloon. "Cripes! You back already? Ain't the bank open yet?"

"I didn't go. I——I——" Ivan's face was ashen.

"What in hell's wrong with you?" Nevada frowned. He scrutinized Ivan through bloodshot eyes. "You look like you'd seen a ghost. Speak up, dammit! You gone dumb?"

Ivan and Nevada were the only customers. Back of the bar Turk Raven was still rubbing sleep from his eyes, the better to see Ivan and make out what had gone wrong.

"It's—it's Piper!" Ivan blurted out. "He just rode into town. My Gawd, Nevada! What'll we do?"

"What'll *we* do? This is your fight, Ivan. Nick may take on your battles, but not me. I dunno, though, I'd sorta like a crack at that redheaded devil. He's caused just about enough trouble around here. But, hell, what are you talking about? It can't be Piper. You told me you'd left him with Larry and Steve and that they would take care of him."

"I tell you it is him!" Ivan sounded frantic. "Something may have gone wrong."

Turk Raven approached the bar. "What's the trouble?"

Nevada turned angrily on the man. "Nothing that concerns you, Turk. Get back to your glass polishing. This is between me and Ivan. You hear me? Get away from us!"

"Just as you say, Nevada," Turk gulped and busied himself at the back of the room, carting some empty beer cases through the rear door.

"Damn right it's just as I say," Nevada growled. He looked contemptuously at Ivan. "Pull yourself together, you fool. Did your first drink of the day go to your head? You should have put away what I drank last night." He grinned uglily. "Then you might really be seeing things."

"Nevada! Nevada! Listen to me," Ivan pleaded. "I'm talking straight. Piper is just across the street. What'll we do if he comes here?"

"You're crazy!"

"I'm not crazy! Look for yourself."

Nevada looked disgusted. He turned and strode toward the doorway, peered out above the swinging doors. When he came back into the room his features were set in disagreeable lines. "It's him all right. Thought you told me you'd arranged with Larry——"

"I did! I did! But something's gone wrong. Nevada, you've got to get me out of this!"

"I've got to get you out? You yellow rat, Ivan! I'll help if Piper comes here, but you'll stay and fight too. Remember that! You've got to help yourself! Hell! He only carries one gun. I've got two. Yours makes three. I'm commencing to like this setup. That redhead has needed his comeuppance for some time. If he comes in here he's going to get it. Get over there across the room. We'll get him between our fires."

"Don't start no fights in here,——" Turk Raven said from the back of the room. "Look, boys——"

"Get outside in your alley," Nevada snarled. "This fight is just about started, Turk. It's too late to stop anything now."

With a cry of fright Turk turned and ran outside. At the same instant a steady step was heard on the saloon porch. The next instant Pete pushed through the swinging doors. He paused just inside the entrance, hands swinging at sides. For an instant no one spoke, then Pete said, "Heard you were here, Ivan, I want my quirt. And you're under arrest——"

"What right you got arresting anybody?" Nevada bellowed.

"Ain't got your quirt——" Ivan commenced weakly.

"Aw, let the bustard have it!" Nevada snarled and reached

for his guns. At the same moment Ivan stabbed one hand toward his holster.

Pete's right hand spoke first, then his left, then his right again. Nevada was hurled back against the bar by the impact of the shots. Ivan let out one agonized yell and pitched toward the floor, his first shot going wild.

Nevada righted himself. Streams of fire poured from his gun muzzles, but his thin form had commenced to wilt again almost the instant he regained his balance. His bullets ripped into the flooring at Pete's feet. Orange flame spurted from Pete's left hand.

From the floor Ivan threw another shot, the breeze of which fanned Pete's cheek. Pete's right-hand gun spoke again, then his left. Ivan's head hit the floor with a loud bump and he lay still.

Nevada was in a sitting position, his shoulders resting against the bar. He tried to lift his guns, laughed weakly and said, "Damned if you ain't fast, redhead," and died.

The barroom was swimming with smoke. Pete glanced at the two men sprawled on the floor, then strode across to Ivan and turned him on his back. Ivan's eyes were already glazing. Pete ran his hand over the man's body, then nodded grimly. "Thought that's where I'd find it," he said. He ripped open the front of Ivan's shirt, thrust one hand inside, and drew out the crimson quirt. "And that is that," he said tonelessly, slipping the quirt back on his wrist. He noticed the handle was wet and removed it again to wipe it on Ivan's shirt. "It's a crimson quirt, all right," was the thought that flashed through his head. As he replaced the quirt on his wrist he noticed that one of his bullets had grazed the round knob, without doing the quirt any lasting damage however.

Yells sounded outside. Deputy Homer came rushing through the open door. He paused just inside, and a wave of relief passed over his features. "My Gawd," he said in awestriken tones. "you're fast! You hurt any?"

"Not any," Pete responded. He plugged the empty shells out of Homer's cylinder, reloaded the weapon, and handed it back. "I might have been, though, if it hadn't been for your gun." He started to reload his own six-shooter.

Homer looked sheepish as he took his gun. "That's one reason I didn't come in sooner," he explained. "I'd been no good without a gun. I waited just outside. Cripes a'mighty! It sounded like a whole arsenal explodin'!"

Men started pouring into the saloon. Somebody yelled, "Nevada Norton's killed!"

"Ivan Traxler too!" came another voice.

Men crowded around, asking questions. Pete made brief explanation: "Ivan stole something of mine. When I went to get it back he pulled his gun. Nevada pitched in to help."

"And *you* got both of 'em?" somebody demanded "Didn't Homer help?"

"Homer didn't come in until later. I was lucky," Pete said.

Turk Raven had come back into his saloon. He looked white, shaken. He cast nervous glances at the two bodies on the floor, then moved quickly behind the bar and took a long drink. Somebody else asked for liquor. Pete said, "Come on, Homer, let's get out of here. I hate killing."

As they moved toward the door Sheriff Perkins came bursting in. He stopped short, his eyes widening at the sight of the dead men. "In Gawd's name," he commenced, "what's been doing here?"

Pete pushed him out on the saloon porch. He said, low-voiced, "I tried to make an arrest, Ethan. Ivan wouldn't have it that way. Nevada came into the fight——"

"*You* tried to make an arrest?"

Something glistened brightly in Pete's palm under the sheriff's gaze. Pete said, "Take charge, will you, Sheriff? And don't talk too much. I want to get across to my room in the hotel and clean up a mite. I'll tell it all later."

Sheriff Perkins nodded, still a trifle wide-eyed. Pete said to Homer, "I'd be obliged if you'd take my pony to the livery and see that he gets a good rubdown and some oats. That pony covered a lot of ground in a mighty small time, and I want to show my gratitude. I'd do it myself, but I had a tough night. I'm nigh dead for sleep. I tell you, Homer, you and Ethan meet me in the hotel dining room and we'll eat dinner together long 'bout noon. I'll give you the whole story then, when I get a few more facts straightened out in my mind. This business is commencing to straighten out some."

"Go ahead, get your shut-eye, Pete." Homer nodded. "We'll see you at noon."

Pete continued on across the street. Just as he was entering the hotel lobby a voice hailed him. Pete looked around, then came back to the sidewalk to greet Graveyard Gratton, who was just getting down from the seat of a wagon he had halted near the hotel hitch rack. Gratton said, "What's the excitement over to Turk Raven's bar?" He rounded the hitch rack and clumped up on the sidewalk.

"I understand there was some shooting," Pete said carelessly. "Did Cressy come?"

"It's a wicked, wicked world," Graveyard said sadly, shaking his head. "Shootin', huh? Probably somebody was hurt; mebbe killed."

"Probably," Pete said. "Did Cressy come in with you?"

"Just so long as fellers are allowed to tote shootin' irons," Graveyard commented sourly, "they'll be a-shootin' of 'em. Everybody should just be allowed to load with blank ca'tridges."

Pete forced a tired grin. "In that case there'd be some mighty bad powder burns, I'm betting."

Graveyard nodded dejectedly. "And there'd be bad cases of lockjaw and such from said burns. Well, reckon I'll go over to Turk's place and see——"

"Just a minute." Pete caught his arm as he was turning away. "Did Cressy come in with you?"

"Think I'd come to a place where there's so much sinnin' goin' on," Graveyard stated drearily, "less'n she made me come? Tried to talk her outten the idea. Figured it might rain"—there wasn't a cloud in the sky—"but she insisted she had to come in for her trunk at Missis Fogarty's——"

"She's here, then!"

"Certain she's here. Nothin' for you to get so excited about. You don't need to squeeze the arm off'n me."

"Where is she?"

"Down to the Emporium Dry Goods & Notions." Graveyard gave the information in hopeless tones. "Says she's got to make over a dress. Don't know why she should need a dress made over. One she's got has looked good enough to me for past couple years."

Pete had started to leave, then, realizing how he looked, came back. "Tell her——" he started.

"I'll tell her nothin'. She already told me what to tell you. She says to tell you if you want to buy that dinner you promised, to call for her at Missis Fogarty's round noon. She'll be busy until then."

"I'll do that, Graveyard. You'd better eat with us. The sheriff and Homer will be eating too."

Graveyard shook his head. "I dunno if I should. Boughten-out vittles don't agree with me. I got a delicate stomach."

"Well, you think it over, leastwise. I've got something to tell you folks. And tell Cressy I'll call for her about noon."

Without waiting for Graveyard's reply Pete turned away and entered the lobby. He went straight to his room, peeled off his clothing, and slept like a log until eleven o'clock. At the end of that time he rose, shaved, and dressed, then walked, with singing heart, in the direction of Mrs. Fogarty's boardinghouse.

20   Pete Explains

CRESSY STILL LOOKED worried as she and Pete turned from Taos Street onto Tonto and headed in the direction of the hotel. The girl was wearing a dress of some brown light woolen stuff, with a high bodice and a small waist. There was a small hat perched on her pale gold hair and a bit of lace at her throat and wrists.

Pete glanced admiringly at her. "Helen of Troy looked like a seven-year-old canner cow, compared to you, Cressy, and that statement also includes Cleopatra, Joan of Arc, the Venus de Milo, and all the other queens of history."

"Pete, don't talk nonsense. You were nearly killed this morning."

"*Nearly* doesn't count. Gosh, Cressy, it just isn't in the books for me to be killed, with you loving me and——"

"I've never said that! Pete, why can't you be serious?"

"It doesn't pay. Look at Graveyard. He's always serious. Only for him running to you with the story, you wouldn't be serious now, either. He got you all worked up with his story of the shooting. You shouldn't listen to men like him. After all, he didn't get that story firsthand, It wasn't near as bad as he made it out. Nothing to it, really——"

"With two men dead, you can say that? I know they were trying to kill you. Oh, Pete!" Her words ended in a wail.

"Oh, Cressy!" Pete mimicked, grinning. "Forget it, girl. These things happen in this country. They'll continue to happen until the crooks have been civilized or put away. You mustn't brood over conditions that you can't help."

"I don't care. That red quirt of yours has caused more trouble——"

"It goes deeper than just the red quirt, Cressy."

"Pete! Where is your quirt?"

"Left it in the room at the hotel. Thought I wouldn't wear it while we were eating dinner. Don't worry, I've got it hidden where nobody'll find it—not in a short time, leastwise. Now, look at me. Smile, please." Cressy smiled. Pete said, "Golly, your smile does things to me. Just keep smiling. And don't pay any more attention to Graveyard's tales of woe. Nothing's going to happen to me. You listen to Graveyard and he'll convince you the world is likely to end any minute. I never saw such a pessimist! He's the kind of a sour puss that if he stubbed his toe over a ten-pound gold nugget laying loose on the range, he'd sit down and start nursing his toe, without ever thinking of the good luck the gold would bring him."

Cressy was laughing now. "All right, you win, cowboy."

"Sure I do. It's a habit I picked up someplace."

They turned into the hotel. Sheriff Perkins, Homer, and Graveyard were waiting for them at a large table in one corner of the dining room. They greeted Cressy and Pete. Pete said, "Graveyard, you decided to risk your stomach after all, eh?"

Graveyard gulped and looked sad. "It's risky," he stated "I'll just eat some light snack."

Thereupon, when the waitress arrived, Graveyard ordered portions of roast beef, roast pork, fried potatoes, boiled potatoes, ham and eggs, coffee, and pie. The others asked for various dishes from the day's menu, hiding their smiles from view of the long-faced Graveyard. Within a short time the food was brought to their table and they commenced eating. Pete, sensing their curiosity, started to tell his story.

"In the first place," Pete commenced, "I want to show you something. Ethan and Homer both know. Cressy and Graveyard might as well be in on the secret too." He slipped one hand in a pocket and produced a small badge which he displayed to the others. Cressy's eyes widened. Graveyard's jaw dropped. Homer picked up the badge and studied it.

"Didn't get a good look at it this mornin'," he explained. "Artexico Cattlemen's Association, eh, Pete?"

"Just a cattle dick, that's me." Pete grinned. "I resigned from the organization a while back. I had an idea I wanted to get an outfit of my own. Couldn't find exactly what I wanted, though. Went looking down in Mexico. While I was there I got a telegram from my old chief. He wanted me to take on just one more job. I wired back I would. That's what brought me over here. It was Joe Dunlop, of the Ladder-D, who was yelping for help. The cow rustlers really have been cutting in on his profits. So now you know what brought me here. I came to help Dunlop and stumbled right into a red-quirt murder mystery. I've a hunch the same hombres are back of both rustling and murder. I hope to clean up both problems before I get through."

"I hope so," Ethan said fervently.

Pete continued, "Yesterday I rode over to the Ladder-D to let Dunlop know who I was, so he wouldn't think the association was asleep on the job. Nice hombre, Dunlop. Cressy, I must take you out to see his place someday. It'll give you ideas. Anyway, after I left Dunlop . . ."

From that point on Pete told of the previous day's and night's happenings, while Cressy's eyes grew wider and wider. "Of course," he broke in once, "I imagine Ivan and Steve and Larry went through my pockets and found my badge. That tipped them off to what I was, of course. However, even if Ivan told Nevada, they're both dead now, so they can't pass the word to Nick Traxler. Oh, Nick's at the head of the rustling all right, but we've got to get more proof before we can bop down on him. I don't want to go too fast until I've found out just what the red quirt stands for."

"Larry and Steve," Homer speculated. "That must be Larry Kurtz and Steve Barton. They're both Diamond-T waddies. Come to think of it, I haven't seen those two in town for quite a spell. Yep, it must be them all right."

"No doubt of it." Pete nodded. "The big cattle rustlers work that way sometimes. Send out a few men to look over the country in which they plan to operate. In that way they can get a line on the various herds, water holes, distance to county lines, and so on. Then when their plans are all set they drop down like a thunderbolt and clean out the unsuspecting cattle owner before he realizes what is going on."

"You didn't say," Graveyard pointed out, both cheeks crammed with foods, until his words were almost unintelligible, "what you done with Larry and Steve Barton."

"I'm getting to that," Pete said. "Of course when they went through my pockets they discovered I was an association man. That's why Larry was so ready to rub me out. Luckily they left all my things in my pockets—especially the knife. But they had to do that. You see, they'd planned to make my killing look like a suicide. Somebody's suspicions might have been aroused if it was discovered anything was missing from my pockets."

"Good grief!" Cressy shuddered. "It makes me shiver to think of it."

"Just contemplatin' this world," Graveyard said sadly, "is enough to make anybody shiver. Pass them biscuits again, Ethan."

"This is certainly a vale of tears all right," Pete agreed dryly. "When a man can't get outside of more'n three plates of biscuits, the old universe is plumb on the downgrade."

"Pete," Cressy interposed, "we're still wondering what you did with the Larry and Steve murderers."

"Would-be murderers," Pete corrected. "Well, after I had 'em both tied in saddles I drove 'em before me to the Ladder-D. Dunlop was up, eating breakfast when I arrived. He was sure surprised to see me again so soon, and more surprised when he saw the visitors I was bringing and heard my story. Steve and Larry are being held at the Ladder-D under heavy guard until I say the word to put 'em in jail."

"Held at the Ladder-D?" Ethan frowned. "Why not bring 'em in and put 'em in jail pronto?"

"In the first place, Ethan," Pete explained, "their crime took place in Rhys County, where you have no jurisdiction. I'd hate to have a case thrown out of court just because I'd brought in peace officers, or even used their jail, from Trabadura County. Some lawyers would take advantage of such technicalities."

"That's true," Homer agreed.

"In the second place," Pete continued, "if I brought those two here to jail, they'd get in touch with Nick Traxler, and Nick would get them out on bail in no time. The same thing would happen if I took 'em to the Rhysville jail in Rhysville County. And once Black Nick had communicated with 'em, he'd learn what I was doing here. I'd sooner keep him guessing for a while—and he'll sure do some guessing when his two punchers fail to put in an appearance."

"Ivan Traxler——" Homer began, then checked the words.

"Ivan Traxler is dead," Pete pointed out, "like I mentioned before, so he can't tell Nick anything, nor can Nevada Norton, for the same reason. Apparently Black Nick sent Ivan to check up on Larry and Steve, but he doesn't actually know that Ivan obeyed instructions, unless some of us tell him—and I don't reckon we will. Not right away, leastwise. Nope, we've got to keep Black Nick guessing. The longer he guesses, the more anxious he'll become. When he gets just so anxious, that's when he'll make a careless move and we've got him. He'll probably hit the ceiling when he hears that Ivan is finished.

"I sent a boy riding to break the news about Ivan and Nevada both," the sheriff said. "Figured Black Nick was entitled to know."

Pete nodded. "He'd have to know sooner or later. The sooner the better."

"Pete," Cressy asked, "isn't Traxler likely to send other men to check up on Larry and Steve when he fails to hear from them? I would in his place."

Pete smiled. "I thought of that too, Cressy. I've arranged with Dunlop to keep his riders moving around on Ladder-D range in pairs for a few days. Anybody they happen to encounter who admits to being from the Diamond-T will be taken captive and held until I can question them. We should cut off quite a few of Traxler's men in that way. Besides, I have hopes of breaking down Larry and Steve's resistance before long. Right now they won't talk. They're plumb stubborn, figuring that Traxler will get to help them out someway. But if Traxler doesn't know where they are he can't help them. Eventually those hombres are going to get the idea that Traxler has given them the go-by. Once that happens, they'll get mad and talk plenty I'm betting. When they do that we'll at least clean up the Ladder-D rustling—and that will be a long distance toward our goal."

The sheriff said, "Pete, you've accomplished a whale of a lot in the few days you've been here. I just wish you'd been on the job when Cressy's brother was killed."

"Maybe that can be cleaned up too," Pete replied. "I haven't given up hope yet."

Graveyard finally pushed back his chair and reached for his "makin's." The other men had lighted up quite a few minutes before. Graveyard said dolefully, "A man's a fool to eat away from home. Restaurant folks fix things up fancy to tempt you, and then you eat too much. I'll probably be sick half the night."

Homer grinned. "Well, if you ain't, you deserve to be, the

amount of fodder you stowed away. Where do you put it, Graveyard?"

"Leave Graveyard alone." Cressy smiled. "We need his clouds so we can appreciate the sun when it shines through."

"And I'm expecting it to shine plenty before long," Pete said. "Something else I want to bring up: Ivan Traxler announced when he left this morning that he was going to sell my red quirt for a pretty penny. Those were his words. Homer, you said he was waiting to get into the bank."

Homer nodded. "I saw him when he first rode in this mornin'. He'd been poundin' his pony hard. He went to the bank first. Haines hadn't arrived to open it up yet, and neither had the cashier, Kilby Ward. From the bank Ivan went to Turk Raven's Saloon, where he met Nevada. You know the rest, Pete."

Cressy said, frowning, "You don't think Banker Haines has anything to do with all this trouble, Pete?"

Pete said, "I don't know. I don't know Banker Haines, either, nor his cashier. I just know one thing, I'm suspecting everybody I'm not sure of."

"But Haines!" Cressy protested. "He's a big businessman. He's respected in Beauregard City. I never cared for him, myself; I think he's too hard in his methods, but, after all, that's nothing, legally, against him. There are plenty of people who do like him."

"Pete is right," Graveyard put in in depressed tones. "He should suspect everybody."

"First time I ever heard you agree with anybody, Graveyard." Pete grinned. He sobered and went on, "Something else I want to do is run over to Rhysville one of these days."

"Why Rhysville?" Ethan asked.

"That's where Joadie Tate was heading——"

"Joadie Tate?" the sheriff interrupted.

"You know, the feller with the wagon I told you stopped at the Ladder-D the same morning Munson was killed."

"I'd plumb forgot him," the sheriff confessed. "You think it was his rocking chair that Munson was found in?"

"I don't know. If I can find Tate I want to ask a lot of questions."

They finished, both with talk and food, finally, rose and drifted out to the street. Pete had but a few minutes alone with the girl while the others talked.

Pete said, "I wish I could think of some way to keep you in town, beautiful."

"I can't, Pete. I promised Father we'd be back early. With things as they've been, he worries every instant I'm out of his sight. No, Graveyard and I will pick up my trunk at Mrs. Fogarty's; then we'll get rolling on the road back. But be sure to come out and let us know what's happening."

"Suppose nothing does happen?" Pete asked.

"If you really mean"—the girl smiled—"just one half the things you've been saying to me since we first met, you'll make things happen."

"Do you mean that?" Pete grinned.

The girl suddenly sobered. "Pete! I don't mean you should make shootings happen. You know I didn't mean that. Oh, I'm so empty-headed at times!"

"First girl I ever knew," Pete stated fervently, "who had brains and beauty both——"

"Cressy!" Graveyard's voice came from a seat on the C-Bar-A wagon at the hitch rack. "You comin' with me, or are you goin' to stay there and let Pete talk you into somethin' you'll mebbe regret later? Remember, we told your paw we'd get back early—and it's gettin' later every minute."

Cressy hesitated a moment longer, her hand warm in Pete's palm. "And even if you did talk me into something," she was saying breathlessly, "I know I wouldn't regret it later, or any time."

And with that she fled toward the wagon. Pete followed, caught up in time to help her to her seat, then stood back while Graveyard backed the horses, wheeled, and turned over toward Taos Street.

Homer said dryly after a minute, "All right, Pete, you aimin' to stand there grinnin' like a hyena all day, or are you ready to come along with me and Ethan and sample some of Beanpole's beer?"

"Beer, by all means," Pete said joyously. "At a time like this it will seem like nectar of the gods!"

Homer said to Ethan in pretended disgust. "That's what a girl can do to a hombre. Pete's gone plumb daffy! Imagine talkin' about a necktie for Jupiter and some of them other foreigners who's worshiped in far-off countries. Pete's sure got female trouble!"

21   "Jerk Your Iron!"

SHERIFF PERKINS STOPPED for one drink at the Lariat Saloon. Leaving Pete and Homer at the bar, he proceeded along Main Street to his office. Just as he arrived Nick Traxler and his brother Luke came riding furiously up to the hitch rack and called his name. The ponies came to a long, sliding halt and sent dust and gravel flying in all directions.

The sheriff eyed the two men glowering down at him from their saddles, then said in a steady voice: "I thought you'd like to know. That's why I sent that feller riding to your place, Nick."

"You really mean it?" Traxler snapped. "Ivan's dead?"

"The undertaker's over yonderly," Perkins pointed out. "You don't have to take my word for it. You'll fine Nevada with Ivan."

The two Traxlers dropped from their horses and ran across the street. The sheriff entered his office, fussed about his desk a few minutes, then came out to the sidewalk again. He had it timed about right. Black Nick and Luke were just emerging from the undertaking establishment. They came striding across the street, Nick's face like a thundercloud; Luke was white as a sheet.

They approached the sheriff, breathing hard, enraged. Black Nick said shortly, "All right, Sheriff, I want the straight of this. Your note just said Ivan had been killed. Who did it?"

The sheriff considered. "Nick, I'm sworn to keep the peace, so far as it lies in my ability to do so. I don't know as I should tell you, considering your present frame of mind. You go home and calm down. Come back tomorrow——"

"By God!" Nick thundered. "The undertaker told me to see you when I asked him. Said he didn't know——"

"Don't blame the undertaker. He was working under my orders. I'm trying to keep down trouble in this town."

Nick whipped out his gun and levelled it at the sheriff. "You'll tell me, by the Almighty, Sheriff, or —lawman or not—I'll——"

"Put that gun away, Nick," Perkins said sternly. "You wouldn't get anyplace by shooting me."

"Nick," Luke said nervously, "you're not aiming to shoot the sheriff——"

"Shut up, Luke!" Nick snapped. Reluctantly he slipped the gun back in its holster. "I ain't apologizing, Perkins. I'm mad clear through. Nobody kills a Traxler and gets away scot-free. I'm aiming to get to the bottom of this business. I'm admitting I can't scare the information out of you. Now I'm asking for it."

The sheriff sighed wearily. "All right, Nick, I'll tell you. But I warn you, if you start any gunplay in town——"

"Tell it!" Nick snapped uglily. "Never mind your warnings. If I break any laws I'll stand the penalty—if necessary."

"Pete Piper killed him," Perkins said quietly.

"Piper! That redheaded son! I'll blast——" Black Nick paused suddenly. His voice changed. "What part of the range was Ivan's body found on?"

"Ivan's body wasn't brought in from the range," the sheriff said. "It happened right here in town."

"Don't lie to me, Perkins," Nick snapped.

"I'm telling you straight, Nick. I'll overlook your manner. I realize how you feel—your own blood brother——"

"Cut the palaver! I'm asking for information!"

"I'm giving it to you," the sheriff said coldly. "Giving you the same information you can get from any twenty or fifty men in town. There's no secret about it. That's one reason I told you who did it, when I saw I couldn't persuade you to go back home. There was quite a crowd present right after it happened. Get around town; talk to any of the men that made up that crowd. They'll tell you I'm not lying."

"Nick," Luke said dumbly, "Ivan couldn't have been shot here in town. You sent him over to the ——"

"Shut your mouth, Luke!" Nick said savagely. "I'll do the talking." He swung back to the sheriff. "What time did Piper murder Ivan?"

"It wasn't murder," Perkins replied, "Ivan went for his gun first——"

"Who says so?"

"I've got Piper's word for it."

"That don't mean anything to me. What time was it?"

"Shortly after eight-thirty this morning."

"Eight-thirty! Christ, it couldn't be! Ivan wasn't in town at eight-thirty."

"Why ask me questions if you know it all?"

Black Nick's frown deepened. Something queer here, he thought. He'd better feel his way carefully. A short, ugly laugh left his throat. "All right, Perkins, for the sake of the argument I'll admit it was eight-thirty. What time was Nevada killed? Who did that job? Who else was in the fight?"

"About the same time. Piper did it."

Black Nick looked incredulous. "You mean to tell me Piper took on Nevada and Ivan at the same time? No, no, Perkins! I can't swallow that. Hell! Piper wasn't a match for Nevada, alone. And with Ivan throwing lead too—say, what kind of a story are you making up?"

"I'm giving it to you straight, Nick."

Luke interrupted furiously, "Don't you believe him, Nick. He's lying to us."

"Nick," Perkins said quietly. "If you don't shut up that brother of yours I'm going to slam him in the hoosegow. He's disturbing my peace. I'll answer civil questions in a civil manner, but I don't have to put up with him."

"You hush up, Luke," Nick snapped. He turned back to the sheriff." "All right, you claim Piper killed both Ivan and Nevada in a fair fight. I don't believe it, but we'll let that pass. Maybe you're mistaken. Maybe Piper used some more of his tricks. Now, what started the fight, what brought it on? Ivan isn't quarrelsome. He wouldn't——"

"Ivan stole something belonging to Pete Piper. Pete got it back, that's all."

"Ivan—stole—something? What are you talking about, Perkins? What kind of a job you framing up? I want the truth."

"Nick," the sheriff said testily, "I've tried to keep my temper. Maybe you'd better not ask me any questions. You don't believe me, anyway. Go down and talk to Turk Raven. The fight took place in his saloon; or ask anybody else about it. Maybe you'd better ask Pete Piper."

"Where is Piper now?" Black Nick snapped.

"I wouldn't tell you if I knew, and I'm not sure I know. I'm warning you, Nick. I don't want any gunplay in this town now —or any other time. If I hear of you starting anything—well, I'll just have to figure you're the aggressor and act accordingly. I'm just about out of patience with you Traxlers."

"So?" Nick sneered. "Giving Piper special protection, eh? Well, I don't give a damn about you or anybody else, Perkins, and——"

Nick suddenly broke off. The sheriff had turned his back and disappeared in his office.

Nick swore at him. Luke started to say something. Nick swore at him too. The sheriff didn't reappear. Cursing, Nick climbed back in his saddle, followed by Luke.

"Come on," Nick said furiously. "We'll go talk to Turk and see what he says. I'm going to get at the truth of this business. There ain't no man living could down Ivan and Nevada, too, in the same fight."

They had scarcely left the hitch rack when the sheriff reappeared on the sidewalk. He settled his sombrero more firmly on his head and walked quickly in the direction of Beanpole Ridge's Lariat Saloon. Here he found Pete and Homer standing at the bar sipping beer and talking of things in general.

Pete asked, "Back for another scuttle of suds, Ethan?"

The sheriff said no and added, "Pete, things seem pretty quiet. Why don't you run out and see Cressy? I've got a note for her father, and I'd appreciate your taking it——"

"Cripes!" Homer protested good-naturedly. "It's only about an hour since Cressy left here. You aimin' to spoil a good drinkin' man, Ethan? Leave Pete alone."

"Homer, you keep your mouth shut," Perkins snapped.

"Sure, I'll be glad to deliver your note, Ethan——" Pete commenced, then paused. "Hey, what's up? Why you so short with Homer? Ethan, what you cooking up? No, I don't think I do want to deliver any note for you—not until I know more."

"All right." The sheriff wilted under his steady gaze. "I was only trying to get you out of town, Pete."

"Why?" Pete was serious now, frowning.

"Black Nick just got into Beauregard. He's mean. I figured I could mebbe forestall more bloodshed."

Homer whistled softly. Pete nodded. "Thanks, Ethan. I

couldn't leave now. You understand that. But thanks for warning me. I'll wait. If Black Nick wants trouble he's entitled to that much consideration. I'll wait."

"I was afraid you might take it that way," the sheriff sighed. He removed his sombrero and mopped his brow with his bandanna.

Meanwhile Nick Traxler and Luke had Turk Raven cornered at one end of that worthy's bar. Turk was pale. "I tell you, Nick, I don't know much about it. Nevada ran me out of here. You wouldn't expect me to face Nevada, would you? He was plenty ugly this mornin'."

Nick's cold gaze threatened Raven. "Don't stall me, Turk," he said coldly.

"S'help me Gawd, Nick," Raven whined. "I can't tell you nothin' much. Ivan and Nevada was in here. Ivan was waitin' for the bank to open. I heard him say it——"

"What was he going to do at the bank?" Nick frowned.

"I ain't the least idea."

"I'll find out, dammit. I'll see Haines and—— Never mind; go on."

"Ivan went to my door and came back, white as a bar apron. He says to Nevada, 'Piper's out there. You got to help me.' They talked some more; then they both got ready for Piper to come in, so they could catch him in a cross fire. About that time I said, 'Let's not have any fightin' here.' Then Nevada run me out. I beat it for the alley; then I heard shots. That's all I know, until I come back and see them both on the floor, dead."

Nick's right hand shot across the bar and seized Turk's throat. "Don't lie to me, you bustard! Look me in the eye!"

Despite his frantic gurgling and choking, Raven managed to look Nick straight in the eyes. After a second Nick released him. "I still can't believe it. How could Piper down both of em?"

Raven gulped and fingered his throat. "Maybe you'd better ask Piper to explain it. I can't."

"Do you know where Piper is?" Nick flashed.

"How would I know? He never comes here. Somebody said he goes to the Lariat Saloon occasional."

Nick swore at Raven, then gave Luke a push toward the doorway. "We'll try the Lariat first. So help me. I'm going to find that devil and blast him wide open. Come on!"

They pushed through the swinging doors. Back of them, in the bar, two other customers who had witnessed Nick's brutal treatment of Raven immediately commenced to ask questions of the saloon proprietor. Raven shook his head, said nervously, "Don't ask me nothin', boys. I don't want to talk. Black Nick's on the prod, and when he's that way it's best not to cross him. I got trouble enough keepin' my own rep clear, without I do anythin' to get him sore at me."

Nick and Luke had reached the porch of the saloon. Suddenly Nick halted, pointing an angry finger west along Main Street. "Wait a minute, Luke; there's Sheriff Perkins now, just coming out of the Lariat bar. Ten to one he's been warning Piper."

Luke's gaze followed the pointing finger. The afternoon sun was commencing to make long shadows along the street. The sheriff left the sidewalk in front of the Busy Bee Restaurant, glanced both ways along the thoroughfare, then started in a long diagonal direction across Main.

Nick spoke through clenched teeth. "He's coming here, probably looking for me. Come on, Luke, I don't want to hear no more of his warnings."

He seized Luke by the shoulder and pushed him back into the saloon. As the two re-entered Turk and his pair of customers glanced up in surprise. Nick spat quick words from one corner of his mouth as they moved down the long room: "We're leaving by your back door, Turk. We haven't been here, see? You don't know where we are! Get it?"

"I get it." Turk nodded dully. "You haven't been here. Say! How about your broncs? Are they out in front?"

Nick paused, face flushing angrily. "What if they are? That's no sign we came in here."

"Just as you say, Nick." Raven shrugged his narrow shoulders.

Nick, still pushing Luke before him, paused at the rear door to speak to the two customers. "You two! You haven't seen us either—understand? And I don't like double-crossers. If you can't be on my side maybe you'd better get out!"

The two paled and nodded without saying anything. Nick and Luke opened the door, slipped out to the alley, closed the door again. The two customers looked at each other. One of them nodded shakily.

Turk said, "How about a drink on the house, boys?"

"I ain't thirsty," one of the customers said. The other spoke nervously. "I got to be getting along, Turk." With one accord they turned and ran for the door, almost colliding with the sheriff as he stepped to the porch. Perkins looked queerly after them as they hurried down the street, then pushed through the swinging doors.

Meanwhile Black Nick and his brother had darted through the alleyway to Tonto Street, then turned over to Main and started toward the Lariat bar. Outside the Lariat doorway they paused. Nick peered in above the swinging doors.

"Is he there?" Luke whispered hoarsely.

Nick nodded. "Just a few yards from the entrance. He's standing at the bar. Homer Pritchard is between him and this doorway. He won't see me when I come in."

"Who else is in there?" Luke asked. His voice shook.

"Three or four other hombres. People who live in town. They won't take no part. Don't you, either, unless Pritchard goes for his gun. This is between me and Piper. When I go in my hand is going to be on my gun. I'll invite Piper to draw. The instant he starts a hand toward his holster I'll draw and let him have it! He won't have a dawg's chance. Come on!"

With his right fingers wrapped on the butt of his six-shooter Black Nick employed the left hand to push back the swinging door. Just inside the entrance he paused to let Luke come in.

A few feet away stood Homer Pritchard. Standing close to him was Pete. The two had bottles of beer before them. Farther down the bar Beanpole Ridge was engrossed in conversation with some other customers. So silently had the Traxlers entered, that no one had heard them yet.

"All right, Piper," Nick snarled, "jerk your iron!"

The men at the bar stiffened. A couple of those at the farther end looked around; then their jaws sagged. Pete didn't turn at once. His form was partly concealed from Nick's view by Homer's body. Nick stood there, legs spread wide, a vicious snarl of hate on his swarthy features, his right hand clenched on gun butt.

"Jerk your iron, damn you!" Nick rasped. "You murdered Ivan, and I'm aiming to blast you to hell."

He paused suddenly. Pete had swung easily around. Nick's jaw dropped as he heard Pete's cool laugh. Pete's gun, concealed by Homer's body, was already out and bearing directly on Nick's middle. Nick's gun, though ready, still reposed in his holster.

"It's already jerked, Traxler," Pete was saying softly. "Now do we go on from here or call it quits? You arrived plumb quiet, but I've been expecting you. Besides, this bar mirror is a big help in spotting customers as they enter."

"Damn you, Piper!" Traxler spat.

"Calling names won't help," Pete said quietly. "You came here with a job in mind. Do you want to go throught with it, or don't you? If you do, I'll put my gun away; we'll both put our hands in the air and start from scratch."

"Look, Piper," Luke commenced in a shaking voice, "you got us wrong. Nick didn't mean anything."

"Don't be a fool, Luke," Nick said angrily. "Piper knows what I had in mind. I've still got it in mind."

Black Nick hesitated. Slowly his fingers unwrapped from his gun butt; then he dropped his arms at his side. "Not now"—he shook his head—"but I'll get you yet. You murdered my brother."

"I killed him in self-defense," Pete said sternly.

"The same goes for Nevada Norton," Homer put in.

"Ivan stole something from me," Pete continued. "I had to get it back, Traxler."

"I don't believe it. Ivan was no thief. What did he take from you?"

"My red quirt, Traxler."

Traxler's gaze darted to Pete's left wrist. The quirt wasn't there. A gleam of sudden hope showed in Traxler's eyes. "Didn't you get it?" he blurted impulsively.

"I got it," Pete said. "It's put where you can't find it."

"Aw, why should I want your quirt?" Nick growled. "Look, Piper, maybe I've been hasty on this thing. I didn't know the situation. Maybe you and I can be friends yet——"

"I doubt it," Pete cut in. "But just to make sure you don't fly off the handle again, I figure you and your brother better let Homer have your guns."

"T'hell we will!" Traxler exclaimed.

"Get their guns, Homer," Pete said quietly.

Despite their profane protests, Homer approached and lifted the six-shooters from Nick's and Luke's holsters. At that moment the swinging doors banged open and Sheriff Perkins came barging in, panting heavily. "Got here in time," he wheezed. "Nick, your broncs are in front of Raven's Saloon. Raven said you hadn't been there, but I know he lied. You'd better slope back to the Diamond-T if you know what's good for you. I warned you I didn't want any gunplay——"

"Homer's taking care of that now." Pete laughed softly. "Sheriff, will you hold the Traxlers' guns until tomorrow? Maybe they'll cool down by that time. They're in no fit mood to possess firearms today."

Luke hurried from the saloon. Nick paused just inside, eyes glaring with hate. "I'll catch up with you yet, Piper," he threatened. "When that happens——"

"I hope you will." Pete smiled coolly. "I'm not yet done with you either, Traxler. And I'm just as anxious as you to have things settled. Keep that in mind!"

Traxler cursed and hurried outside to join his brother.

22 | Banker's Bluff

Two mornings later when the fast express stopped at the raised-dirt platform, on which the Beauregard City depot was situated, Pete Piper swung down from one of the coaches. He said good-by to the conductor, walked over Tonto Street to his hotel, procured the red quirt from its hiding place among the bedclothes, and slipped it on his left wrist. Then he once more descended to the street and walked along

Main until he had reached the sheriff's office.

Homer was seated before the sheriff's office, engaged in his perpetual whittling. When he saw Pete he gave a smile of welcome, closed his knife, and stood up.

"Any luck?" he asked.

"No and yes. I didn't see Joadie Tate, if that's what you mean. Had a bit of trouble running him down. Where's Ethan?"

"Here he comes now. Been down to the Lariat for his mid-morning tonic."

The sheriff arrived and said hello and shook hands. He, too, asked, "Did you have any luck, Pete?"

Homer rose and gave the sheriff the tilted-back chair, then joined Pete at the edge of the sidewalk, where they lounged with their backs against the hitch rack. Pete told his story:

"I was just telling Homer that I had a bit of trouble running down Tate. I went around asking for a man named Joadie Tate, who, I figured, had arrived in a wagon long about last Saturday. Tate's from one of the farming states back East. Him and a lot of his friends came to Rhysville a year or so back. I guess farming land is none too good over that way, and Tate and his people took a skinning from some tinhorn realtors. Anyway, they're plumb suspicious of all Western folks now, and none of 'em is anxious to talk much. There's a whole colony of Tate's kind living out at the edge of town, and when I commenced asking for the whereabouts of one Joadie Tate they all shut up like a clam. There were several hints that I get out and mind my own business."

"T'hell you say!" the sheriff ejaculated.

"T'hell I do." Pete grinned. "It sure looked like they had me hawg-tied; then a streak of luck came my way. I happened to be crossing the street when a runaway occurred. Fool horse went hawg-wild and bent bouncing along the street with a buggy on behind. What made it bad, there was a little kid in the buggy—probably four-five years old. It wasn't any trouble to put a stop to that fool horse's running, so I did it. Then a feller rushes up and grabs my hand with tears in his eyes and allowed how I'd saved his little boy from a terrible death."

"Always the hero, huh?" Homer chuckled.

"Anyway, this feller says so." Pete smiled. "His name was McCoy, and he turned out to be Joadie Tate's brother-in-law. Took me to his house—it wasn't little more than a shack—and insisted I stay to supper. I met his wife. And stayed to supper. Didn't have the nerve to eat much, though. There wasn't much. Potatoes and watery gravy and weak coffee. Cripes! Those folks are poor as church mice but proud as all get out just the same. They're pretty much close-mouthed, too, and don't like to talk to strangers."

"But where was Tate?" the sheriff asked.

"I'm coming to that part. McCoy told me about Tate. Seems, back about eight months or so, Tate loaded his wagon and started out to take up new farming land someplace 'way up north of here. McCoy was agin the idea. I gathered him and Tate had some words about it. Anyway, Tate and his wife and his little girl pulled out. That's the last the McCoys heard of 'em until last Saturday night when the wagon pulled in, with Tate's wife mighty sick. She died that same night."

"Tough," Homer muttered.

"They buried the wife the next day. McCoy and Tate still weren't on what you'd call strictly good speaking terms, and what with Tate's wife dying and the funeral and all, Tate and McCoy hadn't chinned much. But McCoy gathered that Tate had run into some sort of trouble over this way."

"What gave him that idea?" the sheriff asked.

"Something Tate had dropped about having trouble and about losing a rocking chair."

"There's the rockin' chair Munson died in, I'm bettin'!" Homer exclaimed.

"Maybe so." Pete nodded. "Anyway, Tate had heard where he could get two days' work in the next town, and he'd gone to take it, taking the little girl with him. And why do you suppose he wanted that two days' work?"

"I'll bite?" Homer said.

"So he could raise the railroad fare and come back here and square an account. Can you beat that?"

"Is that what McCoy told you?" the sheriff asked.

"That's the story as I got it," Pete replied. "Tate also intended to buy some buckshot, so I reckon he won't be coming peaceable-minded when he arrives."

"Well, I'll be damned!" Homer exploded. "If that ain't the damnedest! Mister, he must love that rockin' chair."

Pete said, "Those folks hang onto anything they got—that's how poor they are. I left 'em some money and told 'em to tell Tate to wire me when he was coming and to be sure and come; that I'd make it worth while."

"Just left 'em enough money for the telegram, I suppose," Homer said dryly.

Pete flushed. "Hell, that kid needed some milk and eggs. And I hope they bought some thick steaks too."

"You don't know exactly when Tate will arrive, eh?" Homer asked.

Pete shook his head. "He was to have two days' work, but they weren't sure but what he might land some other work. That's why I didn't wait for Tate's return. How've things been in town?"

"Peaceful as a church," Homer said. "The Traxlers came in yesterday and asked if they could have their guns. Ethan let 'em have 'em—and he tacked a warnin' onto the givin'."

"Black Nick seems right subdued," the sheriff said. "Said he realized he was wrong in what he attempted the other night. Pleaded mitigating circumstances, his brother's killing and so on. Asked me to overlook it and hoped you'd do the same, Pete. Says he'd really like to be friends."

"How in hell," Homer demanded, "can a man be friends with a diamondback?"

Pete frowned. "Maybe a diamondback is most dangerous when he pretends to be friends. I'd hoped to keep Nick Traxler on the run a little bit, so he'd get careless and make mistakes. I don't like it when he settles down and waits for me to make the moves." He considered a moment. "So far I've kept secret that I was a member of the Artexico Association. It's been a good thing, to date, but I reckon I'll have to see if coming into the open won't help matters a bit. From now on, should anybody ask you, tell 'em who I am."

"What you got in mind, Pete?" the sheriff asked.

"I'm not rightly sure, but any move is better than being worked into a stalemate. I've got business, important business, ahead of me, and I don't want to get bogged down in one place too long."

"That important business wouldn't have anythin' to do with Cressy Alexander, would it?" Homer laughed.

Pete grinned. "If I told you, you'd know as much as I do." He changed the subject. "Seen Nick Traxler today?"

"Yeah," Homer said. "He's in Raven's bar at present, him and Luke. Got one or two of their hands with 'em too."

Pete considered. "You know, I keep thinking about Ivan Traxler saying that he could get a pretty penny for my quirt. And then the instant he got to town that morning he headed right for the bank. Who in the bank would be likely to buy that quirt?"

"There's only two men there—Banker Rudolph Haines and his cashier, Kilby Ward. But I can't see how they'd be mixed into that quirt business, Pete," the sheriff said, slowly.

"I don't either," Pete admitted; "but how can I tell until I've had an opportunity to meet those two hombres? That's a job I've put off long enough. I reckon I'll take care of it now. See you later, gentlemen."

Pete walked down to the corner of Main and Tonto streets, where, cater-corner from the hotel, stood a solid-looking brick building with double doors and a window on either side of the entrance. Painted on the windows were the words: RUDOLPH HAINES—BANKING & LOANS. Pete entered the bank, closing behind him the door through which he'd come in. The front half of the bank was partitioned off by two grilled windows, one of which was now closed, and a small, waist-high swinging gate. On the other side of the partition a huge steel vault stood in one corner. The rest of the room was given over to an office, on which was a door marked PRIVATE. Against one side wall, not far from the entrance, was a breast-high wall desk, on which were a smeary bottle of ink and a couple of pens in holders, together with a much-used blotter.

There weren't any customers in the bank when Pete entered. He approached the man behind the open grille window and asked if Rudolph Haines was in.

"He's pretty busy right now," the man said. He was about thirty, with thin, slicked-down hair, hollow chest, and thin cheeks. "Can I help you sir? If it's something in the way of a loan I'll be glad to take it up with Mr. Haines."

"There's always something in the way of my loans." Pete grinned. "No, I didn't want to borrow any money. I want to see Haines on business."

"If you'd care to tell me——?"

"I wouldn't—or wait, I want to talk to you too. You Kilby Ward?" The cashier nodded. Pete went on, "What time did Hugh Alexander come into this bank the day he was murdered?"

The question came so unexpectedly that for a moment the cashier could only stammer. Finally he endeavored to make himself clear. "Alexander—oh, yes, Hugh Alexander. I remember now. Why, he wasn't in here at all that day, Mr.—Mr.——"

"I understood he was."

"I'm sure he wasn't. Of course if you care to talk to Mr. Haines I'll see if——"

"Told you I wanted to talk to Haines in the first place."

"I'll—I'll see." The cashier hurriedly left his window, approached the door marked PRIVATE, knocked, and then went in. The door closed again.

Pete chuckled softly to himself. "Surprising how a few words will make a hombre jump sometimes."

At the end of five minutes' time the door marked PRIVATE was opened and Kilby Ward appeared again. He seemed less flustered now; his voice was steadier. "Mr. Haines will be able to spare you some time, after all," he announced. "Just come through that gate."

Pete pushed through the swinging gate and entered the office. Ward closed the door and returned to his grille.

"Rudolph Haines?" Pete asked.

The big man behind the desk nodded heavily, importantly. "I'm Rudolph Haines." He was potbellied, with ponderous jowls and a bald head. A thick cigar jutted from one corner of his wide-lipped mouth. Light entered through a barred window behind his chair at the desk.

"I'm Pete Piper."

"Have a seat."

Pete seated himself across the desk. Neither he nor Haines had offered to shake hands.

Haines said slowly and deliberately, "I understand you wanted to see me in regard to that Hugh Alexander case. Are they reopening that again?"

"I didn't know it had ever been closed."

"Closed or not," Haines said, "I know nothing about it. Why are you interested?"

"I'm here on behalf of the Alexander family, and here's my authority." Pete pulled his badge from his pocket, displayed it momentarily to Haines, then put it back again. Haines hadn't had an opportunity to read the words on it.

His eyes narrowed a trifle. "You're connected with the Pinkerton organization?"

"I didn't say that," Pete countered coolly.

"At any rate, you're a law officer," Haines said testily.

"I'm asking you to keep that secret for the present," Pete said.

"Certainly, by all means. I quite understand. Now what was it you wanted to see me about?"

"I want to ask you if you're quite sure Hugh Alexander didn't come into your bank that morning?"

Haines said stiffly, "I've already made a statement to that effect. Are you doubting the truth of——?"

"I'm asking you if you're quite sure."

Haines's features crimsoned. "I'm not in the habit of having my word doubted. Practically everyone in this town was questioned. No one saw Alexander enter this bank."

"How do you account for him not coming to pay you that money, when that was his sole reason for coming to town?"

"I made no attempt to account for it," Haines snapped. "That part is none of my business. Now if that's all you have to say, Piper, I'll be pleased if you——"

"One minute, Mr. Haines. You don't mind my questioning your cashier, do you?"

"I see no reason for taking up his time. He has his duties to attend——"

"You refuse, then?"

Haines's face flushed darkly. He put down his cigar and went to his door, jerked it open, "Kilby!" he called. "Come in here a minute."

The cashier came back to the office. Haines went on, "No, don't close this door. You have to keep an eye on your counter, you know. Someone might come in. Kilby, this is Pete Piper. He wants to know if you saw Hugh Alexander come in the bank the morning he was killed and robbed."

Kilby Ward said, "No, I didn't."

Pete asked, "What time did the bank open that morning?"

"Shortly before nine," Ward replied promptly,

"Was Mr. Haines here at the time?" Pete asked.

Ward's gaze went quickly to Haines. Haines nodded slightly. Ward said, "No, he wasn't. I opened the bank. Mr. Haines came in two or three minutes later."

"Then if Hugh Alexander had come in he'd have had to wait for Mr. Haines, wouldn't he, or would you have sent him right into this private office?"

"I couldn't have done that," Ward replied. "The office wouldn't have been unlocked until Mr. Haines arrived. He had the key."

"What are you driving at, Piper?" Haines demanded.

"Just this. If Hugh had to wait for you in the front part of the bank somebody must have seen him."

"Not necessarily," Ward put in quickly. "There aren't always customers here when we first open——"

"That's enough, Ward," Haines interrupted. He seemed suddenly angry. "Go back to your desk. I think somebody just came into the bank."

Ward quickly departed and closed the door again. Pete sat quietly, a thin smile on his lips. Haines's fingers trembled slightly as he picked up his cigar and puffed vigorously on it. When he spoke his voice was tense with suppressed anger. "The fact remains, Piper, that Alexander didn't come in here that morning. Now are you satisfied?"

Pete shook his head. "No."

"Why aren't you?" Haines snapped.

Pete said, "I've talked this business over quite considerably with Sheriff Perkins. He made a pretty thorough investigation, and I understood that you and your cashier both swear there were a number of people in your bank that morning at opening time. Now Ward just informed me that there aren't always people on hand when you open."

Haines half rose from his chair. "This has gone far enough," he blustered. "That a man of my reputation and integrity in Beauregard City should be submitted to suspicion, questioning ——Well, I have no more time for you. If you've quite finished I'd be obliged if you would——"

"Haven't finished," Pete said quietly. "Mr. Haines, what would you say if I told you I could produce a witness who saw Hugh Alexander enter your office that morning?"

The cigar tumbled from Haines's open mouth, struck the desk, and fell to the floor. Haines sat back in his chair, his face white. "Wha-what's that?" he gasped.

Pete repeated his words.

Haines swallowed hard, bent down to pick his cigar from the floor, and spent plenty of time doing it. When he straightened up again his features were more composed. "That's ridiculous," he blustered. "Who is this witness? I dare you to produce him."

"Didn't say there was one," Pete drawled lazily. "I just asked what you would say if I told you I could produce one."

Haines drew a long breath of relief. "Are you trying to bluff me?" he demanded.

"I didn't say that either." Pete got to his feet. "Just think it over, Mr. Haines. Maybe I'll have a surprise for you one of these days—soon."

Haines looked rather sick. He didn't know what to think now. "Of course," he said weakly, "there is always the possibility that someone saw somebody they *thought* was Hugh Alexander——"

"That's probably it," Pete said lightly. "Good-by, Mr. Haines. You'll probably hear from me again." He opened the door, closed it, walked through the bank, nodded to Kilby Ward, and stepped out to the street.

Homer Pritchard was standing on the hotel corner. He hailed Pete with a whistle. Pete crossed over. Homer said, "Any luck?"

Pete said carefully, "I think so." He told Homer what had happened, concluding, "Of course we were both bluffing, but I've got a hunch I've a lot more chance of calling that banker's bluff than he has of calling mine."

"You don't really know anybody who saw Hugh enter the bank that mornin', then?"

"No, I don't, Homer, but—cripes all fishhooks!—there *must* have been someone who saw him go in. I'm aiming to find that someone!"

Homer said suddenly, "Look—over there."

Pete looked. Banker Rudolph Haines had just emerged from the bank, a derby hat on his head. Without either looking right or left he crossed Tonto Street and walked along Main until he reached Turk Raven's Saloon. Here he turned in and disappeared between the swinging doors.

Pete said soberly, "Seems sort of funny that a man in Haines' position would patronize Raven's grogshop. The hotel bar should be more Haines' style."

"It usually is," Homer chuckled. "Yeah, it's funny all right. I just come from Raven's Saloon before I saw you. What makes it funnier is—Black Nick Traxler is in Raven's place at present."

23   A Cage for a Canary

PETE'S EYES NARROWED. "Do you figure there's a tie-up between Haines and Black Nick?"

"What do you think?"

"Well, I've sort of suspected it. Still, it may just be chance that takes Haines into Raven's Saloon instead of his usual place, the hotel bar. You know, Homer, now that I think of it, Haines kept glancing at this red quirt I'm carrying. Didn't think so much of it at the time. I was too busy questioning him. I reckon, Homer, I should drop into Raven's place. I haven't been in there, except once—the morning I crossed guns with Ivan Traxler and Nevada."

"I'll trail along," Homer suggested.

Together they crossed the street and entered Raven's Saloon. Turk was behind the bar when they pushed through the swinging doors, in the act of serving drinks to Canary Sloan and Luke Traxler. Canary, since Nevada's death, had been elevated to the position of Black Nick's lieutenant and felt his importance keenly. At present he was slightly under the influence of liquor.

Farther down the bar Rudolph Haines and Black Nick had their heads close together. They were talking in low voices. Haines looked worried; Nick was frowning, as though he'd heard bad news.

Pete and Homer stopped at the bar not far from the entrance. Turk Raven approached. "Howdy, Homer? H'are you, Piper? What you drinkin'?"

"Beer," Homer said.

"Bottle of beer," from Pete.

Haines and Black Nick hadn't noticed them enter, but Luke Traxler and Canary Sloan had. Luke whispered something to Canary. Canary looked startled, then moved down the bar to say something to Nick and Haines. Nick raised his eyes slowly; Haines looked guiltily around, then stiffened upon meeting Pete's eyes. He stood hurriedly back from Nick, saying in a pompous voice, "Well, I just wanted to explain the conditions of such a deal, Mr. Traxler. Of course it will be convenient for you to arrange a loan under those terms. I'll be glad to help you. Good day!"

Turning, he strode hurriedly toward the door. Homer said, "Hi-yuh, Mr. Haines! Don't often see you in here."

"Why, hello, Homer. How de do, Piper. I didn't see you men come in." He forced a self-conscious laugh. "No, I don't often come to Mr. Raven's bar. Just dropped in to talk over a little business with Nick Traxler." He nodded again and moved swiftly through the swinging doors.

By this time Black Nick had joined Luke and Canary Sloan, and the three stood conversing in low tones.

Pete and Homer occupied themselves with their bottles of beer. Homer said in an aside to Pete, "What do you think?"

"I think maybe we scored a bull's-eye." Pete smiled. "When the leading banker of a town stops to explain to an outsider just why he has entered a certain saloon and mentions a deal under consideration with his client—well, I'd say said banker is a mite upset. Oh, there's a connection between the two all right, Homer."

"That's as I figure it," Homer said quietly.

Canary Sloan and the two Traxlers were talking louder now; not paying any particular attention to Pete and Homer, just trying to give the impression they were acting naturally.

Pete said to Homer, "Who's the yellow-haired hombre? I don't remember seeing him before."

"That's Canary Sloan. Just another of the Diamond-T crew. Pretty fast with his gun. Can't make up his mind whether he wants to be a bad man or a tenor singer. I've heard him sing. Frankly, I prefer the bad man. I reckon you've never run into him before, though he's in and out of town quite a bit."

Pete frowned reminiscently. "Nope, I reckon I never met him, but his voice sure sounds familiar." He stared into his glass of beer which was going flat. That voice of Sloan's had a reminiscent tone. Where had he heard it?

Black Nick Traxler's voice broke in on his meditations: "Say, Piper, I've been wanting to talk to you. Been out of town for a couple of days, haven't you?"

"Pretty close to it." Pete swung around to face Traxler. "What's on your mind?"

Traxler acted embarrassed. "Nothing much, only I thought I should say something to sort of square myself for the other day—you know, right after Ivan had—well, you know——"

"Forget it, Traxler," Pete said coolly. "It's not the first time my life has been threatened—nor the last, I expect."

"I sort of lost my head for a spell," Traxler said frankly, "or I wouldn't have acted that way. I thought a lot of Ivan. What I wanted to say, I've done some investigating since, and I guess you couldn't do any different than you did. Ivan was at fault. I'm pretty sure of that now. Nevada probably put him up to acting that way. To tell the truth, I can't feel friendly toward you, but there's no sense you and me going on the warpath every time we meet."

Pete shrugged carelessly. "Suits me. I get along pretty well with folks, as a rule, so long as they don't tread on my toes."

"Right!" Canary Sloan cut in on the conversation. "If everybody acted that-a-way there wouldn't be no gun fights." Canary was commencing to show the effects of his drinks, and his words were somewhat thick.

"Better keep out of this, Canary," Black Nick said shortly.

"Why should I?" Canary demanded with owlish surprise. "Ain't we all go' be frien'ly? Let's have another drink, an' then I'll shing 'My Wil' Irish Rosh.'"

"You better mind what Nick says, Canary," Luke put in.

"Aw, Nicksch aw right." Canary grinned, brushing Luke

aside. "Me'n Nicksch goo' frien's. So's Piper and Homer. Jus' one lil drink togesher—then ever'shing will be hunky-dory."

"Shut your trap, Canary," Nick snapped.

The venom in the tones penetrated even Sloan's alcohol-befuddled mind. He quieted and moved away.

Pete's forehead was furrowed with tiny ridges. Where had he heard that voice before? Hunky-dory, hunky-dory.... Everything will be hunky-dory....

Suddenly Pete smiled. He had it! He turned to Homer. "Homer, have you got a cage for a canary down to the jail?"

"Huh? Cage for a canary? Say, what you——?" Light suddenly dawned on Homer: Pete wanted an arrest made. "Sure, but what's the charge?"

"Holdup," Pete said.

"Say, what is this?" Black Nick frowned. "What charge——?"

Pete faced him. "Homer's arresting your friend Sloan."

"What's the charge?"

"I just told Homer. Holdup. Sloan and two others stuck up Miss Alexander and me one night. Stole a quirt of mine."

"Have you gone batty?" Traxler demanded.

"You're crazy!" Sloan protested. "I never done no holdup."

"Don't lie, Sloan!" Pete snapped. "I'd recognize that chirpy bird voice of yours among a million—especially when you say 'hunky-dory.' The scut that held the gun on me that night told us if we'd be quiet, 'everything will be hunky-dory.'"

Homer said, "Canary, that song plumb knocked you off'n your perch. You comin' quiet, or do I have to use bracelets?"

"Nobody's goin' t' arresht me." Sloan took an uncertain backward step and started to feel for his gun. Like a flash Homer was on top of the man. Whipping the gun out of Canary's holster, he struck him a sharp blow with the barrel alongside the head. The rap wasn't hard enough to knock out Sloan, but it did take all the fight out of him. He stood quiet while Homer clapped handcuffs on his wrists.

"Deputy Pritchard, you can't do this," Black Nick protested angrily. "I won't stand for it!"

"How you aiming to prevent it?" Pete asked coolly, facing Traxler. Homer added shortly, "Hell! It's done!"

Luke Traxler blurted hotly, "Piper, you cant' push us around, even if you are a detective. We got our rights——"

Furiously Black Nick turned and struck his brother a backhanded blow across the mouth. "You keep your trap shut, Luke!"

Pete laughed softly. "And who told you I was a detective, Traxler?" Haines had promised to keep that fact secret.

Luke didn't answer. He kept watching his brother, waiting. Nick laughed uneasily. "It's just some fool rumor that's around town, Piper. Luke's just talking to hear himself. But that's whatever. You can't arrest Canary without a warrant."

"There'll be a warrant sworn to when we get him in jail," Homer snapped. "And you, nor anybody else, can't stop me from takin' him there, Nick. Now use your head. Don't be foolish."

"Nick, you won't let them take me——" Canary cried.

"You go along with them quiet, Canary," Nick said. "I'll have you out on bail in no time. They can't make a charge either. Don't confess to nothing. I'll get a good lawyer. We'll have you out, Canary, in jig time. I'm going over and see the J.P. right now."

And with that Black Nick, followed by Luke, rushed from the saloon. Canary eyed Homer defiantly. "All right, lawman, take me down to your tin-can jail. But I won't be there long."

"Maybe," Pete said grimly, "you'll be willing to stay long enough to tell us who your two pals were that night."

"I didn't have any pals. I don't know what night you're talkin' about; I don't know nothin'," Canary said sullenly. "Now try to make me talk."

"Canary," Homer warned, "you're askin' for somethin'."

They started out of the saloon, Canary walking reluctantly between Homer and Pete. Turk Raven stared after them openmouthed, then, from sheer force of habit, said, "Come again, gentlemen."

Pete looked at him and laughed. "You really mean that?"

"I'm damned if I do," Raven growled. "You only been in here twice, and each time it spelled trouble. If I never see you again it'll be too soon!"

24   A Shotgun for Scoundrels

THE NEXT THREE days passed uneventfully. As Pete had expected, Nick Traxler had arranged for bail for Canary Sloan almost immediately. At any rate, Pete had the satisfaction of knowing that Sloan would be brought up for trial in due time; by then he hoped to have learned who were Sloan's accomplices the night of the holdup. In the event Sloan jumped his bail, it would only prove his guilt. Sloan had had sense enough to stay away from town for a few days at least, or maybe he was working under Traxler's orders. Traxler himself had come into Beauregard every day; he looked worried and was continually asking if one or another of his men had been seen in town. Pete smiled to himself when he heard this; his scheme was apparently working; Dunlop was carrying out orders.

On Sunday Pete rode to the Ladder-D and talked with Joe Dunlop. Dunlop informed him that he now held, under guard, no less than eight Diamond-T punchers whom his men had picked up riding Ladder-D range. Dunlop was getting worried. "I don't know how much longer we can hold them, Pete. I'm afraid it isn't really constitutional."

"Don't worry, Mr. Dunlop," Pete had replied. "I'm the one who's responsible. Eventually those hombres will break down and commence talking. That will happen when I've got Nick Traxler completely roped and thrown. Right now he's worrying plenty. He's sent men out looking for Steve Barton and Larry Kurtz. Those men just disappeared when your men grabbed them. The same thing happened to other Diamond-T punchers Traxler sent out. If I put 'em in jail Traxler would just bail 'em out. On top of that, he'd learn just how we're whittling down his crew. Our advantage lies in secrecy. And just remember, if those men were free they'd be running off your cattle."

"By the great Jehovah! You're right, Pete. All right, I'll leave it to your judgment. You've shown, so far, you know what you're doing."

"Thanks, Mr. Dunlop."

From the Ladder-D, Pete had cut across the range to the C-Bar-A, arriving there in time for supper Sunday night. He spent a pleasant evening with Cressy and the rest, then, as there was a full moon that night, he spent the rest of the evening with Cressy. The following morning he rose early and returned to Beauregard.

Homer, as usual, was whittling on the porch in front of the sheriff's office when Pete rode up to the hitch rack and dismounted.

"Hi-yuh, Pete!"

"Hi-yuh, Homer! Anything happened?"

"Nothin' unusual." Homer grinned. "Black Nick Traxler was in town yesterday. Seems a couple more of his cowboys have disappeared. Been gone since Friday night. He figures they must have quit their jobs."

Pete and Homer exchanged knowing grins. Homer continued, "Oh yes, there's a telegram was delivered for you from the depot a spell back. Ethan's got it."

The sheriff appeared in his doorway. "Hello, Pete. I didn't hear you ride up. Wondered who Homer was talking to. I got a telegram here for you." He reached into his office and handed Pete a sheet of paper.

Pete read the wire, then looked up. "It's from Joadie Tate. Says he's arriving on the eleven fifty-seven this noon. I'll be right glad to talk to that hombre——" He broke off; suddenly: "Dammit! I'm a muddlehead! I intended to get a picture of Hugh Alexander when I was out to the C-Bar-A; then I plumb forgot it."

"What do you want a picture of Hugh for?" Ethan asked.

Pete explained: "Last couple of days I've been asking all over town if anybody had seen Hugh enter Haines' bank that morning. It's surprising how many people I talk to that didn't even know what Hugh looked like. If I had a picture of him I could show, it might refresh their memories."

"Only one man takes pictures in this town," Homer cut in. "That's Willie Dabbert. We might drift down to his photograph parlor and see if he'd have a picture of Hugh."

"It's an idea," Pete said instantly.

Together he and Homer walked along the sidewalk until they had reached a small shop in the middle of the next block. On the front was a sign that read: WILLIE DABBERT —ARTISTIC PHOTOGRAPHS—GROUPINGS A SPECIALTY. Homer and Pete entered and found themselves in a room containing a worn carpet, two chairs with a great deal of ornate woodwork, an imitation potted palm, a small table with spindly legs holding a Bible, and several other accessories. There was a skylight overhead. Photographs decorated the walls. There were a couple of the large painted canvases, stretched on frames, known as "backgrounds." One background represented a desert scene; the other a waterfall with tall trees and ferns at the side. A third, smaller background was simply painted with varying shades of gray and black that blended together. A large box camera, the rear half of which was covered with a black cloth, stood on a tripod in one corner.

Willie Dabbert entered from a back room. He was a small man with heavy eyebrows and chemically stained hands. "Something in a nifty photo, gents——" he commenced; then, "Oh, it's you, Homer." His face fell; then he cackled, "Nope, I guess I wouldn't want to chance on you breaking my lens again."

Homer introduced Pete and told him what they were looking for. Dabbert considered a moment; then his face cleared. "Yes, I remember taking a picture of young Alexander shortly before his death. I keep copies of everything I do, for a record, in my album."

He procured a large weighty book from the floor in one corner, blew the dust from it, and placed it on the table. Then he commenced to turn the thick pages, heavy with the various photos pasted in them. Pete and Homer stood at either shoulder.

Ten minutes later, when they left Dabbert's photograph parlors, Pete had a picture of Hugh Alexander. What was fully as important, in running through the pages, Pete had noticed one picture in particular. This, too, he had purchased and sworn Dabbert to secrecy. The picture showed Tiger-Eye Munson, Luke, and Ivan Traxler, dressed in what they considered their Sunday best. As Dabbert explained it, the three had arrived in town one day, drunk, and insisted on having their photo taken. What impressed Pete was the fact that despite the dress-up clothing, including derby hats and heavy watch chains, there was, on Tiger-Eye's left wrist, a riding quirt. Naturally it didn't appear red in the picture, but Pete was certain it was the same quirt.

On the street Homer said, "What did you want that picture of Munson and the two Traxlers for?"

"I'm not sure yet," Pete said slowly. "Just took it on a hunch, I reckon. It struck me as queer that, in spite of being dressed up, Munson kept his quirt close to him. Makes it look like a valuable sort of quirt."

"Well, I'll be damned!" Homer exclaimed. "Pete, maybe that picture's a clue."

"That's what I'm hoping."

"It's queer I never saw Munson with that quirt around town."

"Can't tell what he had in mind. Dabbert said they got drunk out to the Diamond-T, then dressed up and came to town. A drunk does funny things sometimes. Maybe that was the only time he ever wore it."

"Maybe so."

Shortly before twelve o'clock Pete headed down toward the railroad depot to await the arrival of Joadie Tate. On hand to meet the same train was Luke Traxler, accompanied by Ducky Drake. Luke was expecting a pair of fancy boots he'd ordered from a mail-order house in Kansas City. He nodded to Pete in rather surly fashion; then he and Ducky walked down the platform to wait near the freight depot.

Finally the rails commenced to hum. Far down the tracks came the sound of a locomotive whistle. The train came on with a steadily increasing roar and clanging of the bell. Then all of a sudden it seemed to close in on the tiny station on the raised-dirt platform and pant to a shuddering, smoke-and-steam belching stop. Cinders showered down. A cloud of thick smoke enveloped the platform, then lifted. A conductor stepped down from the coach nearest Pete.

Only one passenger alighted, a tall, gaunt man with burning eyes and weathered features. His sombrero was a tattered wreck. The coat, over his sweat-stained denim shirt, was a threadbare, rusty green. The legs of his patched, bibbed overalls were tucked into knee-length, flat-heeled, heavy boots. A double-barreled shotgun was cradled in his right arm. His gaze moved angrily about the depot platform.

Pete stepped forward. "You Joadie Tate?"

Tate surveyed him, then extended a gnarled hand. "I reckon how ye're Mr Piper." The words were a drawling monotone. "Got yer message and the money. Thankee. I'll pay ye back soon's I'm able."

The conductor's "All abo-o-a-a-rd!" sounded. The train moved off in a rush of steam, noise, cinders, and black smoke, drowning out Tate's further words that mentioned something about having a "special purpose in comin' to Beauregard, anyway." Pete said, "I see you brought your scatter-gun."

Tate's eyes burned angrily. "Got a score to settle with a pair of fellers. Jest as soon's ye get through askin' them questions ye mentioned to McCoy, I aims to go huntin' me a couple of prime skinks. There ain't no man a-goin' to order Joadie Tate to git outten the country. Only for circumstances, I wouldn't never left on the say-so of that pair of tick-mean scoundrels —— Say, thet's a purty quirt ye're a-wearin'. The red color looks real nice."

"Ever see one like it before?" Pete asked quickly.

"Couple of times. Once when I fust come through Beauregard—— Say, there's one of them fellers now! By the great A'mighty——"

Pete whirled. Luke Traxler was peering around the corner of the depot, just raising his gun. At the same instant there came the jarring roar of a .45 as Ducky Drake moved into action.

25   Buckshot!

PETE LEAPED TO shove Joadie Tate to one side. The movement probably saved Tate's life as Luke Traxler's bullet, aimed for Tate's chest, only succeeded in striking the man's left shoulder. At the same time Ducky Drake's slug had whined far wide of the swift-moving Pete.

Pete's right hand stabbed down, came up in one fast, eye-defying arc. Flame and smoke darted from his gun muzzle. Ducky Drake took one uncertain step, then pitched from behind the shelter of the depot building. Luke Traxler was now in plain view too.

Joadie Tate had been swung off balance by the heavy slug from Luke's six-shooter. He half stumbled, righted himself, then with a superhuman effort pulled the shotgun to his right shoulder and sighted along the twin barrels.

Thunder and black smoke issued from the right barrel, then from the left. Luke Traxler, caught in the act of lifting his six-shooter for another try, was hurled violently back by the double blast and knocked from his feet. He lay moaning where he had fallen.

"Thet's fifty per cent of my score squar'd." Joadie Tate spoke deliberately and spat a long brown stream. "Now if I can only find the other skunk—— " Quite suddenly he lost his balance and sat down heavily on the platform, the gun tumbling from his hands, his left arm swinging limp.

Pete cast a final glance toward Drake and Traxler, then hurried to Tate's side. Tate's face was white through the crop of unshaven whiskers on his jaw. He started to get up.

"Sit still," Pete said. "Take it easy a minute. Know where you're hit?"

"The son of a bustard got me in the left fore quarter," Tate said slowly. There was a hole in the left shoulder of his worn coat. "It ain't no matter, Mr. Piper. I'll be all right come a few minutes or so. But I'll bet a pretty that skunk don't never recover from them buckshots I give him. Did ye get hurted any?"

"I'm all right. Just take it easy."

The stationmaster appeared cautiously now from his depot. Several other people had put in an appearance. There were yells from the direction of Main Street. Pete cast a quick glance at Ducky Drake and Luke. Drake was already dead. Traxler was still breathing but unconscious. Blood welled from his open lips.

The stationmaster shuddered and remarked, "Gawd! What a shambles! You got Ducky plumb through the cheek."

"That's all I had to shoot at," Pete said shortly.

"What started the fight?"

"I'm not sure—yet," Pete replied. He went back to Joadie Tate, who by this time had torn open his coat and was stuffing a wad of chewing tobacco into the bullet hole. Then Tate picked up his shotgun, reached in a coat pocket, drew out two more shells, and reloaded. He struggled to his feet, saying, "Now I'm ready for the other buzzard. Them two took a rocker of mine."

Homer and the sheriff came panting up on the platform, Homer in the lead. "Dang it, Pete!" he exclaimed. "Ain't I ever goin' to be on hand when you do your shootin'?"

The sheriff said, "What started this brawl?"

"I ain't sure yet." Pete frowned. "Oh, this is Joadie Tate; Sheriff Perkins and Deputy Pritchard. I just happened to look up, and there was Luke Traxler throwing down on Joadie. Then Drake took a hand. Drake's dead. Luke's still breathing. I'd like to get him over to Doc Gillett's."

Solemnly Tate shook hands with the sheriff and deputy, then walked across to take a look at Luke Traxler. When he returned Pete said, "Come along to the doctor's with us, Joadie. You'd better get that shoulder fixed up before you look for the other skunk." Reluctantly Tate consented.

The sheriff hailed a man passing with a wagon. Luke was lifted into the body of the vehicle; then the rest climbed on.

Three quarters of an hour later Dr. Gillett had probed out the bullet and bandaged Tate's shoulder. The wound hadn't been very serious, luckily. Then the doctor returned to Luke Traxler, stretched in bed in another room. Pete stopped him as he was leaving. "How long will it be before Luke recovers consciousness, Doc?"

Gillett said irritably, "I wouldn't be surprised if he never came to. Jeepers, Pete! Tate's buckshot nigh cut him in two."

"I'll stick around a spell, anyway," Pete said.

Homer and the sheriff had left to see about removing Drake's body to the undertaker's. Pete and Tate sat alone in the doctor's office. Pete said, "Joadie, I reckon this is as good a time as any for you to tell me just what happened when you were over this way before. First"—drawing out the photograph of the two Traxlers and Tiger-Eye Munson—"have you ever seen any of these hombres before? One I know you have. You filled him with a buckshot a spell back."

Tate looked at the picture, said immediately, "Sure, I've seen all of 'em. This here one"—pointing to Ivan Traxler—"is the other skunk I'm aimin' to gun."

"You're too late," Pete explained. "I already gunned him myself."

"Ye did?" Tate looked crestfallen. "Now I never will get my rocker back."

"I reckon you will," Pete said. "I think it's stored out in Doc's barn at present. We'll see in a little while."

"Thet's mighty satisfactual, Mr. Piper." He glanced again at the photograph. "This old jasper is the one what was wounded thet day—— Say, is thet quirt you got the same's in this picter?"

"I hope so," Pete replied. "You mentioned having seen a quirt like this before. Maybe it's the same one. Will you tell me where?"

"Like's not I'd best start at the beginnin'. Back about eight months or so, me'n Marthy—thet was my woman—an' Josie Ann—thet's my little datter—come through Beauregard on our way north, where I figured to raise some crops. Well, Marthy wanted to buy some flour an' I was cravin' a shot of lightnin' juice. I wanted to change a five-dollar bill so's I could give her some money. We was right nigh the bank which had just opened up. I went inside. There was a likely-lookin' young jasper standin' at one of the winders, talkin' to the cashier. I noted then he had a red quirt on his wrist——"

"Wait a minute!" Pete exclaimed. He whipped from his pocket the photograph of Hugh Alexander. "Don't tell me this is the man you saw in the bank. Lord! If I have this kind of luck——"

"It's the very same." Tate stabbed a calloused fore-finger at Hugh's picture. "It ain't likely I'd forget them steady eyes an' thet solid jaw. Thet's the feller all right."

"This is a break!" Pete exclaimed. "Now, Mr. Haines, we'll see if I can produce a witness——"

"Whut ye sayin' 'bout a witness?" Tate asked blankly.

"Never mind, Joadie." Pete grinned. "Go on. What happened?"

"Nothin' to get excited about. While I stood there, waitin' to git to the winder, a soft-livin' kind of a man come in—you know, with heavy chops an' a fat see-gar. The young feller says, 'Good mornin', Mr. ——' Say, mebbe the name was Haines. Anyway, they talked a minute; then this Haines took him through a door that had a private sign on it."

"What happened next?" Pete queried breathlessly.

"I don't know as to thet. I got my bill changed at the winder an' left to give Marthy some money. Then I went to a bar——"

"You didn't see the young fellow come out of Haines' private office?"

"Nope. I left, like I told you——"

"Were there many other people in the bank?"

Tate shook his head. "Jest me an' the young feller an' the cashier an' this Haines man. I reckon mebbe he was the banker." Prompted by Pete, he went on, "After we left Beauregard we drove on up to this acreage where I cal'clated to raise my crops. Put most all my money in seed an' sech, but it wa'nt no go. The whole kit an' caboodle just shriveled for the want of water. An' there we was, flat broke. On top of thet, my woman got sick an' Josie Ann was ailin'. Marthy allows as how she wants to get back to Rhysville, so we loaded my wagon an' started, with Marthy gettin' weaker every step them horses took."

"You sure must have had a rough trip."

Tate nodded solemnly. "I'd figured to stop in Beauregard and take Marthy to a doctor, but we lost direction. Stopped at a ranch named Ladder-D to do some queryin' an' git water. A man named Mr. Dunlop was there, an' he set me right. We drove on for a couple hours more. Sudden-like I hears rifle shootin'. I don't think nothin' about it, bein' my mind was occypied toolin' my team through the bresh an' trees, ontil sudden-like an old coot with long white whiskers—the one thet's wearin' the quirt in your photygraft——"

"His name was Munson. The other two are the Traxler brothers."

"Now ye mention it, 'pears like I recollect him bein' called Munson by them Traxlers. Like I was tellin' ye, Munson staggers outten the bresh, wearin' a red quirt. I see he'd been wounded. He calls for me to save him. I jerked down my team and lighted. My woman was in the wagon too weak to stir, but Josie Ann, she helped. I goes round to the back of my wagon to unrope a mattress I'm carryin', so's old

Munson could stretch out comfortable. But first I had to unrope my sittin' rocker so's to git at thet mattress. I put the rocker on the ground, an' Josie Ann pulls it over to Munson. Munson drops into it, half dead. Just then we hear hawsses comin' on the run. Munson rouses hisself an' jerks the red quirt off'n his wrist. Then he give it a throw thet sent it a-flyin' outter sight, over the top of the bresh. I hear him mutter, 'They'll never git thet quirt now.'"

"So Munson threw the quirt away, eh?" Pete said softly. "Things are coming clearer."

Tate nodded. "He'd hardly thrun it out of sight when them two Traxlers come gallopin' outten the bresh. They pulled up short alongside my rocker where Munson was restin'. They both started to curse him out an' call him a double-crossin' son. He laughed at 'em, weak-like, when they kept askin' where the quirt was. Then they started to threaten. 'Bout thet time I stepped in an' ask 'em to leave the pore ol' feller be. With thet, they get mad at me an' tell me to get out. Just like thet—pointed their guns at me an' told me to get out an' never come back." He looked solemnly at Pete. "Whut would you a-done, considerin' my responsibilitiss of a sick woman an' an ailin' datter?"

"I reckon," Pete admitted, "I'd have done as you did. I'd have got out."

"If it hadn't been for Marthy——" Tate paused, and his eyes burned angrily. "Yes, I got out, but I give 'em an argyment. I told 'em I wanted my rocker. They said to hell with my rocker—thet rocker thet was Marthy's favorite sittin' chair! When they threatened to shoot th' whole kit an' caboodle of us I drew in my pride an' got back on my wagon with Josie Ann an' Marthy. An' I got out! But I promised I'd come back an' squar up someday. Ain't ary man, or ary two men, goin' to talk thet way to Joadie Tate an' live long to brag on it. I was sure boilin' when I left. About the time we hit thet main road thet runs to Rhysville I hear some more shootin', but I jest whipped up the team an' kept rollin'. After we got to Rhysville, Marthy died. I reckon you know the rest. But I got to git thet rocker. Got to git me another woman too. Josie Ann needs rearin'. An' there ain't nothin' so teasin' to some women as a good rocker to help persuade 'em. Ain't thet right?"

"Some women sure go for a good rocker," Pete agreed.

Tate scowled. "I ain't excusin' myself for bein' so sheep-livered as to run away thet day an' leave Munson; kinder hated myself, even knowin' they wa'n't much I could do."

"You don't need to bother your head about Munson. From all I gather he was a primo scoundrel. Somebody—those two Traxlers, I reckon—killed him that day. It was just a matter of birds of a feather having a falling out." Pete continued and gave him brief details of what had happened.

Some of the angry glow died out of Tate's eyes. "I reckon I won't fret myself no longer then. I'll be gettin' back to Rhysville, or someplace. Got a livin' to make for Josie Ann an' got to find me another woman. Say, do ye reckon I could see my rocker? It would pleasure me a considerable."

"I reckon." Pete roused himself from speculation. "Joadie, I'm indebted to you for clearing up a pile of things. Don't be in too much of a hurry to leave. I'm figuring to get me some holdings and I'll need a man that can farm, raise alfalfa, and such. And I wouldn't be surprised if you could find a woman hereabouts to help you bring up Josie Ann."

"Thet's right kind of ye, Mr. Piper. I'm bounden to ye for the favor. . . . Where did ye say my rocker was at?"

Pete said, "Out in Doc Gillett's barn. You can go straight through the house." Tate rose and, carrying the shotgun, departed.

Within a few minutes he returned. Many of the angry lines had already been erased from his leathery features. "Thet's sure a purty rocker," he stated. "Don't seem to be harmed none. Well, this fore quarter of mine is thumpin' some. Reckon how I'll go out an' git me a shot of lightnin' juice to numb the sting."

"Better go to the Lariat Saloon; it's the best. Should you happen to go to Raven's bar, you might run into Black Nick Traxler. He won't be feeling so good about Luke."

Tate paused in the doorway. "First names don't make no difference," he said solemnly. "Traxlers is all the same to me. Ain't seen ary man yit what can contend with a charge of buckshot."

"You're right, Joadie, but Black Nick Traxler is my meat."

"Thet makes it different. I don't cal'clate to cut in on ary other man's feudin', Mr. Piper. Where will I be seein' ye?"

"Either at the sheriff's office or the hotel. You'd better go to the hotel when you've had your drink. Tell 'em to give you a room and charge it to me."

"I'm bounden to ye. An' thank ye for the restorin' of my rocker."

"Don't mention it."

26   The Crimson Quirt's Secret

AFTER JOADIE TATE had departed Pete sat waiting. Dr. Gillett came into the room, went to a cabinet, and procured a small dark bottle. Pete said, "Luke regain consciousness yet?"

Gillett shook his head. "I have hopes he will soon, though.

He can't live much longer. I'll call you in time. Did your hillbilly friend leave?"

Pete smiled faintly. "After he'd had a look at his rocker he felt like having a shot of lightning juice."

"I saw him making his way through the house, dragging that twin cannon with him. He's a tough coot."

"They don't come any tougher."

After the doctor had again returned to the room where Luke was stretched in bed Pete rolled and smoked a Durham cigarette. He was growing impatient at the long wait, but if there were any chance that Luke might make a confession before he died Pete wanted to be there. He slapped the lashes of the red quirt idly against his left boot. Somehow there was a secret connected with that quirt. Already it had caused death. What was the secret? Winchell had died trying to steal it. Its theft had brought death to Ivan Traxler and Nevada Norton and Tiger-Eye Munson—at least it must have been connected with Munson's murder. He had thrown it away that morning that it might not fall into the hands of Luke and Ivan.

Pete remembered the morning he had taken it, wet with Ivan's blood, from within Ivan's shirt. The bullet that got Ivan had nicked the handle of the quirt. Luckily the damage to the quirt hadn't been serious. Pete's gaze strayed to the handle of the quirt, noticing the spot where the hot lead had grazed it. Then he looked a second time, closer. A thrill of excitement ran through him.

The bullet had struck just where the knob joined the handle, cutting away some of the horsehair covering. A bit of the leather on the knob was missing too. Apparently the handle was of wood, covered with horsehair and leather. Pete peered still closer at the tiny bit of wood showing. It started him wondering. "Looks like," he muttered, "as though this knob on the end is just a sort of plug that fits into the handle. Can the handle be hollow?"

He tried to pull off the knob. It resisted his efforts. He examined the handle again. Where the knob joined the handle he saw what appeared to be a small section of screw thread. Could it be possible that the knob screwed into the handle? He gave it a turn. The knob again refused to budge. Then he gave it a turn in the opposite direction. That did the trick!

The workmanship of the screw thread was unusually fine, considering it had been carved by hand, assuring a tight fit between knob and handle. Pete concluded unscrewing the knob and gazed intently into the hollow handle. "Something in there all right," he told himself. "Probably this was intended for a feller to hide a small roll of bills. Plumb convenient. I always felt this handle was larger than was really necessary."

One finger probed into the hollow handle, touching what felt like a rolled sheet of paper. Patiently he worked the paper out of its secret hiding place. At last he had it. An exclamation of surprise and triumph left his lips as he unrolled to be a note for six thousand dollars, written on the stationery of the Haines bank, and signed by Cyrus Alexander. Across the face of the note, in a bold hand, were the words, "Paid in full. Rudolph Haines." Below this signature was the date, giving the day, month, and year payment was received. It was the date on which Hugh had died.

"By Cripes!" Pete exulted. "This is something! Wait until I tell Cressy. And her dad. This proves that Hugh Alexander paid up the note. The C-Bar-A is saved!"

He folded the paper and placed it in a pocket. Picking up the knob to rescrew it into the handle of the quirt, he noticed initials—probably done with a nail or some other sharp implement—scratched on the bottom inner side. The initials were H. A. Hugh Alexander. Pete muttered, "This was Hugh's quirt all right."

At that moment Dr. Gillett entered the room. "What you talking to yourself about? Say, you look like you'd found a gold mine. What's up?"

Pete produced the canceled note. "Take a look at this. And Haines claimed Hugh never paid him. See it, Doc? There's proof. Just in case anyting happens to me you've seen it."

"Say"—Gillett frowned—"what's Haines up to? Looks like he was working some kind of skulduggery."

"That's what I'm aiming to find out." Pete thrust the note back into his pocket and started toward the door.

Gillett caught his arm. "Don't you want to talk to Luke Traxler? He's awake, but he won't last long."

"Reckon I'd better." Pete nodded. He turned and followed the doctor into the other room.

Luke lay stretched in bed, all the color gone from his face. When he saw Pete he said feebly, "You licked us again, Piper. Well, no hard feelin's now."

"You in pain, Luke?"

"No, the doc's got me full of dope. He tells me I'm finished."

"Do you want Nick sent for?"

"Probably couldn't get here in time. It don't make no difference, I reckon. Like's not he'd bawl me out. He was always bawlin' out me and Ivan. He was right hard on us—even if we were brothers. We might have been different if it wa'n't for him."

"Luke," Pete said, "I discovered that paid-up note in the handle of the quirt."

"Figured you would," Luke said in a tired voice, "if you kept it long enough. You're smart, Piper. I guess nothin' makes much difference now. You'll probably get Nick and Haines and all the rest of the boys."

"Luke," Pete asked, "why did you try to kill Joadie Tate —you know, that man on the station platform—today?"

Luke smiled faintly. "It scared hell out of me when I saw him—'specially with you. He was there the day me and Ivan run Tiger-Eye Munson to earth—him and his damn rocker. We run him out—at the point of our guns. I knew if I didn't kill him he'd connect me with—Munson's death."

Dr. Gillett tilted Luke's head and gave him something to drink from a glass. Luke seemed anxious to talk now. "Maybe it will square me a mite for what lays ahead." His voice had grown stronger again. "Maybe," he continued, "if Nick had been just satisfied with rustlin' a few cows now and then we'd not got so jammed up. But Banker Haines was pretty greedy for money. Him and Nick were workin' things together. They wanted to get control of the C-Bar-A. It was a disappointment when Hugh Alexander came in the bank with the money to redeem the note. Haines and Nick were so sure they'd get the Alexander outfit. They needed the water there. Nick tried changin' the course of Torvo River, one time, but his dynamitin' backfired, and he cut the Diamond-T off. We sure needed water bad—and whether we needed it or not, I reckon Nick and Haines would have grabbed everythin' they could get, anyway. Damn that Haines!"

"Luke," Pete asked, "was the cashier, Kilby Ward, in on the scheme too?"

"Yes," Luke admitted. "Haines bullied him into keepin' his mouth shut. Ward was a lunger. He had to have a job. He couldn't do cow work. Rather than lose his job, he done what Haines ordered."

"Who killed Hugh Alexander?" Pete asked next.

"Tiger-Eye Munson, the double-crossin' son." Luke's eyes gleamed angrily for a moment. "Tiger-Eye happened to be on hand when Hugh Alexander bought that quirt from a Mexican peddler. He knew about the secret compartment in the handle. We didn't find it out until a long time later—the day he—he died. That mornin', like I say, Haines was plumb surprised and disappointed when Hugh paid up that note. He stalled Hugh off for a spell, until he could send Kilby Ward with a note to Munson. Munson left town and waited for Hugh to show up. When he came ridin' along Munson killed him and took the quirt. Munson always swore, though, that Hugh didn't have any paid-up note in his pocket; said he'd searched him and couldn't find it. He swore all he took off'n the body was that red quirt."

Pete asked, "How come that Hugh left town that morning without waiting for his sister?"

"That was due to some more of Haines' sly fixin'. He paid a little Mex kid to deliver a message to Hugh, supposedly from Hugh's sister. The message was to the effect that Cressy Alexander had left for the C-Bar-A and that Hugh was to follow at once, as she'd had word that their father was seriously hurt in a gun accident. Naturally Hugh got on his bronc and tore up the road—until he reached the spot where Munson was waitin' with his Winchester. That was the end of Hugh Alexander. Naturally there was a big fuss kicked up. The sheriff made an investigation. But Haines and Kilby swore that Hugh had never been near the bank. The money was gone, and no note could be found. Haines had already had Kilby forge Cyrus Alexander's signature to another note, in case Alexander ever demanded to see the note he'd signed. But somehow he never did. Kilby was right good at forgin' folks' signatures."

"Nice talent for a bank cashier to have," Pete observed. Dr. Gillett gave Luke another drink from the glass.

Luke continued, "That redeemed note bein' missin' caused both Nick and Haines a heap of worry. Finally they come to the conclusion that Hugh must have torn it up instead of takin' it back to his father. They both questioned Tiger-Eye right thorough, but Tiger-Eye denied he'd found any such note on Hugh's body, so there was nothin' that could be done about it. We were all forced to believe him. Nick always trusted Munson more than Ivan and me, though. We did a lot of pallin' around with Munson, and I reckon we knew him better. In fact, me'n Ivan suspected he knew where that missin' note was."

"What was Munson's idea in keeping it?" Pete asked.

Luke shifted a trifle in bed. There was a slight shrug of his shoulders. "I think he kept it to hold over Nick's head if anythin' went wrong. Maybe he planned to sell it to Haines. Haines was worried enough for a spell to pay good money for the note if it could be found. For that matter, I reckon Ivan and me would have done the same thing if we could have got hold of it. Nick never did give us our full profits from the Diamond-T, and we held that against him."

"How did you finally learn," Pete asked, "that Munson had the note?"

"Ivan and Munson and me got to drinkin' out at the ranch one day, and we got pretty high. Finally we all dressed up and came in to town and horsed around. Got our picture took and then did some more drinkin' at Turk's On the way home we got to talkin' about the note. Well, Munson was talkin' free, and he boasted he could get the note if he wanted. Later, when he sobered up, he denied he meant anythin' of the kind. But it started us thinkin', and from then on we watched Tiger-Eye right close."

Luke paused to catch his breath, which was coming with more difficulty now. After a time he went on, his voice fainter. Pete bent near to catch the words as Luke resumed: "The mornin' Munson died, Munson, Ivan, and me were the only ones in the bunkhouse. Me'n Ivan were in our bunks, asleep. I woke up and saw Munson unscrewin' the top off'n that red quirt. He pulled out a paper and looked at it, then had a laugh for himself. He was all dressed, ready to ride, and his bedroll was ready. I saw him put that paper back in the quirt, screw the knob back on, then get up, grab his rifle, and leave the bunkhouse. I don't know what his plan was, but I've got a hunch he was pullin' out for good and probably figurin' to stop in Beauregard and sell that paper to Haines."

"Sounds plausible," Pete cut in, so Luke would catch a momentary rest.

"I laid in my bunk a spell, thinkin' it over; then I woke up Ivan and told him what I'd seen. We decided to take after Munson and get that note, if that's what he had in the quirt. We mounted and hit the trail. Sure enough, he was headin' for Beauregard when we saw him. Ivan yelled at him to stop. I reckon he guessed what we had in mind, because he shoved spurs to his bronc and cut off across the range, with us followin'. We commenced to gain too. First Munson cut loose his bedroll to lighten his pony's load. We kept on gainin'. Finally Munson grabbed his rifle from its boot and let fly at us. Tiger-Eye couldn't be beat, shootin' from the ground with a Winchester, but he never was no good from the back of his horse."

"Lots of fellers are like that," Pete put in.

"Eventually we cut loose with our six-shooters. We didn't have rifles with us. It was a runnin' fight, with our horses gradually tirin'. But none of us would give up. First thing we knowed, we were 'way over near Elephant Ridge. By this time, though, Tiger-Eye had stopped usin' his rifle, and we knowed it was empty. We were closin' in so fast, I guess he didn't want to take time to reload. Maybe all his Winchester ca'tridges were in the bedroll he'd cut loose. On the other hand, we hadn't had much luck with our six-shooters. Then we got a break. I managed to hit Tiger-Eye's horse. That slowed him a heap, but he kept goin'. Then Ivan plugged the horse. Next time I shot at the horse, by accident I hit Tiger-Eye in the shoulder. He dang nigh fell out of his saddle——"

Luke stopped and caught his breath. Again Gillet held the glass to his lips. "Wish—wish—I had a shot of likker, Doc," he gasped.

The doctor waited a few minutes and then held a flask of

whisky to the dying man's lips. A momentary flush of color came back to the chalky features. A long sigh left his lips. "Where—where was I?" he mumbled. Another minute passed, and the breathing became stronger. Luke continued after a little: "Right after I hit Tiger-Eye—he rode his horse—into brush and—and we lost him. Kept on huntin'—though. Knew his bronc couldn't run—much longer. After a while—we came to where the bronc had dropped. Followed tracks———"

A faint smile curved the lips of the dying man. "It sure give us a start when we come on Tiger-Eye—sittin' in that rocker, comfortable as you please—with that wagon—alongside. We told Joadie Tate to get out—and he got—after we'd threatened him—some. Then we asked Tiger-Eye where the red quirt was. He laughed at us—taunted us with the fact— the note was inside the handle. Ivan got mad. Tiger-Eye already had his six-shooter in his hand. Ivan cursed him. Tiger-Eye raised his gun to shoot Ivan. He shot once—but I pushed his arm—made him miss. Then—Ivan—let him have it...." Luke's eyes closed.

For a moment Pete thought he was gone. "Better give him some more of that glass, Doc," Pete said quickly.

"Nothing I can give will help him now," Gillett said grimly. "He's been living on luck for the last ten minutes."

Luke's eyes opened slowly. They'd commenced to grow glassy. "Ain't done yet," he gasped. "More to—tell you— Piper. After Tiger-Eye was dead—Ivan got to worryin' if— the wagon had really—pulled out—and in—what direction. We rode to—top of Elephant Ridge. Through—field glasses —we saw Tate—headin' toward Rhysville. Then—we spotted you—comin' through brush—from the south. Watched you. After a while we saw you—had that—red quirt. Ivan shook a load outten his rifle. I did too. We both missed. I took the field glasses—then your shot came. It shook me—up plenty. We lit out for—Diamond-T. Got there—but Nick wa'n't there. Ivan rode on—to Beauregard. Told Nick—about note —handle of quirt.... Guess you—know the rest—Piper...."

27   Traxler Goes the Limit!

AT TWELVE O'CLOCK that same day Black Nick Traxler was engaged in serious conversation with Canary Sloan and Hump Auringer. The three were seated in the bunkhouse. In the kitchen Soggy Horton was cleaning up a mess of dishes. Black Nick's features were twisted with anger.

"I tell you, I don't like it," he was saying harshly. "What's happened to our crew? They seem to disappear in pairs. Where do they go?"

"That's what I'm wonderin'," Sloan muttered.

"Might be," Hump Auringer speculated, "that those boys are doing a mite of rustling on their own. Maybe they figure our game, being big, is dangerous. It wouldn't surprise me none if they've pulled loose from the outfit and were working from that county north of Rhys."

Nick nodded moodily. "I've thought of that too. They know our connections for selling cows up there. They could run their own little game—but, dammit, it's hard for me to believe the boys would just desert me like this! I've a hunch that redheaded son is mixed into the matter somehow."

"You mean Piper?" Sloan asked.

"I don't mean nobody else. Look at us"—Nick's voice rose hotly—"what have we got left? Just me and Canary and Hump and Ducky Drake and Luke——"

"Don't forget me." Soggy Horton stuck his head through the kitchen doorway.

Black Nick rasped, "T'hell with you. What good are you except for spoiling food?"

"You can give me my time whenever you feel like it," the cook snapped, bridling.

"I'm li'ble to do that too," Nick threatened darkly, "and you'll get some lead along with the silver."

Soggy Horton shut up and withdrew.

Canary Sloan said, "Geez! If Ducky and Luke fail to come back I'll sure know somethin' is wrong."

"They'll be back," Nick said confidently. "Luke went to Beauregard to pick up a pair of boots he'd ordered from a mail-order house. Ducky went along for company. No, it's just the men I send riding to Ladder-D range that disappear. That's what worries me. Where do they go? What happens to 'em?"

"What worries me," Sloan said nervously, "is my trial that's comin' up."

Nick said impatiently, "Forget that. It's five weeks off. I got you out on bail, like I promised, didn't I? I'll get you out of that trial too. We got other things to think about."

Hump Auringer said, "Well, thinking won't get us anyplace. What we going to do about it?"

Nick scowled. "The way I got it figured," he said slowly, "we were doing all right until Piper arrived. Since then everything has gone to pot. Folks in Beauregard don't even act afraid of us any more. The thing to do is get rid of Piper and a few other law lovers that infest this range."

"How you going to do that?" Sloan asked.

"I'm going to hire the damnedest crew of gun fighters you ever saw," Nick promised darkly. "Not just punchers—professional gunmen. I'm aiming to go the limit this time, but

I'll wipe out the opposition once and for all."

"Professional gunmen come high," Hump reminded. "Some of 'em ask a couple hundred a month. That'll run into money. Do you want to spend that much money, Nick?"

"Yeah, I do," Nick snapped. "But it won't be my money. Haines has been collecting profits from our game for a long time without ever taking any risks. It's about time that he helped a mite more. I'm going in and inform him that it's up to him and his damn bank to finance the hiring of about a dozen good lead slingers. Come on, Hump, you and Canary might as well come with me. We may be forced to throw a scare into Haines."

They rose from their chairs. Auringer and Sloan went to saddle three ponies. The cook stuck his head through the kitchen door to ask, "Will you be back for supper, Nick?"

"What business is it of yours?" Nick rasped angrily. "You just see that it's on the table if I do come back—or else." He flung himself angrily from the bunkhouse.

Five minutes later the cook heard the sound of retreating hoof beats. "I ain't a-goin' to take that from no man," he growled and commenced picking up his personal belongings. "It's just about time that one more hand disappeared from this outfit—and I aim to be him." Ten minutes later he had saddled a horse and was riding rapidly west. No one in the neighborhood ever saw Soggy Horton again. . . .

Five miles from Beauregard City, Nick, Auringer, and Canary Sloan saw Sheriff Ethan Perkins riding rapidly toward them. The three Diamond-T men pulled to a halt and waited for the sheriff to draw abreast, at the same time wondering what brought Perkins in this direction.

The sheriff reined in his pony and nodded to the three men, then said, "Glad I met you, Nick. It'll save me a ride."

"What's on your mind?" Traxler demanded.

"I've got some bad news for you, Nick."

Traxler stiffened. "Well, spill it. Ducky or Luke get drunk, or something?"

"Worse than that," the sheriff said. "Ducky's dead. Luke's dying."

"What you talking about?" Nick growled unbelievingly. Hump and Canary didn't say anything. They both looked upset, though.

"I'm telling it straight," the sheriff insisted.

"Piper?" Traxler spat the one word.

"Piper and another man—stranger in town, named Tate. Tate shot Luke—nigh cut him in half with a scattergun. It was Piper killed Drake."

"What was the scrap about?" Traxler asked, his eyes burning.

"Look, Nick," the sheriff said, "there's no use going into that now. If you want to go in and see Luke, that's all right with me, but I want your promise you won't make any more trouble. You'd better send Hump and Canary back."

"You're trying to tell me what to do?" Traxler laughed harshly. "Perkins, I've had just about enough of your meddling. If you don't want to give me the details, all right. But we're going into town and we're going to square a couple of matters—"

"In that case," the sheriff said steadily, "I'm going to have to do what's possible to prevent further trouble. Go on to town, if you like—but you're surrendering your guns to me before you move another step. Hand over your gun, Nick."

Traxler's face flamed. "The hell I will! Get out of the way, Perkins. I ain't to be stopped."

"Better think twice about it, Nick," the sheriff warned, dropping one hand to his gun butt. "Remember, it's the law of Trabadura County that's talking—not me personal."

Canary Sloan said nervously, "I reckon the sheriff's right."

Traxler hesitated, then gave a short laugh. "I reckon," he conceded. "No doubt about you being right, Sheriff. You win." He put his hand to his holster, carelessly drew out his six-shooter—and pulled trigger. White flame spurted from the muzzle.

A look of shocked surprise spread over the sheriff's face. He tried to complete his own draw. One hand clutched at his middle; then he suddenly toppled from the saddle and struck the earth. Powder smoke thinned out, vanished in the breeze.

No one said anything for a minute. The three Diamond-T men sat their saddles, looking down at the still form of the sheriff. Hump Auringer broke the silence first. "You said you were going to go the limit, Nick," he said unsteadily. "I reckon you meant what you said."

Traxler swore. "I've had a craving to do this for a long time," he said coldly. "Come on, we'll get on to town. If anybody asks, we haven't seen the sheriff." They spoke to the horses and moved on.

Canary Sloan gave a reluctant backward glance. "You sure you got him, Nick?"

Traxler laughed scornfully. "You asking *me* that, Canary? You that knows my shooting as well as you do? Don't be foolish!"

They urged the ponies forward and entered Beauregard City a half-hour later. Hump said, "We'll have to ask somebody where Luke is."

Traxler said, "T'hell with Luke. He was always blundering into trouble. I'll find him later probably at Doc Gillett's. But first we got to see Haines."

The three loped through town and stopped at the hitch rack of the bank. It was near the closing hour, and there were only a couple of customers at Kilby Ward's window when they trooped in. "Haines back there?" Traxler snapped.

Ward looked up nervously and nodded. Traxler, with Hump and Canary at his back, shouldered into Haines's office and closed the door behind them. Haines looked up, startled.

"What's the idea of this, Nick?"

"We've got to have a talk, Haines. Sit down, Canary. Hump, you can sit on this desk."

"Just a minute," Haines said angrily. "You know better than to come here like this, Nick. If you want to see me I'll meet you at our usual place tonight. We can't risk———"

"We've got to risk a lot more than you figure," Nick cut in coldly. "We don't aim to carry the load any more, Haines. You've got to help. I'm going to need some money—big money. We're going to hire a crew of gun slingers that———"

"Have you gone crazy?" Haines commenced.

"No, but you have if you don't listen to me. Piper has that red quirt. Luke has been shot. If Luke ever told Piper what's in the handle of that quirt it would mean your neck."

"That part is your concern," Haines blustered. "You swore you'd recover that quirt. You've wasted enough time———"

"I've wasted no time," Traxler interrupted. "I know how serious this business is. You're refusing to face the facts. You're in this with us and you're going to do what I say. Just to wake you up so you'll believe me, I'm telling you that I just killed the sheriff."

"My God!" Haines exclaimed. "Nick, you've gone crazy!"

"Not crazy. I'm just sick of all this shilly-shallying———"

The door of the private office was suddenly flung open. Kilby Ward stood there, white-faced. "Mr. Haines, Mr. Haines———"

"Now what's wrong?" Haines demanded.

"I'm not sure, but I think we're going to have trouble. I was just closing the bank doors, when I looked out and I saw that Piper and the deputy coming here. They were running and they looked pretty mad. Their guns were in their hands———"

Haines leaped from his chair. "Lock those front doors!"

"I did," Ward said in a frightened voice.

Haines turned accusingly to Traxler. "They've learned you killed the sheriff."

"They couldn't have, this quick."

"Well, get out of here. You're not going to make me an accomplice."

Traxler looked toward the single window in the office and noted the iron bars across it. "I reckon we'll all have to stay," he said coldly. "I sure don't intend to go out the front way."

At that moment there came a heavy pounding on the double doors at the front entrance of the bank. Haines moaned, "They're here. I'm ruined!"

"We all are, if we don't do something about it. Haines, I know you have a couple of guns here. You and Ward are going to use 'em. We'll cut down Piper and that damn'd deputy. Hump! Canary! Get your guns out. This looks like a finish fight!"

28   Showdown!

PETE HAD LEFT Dr. Gillett's house and was just turning on Tonto Street when he saw Homer hurrying toward him. Homer started to speak, but Pete said joyously, "Look at this Homer!" He drew from his pocket the Alexander note for six thousand dollars, with Haines's cancellation written across it. "I guess this proves that Hugh Alexander entered the bank that morning. And I got a witness to swear he saw him go in Haines' private office."

"Good cripes!" Homer exclaimed, his own business momentarily forgotten. "Where'd you get it?"

Pete quickly rattled off the story; then, "Say, did you see Joadie Tate? He'll make a good witness."

"He's at the hotel. Had to tell me all about his rocker—and the new woman he's lookin' for—" Homer suddenly paused, his face sobering. "Pete, I'm afraid there's somethin' wrong."

"What do you mean?"

"I'm afraid somethin' has happened to Ethan. He was so set on not havin' any more gunplay here that he went himself to the Diamond-T—at least he started there—to break the news of Luke's shootin' to Black Nick. I offered to go in his place, but he figured he might have more influence with Nick than I would. I think he was wrong, but you know how Ethan is. It was his idea to persuade Black Nick to leave his gun at home when he come to town. I told him you can't persuade a rattlesnake to nothin', but Ethan insisted——"

"I don't know, Homer," Pete said thoughtfully. "The sheriff may know what he's doing. He can put pressure on Traxler and tell him the law orders him not to wear his gun. That should stop him."

"But wait; I was comin' to find you. Nick Traxler, Canary Sloan, and Hump Auringer just rode into town a few minutes back. They were all wearin' their guns. They went direct to the bank."

Pete frowned. "Maybe that don't look so good. Course Nick didn't come to look for Luke, so maybe he don't know about

Luke dyin'. He's dead now, as a matter of fact——"

"Don't you see, Pete," Homer said impatiently, "Ethan went to tell Nick! There's just one road to the Diamond-T. Ethan *couldn't* have missed him. He *must* have seen Nick and told him."

"In other words," Pete said grimly, "they encountered the sheriff somewhere along the road. The sheriff didn't come in with them. That means they left him somewhere out there. Homer!" His words took on a cold, calculating tone. "You said once that you were never around when I did any shooting. We're going to change that right now. I've got enough on Haines to make an arrest, anyway. Come on, we're heading for the bank!"

They broke into a run. Homer panted, "Remember, there's five there, includin' Ward and Haines."

"I'm just sorry there aren't more," Pete spat angrily. "This is a showdown!"

They arrived at the bank and pounded up the steps to find the double doors locked. Pete pounded heavily; Homer followed suit. They waited a few moments before Pete called, "Open up in there!"

Footsteps sounded within, then Kilby Ward's voice: "Sorry, gentlemen, the bank's closed for the day."

"Not to us it isn't!" Pete snapped.

"Dammit!" Homer yelled angrily. "Open up! This is Deputy Pritchard!"

A crowd commenced to collect on the sidewalk before the bank. A volley of questions were fired at Homer and Pete. Neither paid any attention. Pete again called an order to open the doors. There was no more word from within. Pete looked at Homer, caught the suggestion in his eyes. He nodded. "Right. We'll have to bust 'em down!"

They hurled their combined fighting weights against the double doors, which groaned under the impact. The doors were heavy but the locks ancient. Suddenly there came a sharp splintering sound as lock screws were wrenched from the wood. One door started to swing open. Pete gave it a sudden push; then he and Homer jumped to either side. From within the bank there came a roaring of heavy guns as hot lead whined through the entrance. The crowd on the sidewalk scattered frantically.

Pete said, "Come on!" He dived inside, running low, with Homer close at his heels. For a moment he saw no one; then behind the two grilled windows he spotted Hump Auringer and Canary Sloan just raising their guns for second shots.

Shooting by instinct rather than aim, Pete flipped a shot toward Auringer. He heard a yelp of pain as Auringer's face disappeared from the window. Homer's gun roared at the same instant as Canary's. Canary clutched at his throat. Homer staggered back, then sat down violently on the floor.

Somethin like fiery iron ran along Pete's ribs. He swayed to one side but kept his balance as he saw Kilby Ward just raising from behind the waist-high gate that stood between grilled windows and side wall. Kilby's gun was pointed at Homer, struggling to rise and get back into the fight.

A mushroom of smoke and flame spurted from Pete's hand. Kilby uttered a high-pitched scream, straightened to full height, and then went sprawling to the floor. For a moment the shooting ceased.

Pete said, "You hurt bad, pard?"

Homer grinned through his pain. "That Ward bustard got me in the leg. Broke, I reckon. But I ain't through."

"Take it easy!" Swiftly Pete punched out depleted shells in his six-shooter and loaded to full capacity, his eyes on that closed door to the rear, marked PRIVATE. "Take it easy," he said again. "I'll smoke out those other sons!"

Homer struggled again to rise, then sank back, clutching his wounded leg. He sat there, watching Pete push aside the swinging gate, step over Ward's body and continue on toward Haines's private door.

Behind Pete, Canary Sloan rose stealthily into view, lifting his Colt gun. Blood streamed from a spot on Canary's neck, but he was still in the battle.

Homer raised his six-shooter, took careful aim from his position on the floor, and pulled trigger. Canary spun completely around and crashed down.

Peter whirled, saw what had happened, and nodded coolly to Homer. "Nice work, pard." He turned toward the door marked PRIVATE and called, "Better come out Traxler. I want you! And you, Haines!"

There was no reply from Haines. Traxler's snarl came through the door: "Come and get me, you redheaded son!"

"That," Pete snapped, "is an invitation."

He raised his gun. It roared once, shattering the lock on the door. Then he raised his foot and kicked it open. The door swung back. Haines stood at one side of the room, Traxler at the other. There were guns in their hands. Pete's weapon was throwing sharp lances of flame and smoke.

He felt something strike his body and knock him to one side. Then through the haze of swimming powder smoke he saw Haines pitch forward, striking his head on the desk as he fell.

"It's you and me now, Traxler." Pete laughed crazily. He knew he was hard hit, but he kept plunging in. Back of him Homer's gun exploded once more, just as Traxler came rushing toward the staggering Pete. Traxler paused in mid-stride. Pete caught the edge of the desk. God! His gun was heavy. He could hardly lift it. Burned-powder stench stung his nostrils. He was growing fainter every second. With a supreme effort he brought the six-shooter to bear on Traxler just as Traxler released another shot.

"Look out, Pete!" Homer yelled frantically. Again his gun roared.

But the warning came too late. Something like a hot club knocked Pete's head crazily to one side, and he felt himself falling, falling. Even as he struck the floor he remembered releasing his hammer on a final shot.

Then with a strangled cry of agony ringing in his ears, Pete sensed a dense black curtain settle down on his senses. He sighed and lay still. Homer was calling to him, but the words didn't make sense. There came a rush of many feet, excited cries. But Pete was beyond hearing all that now. . . .

29   Conclusion

PETE AWAKENED SLOWLY. For a moment he couldn't think where he was. He seemed to be in a bed—a bed with sheets on it. Through a dim haze he saw a head of pale gold hair hovering above him. He closed his eyes again, opened them. This time they focused more clearly, but the head was gone. He called, "Cressy!" and managed to twist his head to one side. He saw a sunny window with curtains blowing in the cool breeze.

Then Cressy was standing, smiling, above him again.

"Awake at last, eh, cowboy?"

"Cressy, I had the queerest dream. I dreamed I was in a gun fight and——Hey, where am I? What happened?" Even while he was speaking, remembrance of the fight at the bank came back with a rush. His head cleared to a greater extent. A sudden scowl formed on his face. He spoke one word, "Traxler?"

"Traxler's dead," she said. The scowl left Pete's face. "Good grief, Pete! You had us all frightened for a spell. You're coming along all right now, though."

"Was I hit bad?"

Cressy laughed. "It wasn't what they term a slight flesh wound, me lad. And you were hit more than once. You got a nice one over the ear. Just a teeny bit closer and that would have been the end of Mr. Piper's son. Dr. Gillett just left about ten minutes ago. He said he thought when you awakened today your head would be clear."

"My head's always clear," Pete contradicted.

"Not for the past two weeks——"

"Two weeks?" Pete's voice was startled. "You mean I've been lying here for two weeks—delirious? And talking?"

"Particularly talking," Cressy said dryly. "Some of the remarks you've made have brought blushes to Graveyard's face—when he told me about 'em."

"Graveyard?"

"Don't you understand, Pete? You're here—at the C-Bar-A. Gillett thought you might mend faster out here, so we brought you here when it was safe to move you. I've been your day nurse; Graveyard has been tending you nights. Oh, we've all had a hand——"

"The sheriff!" Pete said suddenly.

"Sheriff Perkins is going to live. He had a mighty close call, though. He was found near the road about five miles this side of Beauregard. . . . Yes, it was Black Nick shot him."

Pete asked other questions. He was learning that his body was swathed in bandages. His head was bandaged too.

"Pete, we owe you so much," Cressy was saying. "We found the note in your pocket. Dad was overjoyed. We both are. Oh yes, it was Auringer, Sloan, and Drake that held us up that night. Auringer confessed. No, he didn't die. He's got a long prison sentence ahead of him, as has Rudolph Haines. Haines told everything. Joe Dunlop came to see how you were yesterday. Those Diamond-T punchers he was holding prisoner broke down when they heard Traxler was dead. They weren't stopping to rebrand the Ladder-D cows; they just rushed them in to the county north of Rhys and sold them there after Kilby Ward—who is dead too—forged bills of sale."

"Rustling on a wholesale scale, eh? How's Homer's broken leg?"

"It wasn't broken, after all. The bullet struck a nerve, or something, and just paralyzed him for a time, so he couldn't use it. He's here, now, waiting to see you."

There came a knock at the door. Cressy went to open it. Her father's voice asked, "You aiming to keep Pete to yourself all day, Cressy?"

"Longer than that." The girl smiled.

They filed into the room: Cyrus Alexander, Homer, Graveyard, Pinto Grant, and, last of all, Joadie Tate, still lugging his heavy shotgun. It seemed to go everywhere with him. Homer was on crutches with a bandage showing through one cut-away pants leg. He said, grinning, "Hiyuh, Pete! There's a rumor around to the effect that you finished Black Nick Traxler."

Pete laughed. "If I didn't you did."

"Not me," Homer contradicted. "From where I was sittin'

on the floor I couldn't even see him, until just toward the last. I just kept rollin' lead into that office in the hope it would make him cautious, when I saw you were gettin' groggy. I was sure scared when I saw you go down. Your last shot did it, I reckon."

Cressy's dad was clutching Pete's hand while they talked. His eyes were moist with happiness. He didn't say much.

"Good to see you alive and kicking again, Pete," Pinto Grant said. "You need a shave bad, though."

"I had that," Pete chuckled, "a dang close shave."

Pinto said suddenly, "Look at Graveyard! He's actually smiling."

"Why not?" Graveyard asked. "First time in thirty years I've seen anythin' to smile at. Now we can really commence livin' around here."

Pete said to Joadie Tate, "How's it going, Joadie? Your rocker holding up under all this strain?"

"Might' glad to see ye awake, Mr. Piper," Tate said solemnly. "Yep, my rocker's all right. Got 'er moved to the room at my hotel. But I ain't found no woman yit—an' I shown thet rocker to a passel of women already too. I'd be bounden to Miss Cressy if'n she'd he'p me meet up with some henfolk."

Cressy laughed. "We'll sure have to find you a wife, Joadie, even if we have to send back to your own people to get one."

And then after a time Cressy urged the men out of the room and shut the door again. She returned and sat on the edge of Pete's bed. "You know, Pete," she said, "you once told me you wanted a spread of your own. The Diamond-T can be had cheap now, I'm betting—that is, if you'd like to live so close——"

Pete shook his head. "Nice country over there, but no water. Of course"—nonchalantly—"I might marry you just to get water rights."

"It's an idea," Cressy agreed softly. "I'll think it over."

"Look," Pete said seriously, "I have an inspiration. I'll buy Joadie's sitting rocker for you. Now is it a deal?"

"Sold!" Cressy laughed.

Pete reached up and caught her hand. It was warm in his palm. He said, "You mentioned some delirious talk of mine that made Graveyard blush. What was it?"

Color flowed into Cressy's cheeks. Her head of pale gold came nearer Pete's. He felt her lips warm on his own, heard her whispered words. After a long time he laughed softly. "Oh, *that*. . . . Shucks, lady, that's just a starter. . . ."